THE
HOLLOW
THRONE

TIM LEACH is a graduate of the Warwick
Writing Programme, where he now teaches as
an Assistant Professor. His first novel, *The Last
King of Lydia*, was shortlisted for the Dylan
Thomas Prize, and *A Winter War*, the first in
the Sarmatian Trilogy, was shortlisted for
the HWA Gold Crown Award.

Follow Tim on @TimLeachWriter

THE
HOLLOW
THRONE

TIM LEACH

An Aries Book

First published in the UK in 2023 by Head of Zeus,
part of Bloomsbury Publishing Plc

9 7 5 3 1 2 4 6 8

A catalogue record for this book is available from the British Library.

ISBN (HB): 9781800242920
ISBN (E): 9781800242975

Map design by Jeff Edwards

Typeset by Siliconchips Services Ltd UK

Printed and bound in Great Britain by
CPI Group (UK) Ltd, Croydon CR0 4YY

Head of Zeus
First Floor East
5–8 Hardwick Street
London EC1R 4RG

WWW.HEADOFZEUS.COM

For Emma, Sarah, and Kathy

AD **180**

Antonine Wall (disused)

D A M N O N I

R. Clyde

D A M N O N I I

Island
of Spears

S o u t h e

U

R. Nithe

NOVANTAE

SELGO

Solway Firth

Bil

Alauna

Ma

Gabrosentum

Legend
◻ Roman forts

0   25 miles
0   50 km

N

NORTH SEA

Firth of Forth

OTADINI

VOTADINI

R. Tweed

VOTADINI

Cheviot Hills

a n d s

VOTADINI

R. Esk

E

Hadrian's Wall

Brocolitia   Cilurnum

Banna Aesica   Vercovicium   Vindobala   Segedunum
                                   Onnum
Camboglanna   Magnis Vindolanda   Condercum Pons Aelius
Maia   *R. Tyne*
     Aballava
ncavata   Uxelodunum

B R I G A N T E S

The Pennines

THE MAIMED KING

AD 175

1

Across the hills and through the heather, a broken people wandered to the north.

Many thousands they were, grey-faced with exhaustion, their skin daubed with blood and earth, stumbling and dragging their feet as they walked. They resembled an army of the dead more than the living, as though some ancient barrow had broken open and the corpses had come crawling out in their thousands. Etched upon their shields and upon their skin could be seen the markings of many different tribes – the Damnonii, the Venicones, the Taexali, and many more. Half a dozen tribes of the northlands, who had put aside the ancient wounds of their feuds beneath a single banner and called themselves the Painted People.

No army pursued them, no living enemy could be seen. Only, towering in the distance to the south, the great Wall of stone that marked the edge of an Empire. The Painted People fled from that Wall, and it was as though that army of the dead had fought a monster of stone, and had lost.

But no monster had defeated them, nor had it been the Legions of Rome – that at least would have been a familiar humiliation. This had been a new enemy, a new shame for them to bear. A people from a distant land bound in service to the Empire: warriors who wore dragonlike scales upon their skin, carried great lances in their hands that seemed made to murder giants, rode monstrous horses that fought and killed alongside the men.

What could one do against such warriors, who seemed to have ridden out of a myth? And though the Painted People barely had the strength to walk or even to stand, even so they recited a name, spoken over and over again, like a curse or a prayer: *Sarmatians, Sarmatians.* The name of those who had defeated them. The name they would have to learn to hate.

The Painted People moved like a wounded beast, staggering and bleeding their way across the heather and the hills, a spoor of corpses left behind them as bloodied men stumbled and fell and lay down to die. They fled to a deep forest within a valley of the northlands, one of the places where the secret acts, sacred and forbidden, were done amongst their people. There at last, shielded by the trees from the eyes of men and gods alike, they collapsed to the ground.

No more words, at first. Save for that repeated naming of their enemy, their shame and exhaustion had taken them to a place beyond language, back to the old ways of the heart and the mind, when their ancestors had loved and fought and hated without speech. Gradually, piece by piece, the art of words came back to them. But they needed only one. They spoke nothing but a single name, over and over again.

'*Corvus, Corvus, Corvus.*'

The name of their war chief, the high king of the Painted People. The man who had led them to their defeat.

One day before, they had chanted that name as a rallying

cry upon the battlefield. For he had brought them great fortune in war, taught them well how to hate and destroy their enemy. Now they spoke his name like a curse and a command, demanding that he come and face their judgement.

Summoned by the word, the way that fey creatures are bound to answer the sounding of their true name, a figure stepped into the clearing, the moonlight shining upon his corpse-white skin.

He was tall, taller than any other man there – a fair-haired warrior from half the world away, from the forests beyond the Rhenus at another edge of the Empire. His blue eyes were as still and empty as the waters of the northern seas, his pale skin marked with the signs of the Legion he had deserted long before. He stood before them then, unbowed and seemingly unafraid. He waited to see what those broken people would do to him.

The Painted People gathered about him, murder slowly building in their hearts. The vengeful anger of defeated men, and more than that too – for all the dead that they had left behind in the shadow of the Wall, they knew that a sacrifice was still needed. A curse of the gods must be upon them, to suffer such a defeat. Only the blood of a king would end that curse, and he had been a king to them all.

Corvus knew all this, it seemed. But he did not beg, or curse, or take up a weapon to defend himself. He merely unclasped his cloak and cast it to the earth, pulled away the armour of leather and cloth, unwound the wrappings of his boots. He moved with slow, careless gestures as he cast away his clothes – he might have been a traveller come home after a long journey to warm himself by the fire, or a man going to bed with his lover.

At last he stood there naked, an offering of flesh.

No fire had been struck, for none of them had the strength or the will to build one. But the moon was half full, and the near-ceaseless clouds had cleared for once. The wind lay still; the clearing in the forest was open to the sky. And so the Painted People saw Corvus clearly, just as they saw the knife in his hand.

It would have been the work of a moment, to swarm upon Corvus and cut him to pieces. Yet they held still. Not from fear of what his knife might do to them, for they were too weary to feel any fear of death. Somehow, in that moment, they found themselves afraid of what Corvus meant to do to himself.

The knife rose high, as he offered the blade to the goddess of the moon. Corvus laid the edge of the weapon to his forehead, perhaps seeking some comfort in the touch of the iron, dry and cold, against war-fevered skin. The tip of the knife went to his chest, as though he intended to give himself a quick death, then to the belly, the place of the slow death. The knife drifted down, beneath his manhood, and the Painted People knew then what he intended.

They were crying out then, calling for him not to do it. For all that they had been willing to kill him a moment before, they feared for him now. They felt his pain as their own. He was their brother, and they loved him.

But it was too late. He had already begun to cut.

A ragged screaming broke the silence of the forest – Corvus had borne many wounds on the battlefield, but this was a pain unknowable. His teeth bared, bone white under the light of the moon, the cords of his neck dancing and writhing, his agonised face turned towards the sky.

Then it was done, with a flowing of blood and seed upon the earth. And Corvus was kneeling, red hands cupping and holding himself, as though he feared to let what he had cut away touch the earth. Silence from those around him, who knew that they were witnessing something terrible and holy.

Corvus was speaking then – he gave no prayer to a god to undo what had been done, nor sound out a curse upon his enemies. He simply said: 'Bring it to me.'

For the Painted People, there was no doubting what he meant. There was only one treasure of theirs that he could mean.

It was secret and forbidden, known only to the tribes of the northlands. They had carried it with them on their journey, but had not dared to use it even when they knew they were defeated. Better to die, it had seemed to them before, than to unleash that evil upon the world. But now the word went out, and from the heart of the woods, passed hand over hand with great tenderness, they brought their terrible treasure forward into the clearing.

At first it seemed that they carried a piece of the night itself – a sphere of utter blackness, swallowing the moonlight that fell upon it. But those closer to it could see the old hammer marks on metal that had been beaten to smoothness more than a century before. Those who held it felt the patterned shapes beneath their fingers. The etchings of trees, elm and oak and ash. The faces of men, smiling and laughing and screaming.

It was an old cauldron, forged of black iron. Such a simple, humble thing, the kind that might hang above a cookfire all through those lands north of the Wall. But there were many sacred cauldrons in the tales of their people. The Cauldron of Ceridwen that brewed wisdom as if it were soup. The Cauldron of the Dagda that would never run empty. And this one – the Burning Cauldron, the tomb of long-dead gods.

Each man who held it did so only for a moment, stumbling to pass it on as quickly as he could. Afterwards, all of them would swear that though the cauldron had not felt fire for a hundred years, even so it almost burned their fingers, still hot to the touch.

And so it travelled hand over hand, until it came at last to rest before Corvus. Before the man they would come to call the Maimed King, who reached into it with a trembling, bloody hand.

Within it lay no treasure of gold and silver, no crown of kings or wizard's wand. There was nothing within but ash and soot. And into the Burning Cauldron, Corvus cast that ruined piece of himself. Then he bowed over to the ground and lay weeping upon the earth, all his strength and courage spent.

All at once, the Painted People gathered to their king. One laid a cloak across Corvus to cover his nakedness, and another lay beside him in a close embrace, a brother's embrace. All was forgiven then, for they knew the blood sacrifice he had made. The great offering to the old dead gods – a forbidden, powerful magic that might let them rise again.

The killing spirit had left them now. There was only a kinship of suffering, a quiet grief that bound them together. For there would be no peace, not after such an offering. No retreat to the valleys and the rivers, no peaceful life spent tending herd and field. They were given over to one purpose only – revenge against the Romans and the Sarmatians, those who had wronged them. Revenge for their Maimed King, who had sacrificed so much for them.

It would be a patient revenge, a thing of many years. For now, they were content to disappear into the forest and heather. To tend their wounds, gather their strength, and let the evil in that cauldron grow strong, ready for the time that it would be unleashed upon the world.

All that grows and thrives must first come from the earth – this the Painted People knew. And so, beneath the light of the moon and stained with the blood of their king, they began to dig.

THE BURNING CAULDRON

AD 180

2

When Kai first looked upon the valley, it did not seem like a place of death.

It was the same, familiar Valley of Dùin where he had travelled many times before, hunting deer in the musky dell or grazing a herd at the grass that grew tall by the river. There were no glinting spearheads lurking amidst the trees in the forest, no oathsworn warriors gathered at the ford of the river, no creak of bowstrings echoing from the grey cliffs above. But as Kai looked on the open meadows, the sun cutting through the clouds and dancing on the hillside, some sense of an omen told him that his death was waiting there.

Only one thing was out of place. It was a bright, clear day such as was rarely seen this far north, and perhaps that alone held the omen. It was always said amongst his people, the Sarmatians of the eastern steppe, that a man should always fear a bright clear day, for the bloodthirsty gods of war liked to see the killing done through an open sky. And so he sat atop his tall horse, and waited – perhaps if he listened closely enough, he might hear some whisper from those gods, who sought to lead him to his death.

Behind him, his raiding party stirred restlessly – a dozen warriors, old and young, bearing the tattoos of the Votadini tribe. Most of their horses bore a second rider: a goat trussed and slung across the saddle. Their weapons were bright under the sun, but here and there a spear was darkened with blood, for their enemies, the tribe of the Novantae, had not given up those animals without a fight. No great victory had they won, but though few stories sang of stolen goats, they were prizes richer than iron or gold for a starving people.

And the Votadini were starving. Exiled and driven from their homes five years before by the Romans, they had no fields to till, no winter grazing grounds to keep their meagre herds fed – they lived by the hunt and the raid alone. Each summer, Roman patrols wandered further north. Each winter, the herds grew thinner and fewer, the numbers of the tribe dwindling, dying. That day Kai had led this raiding party further into Novantae lands than he wished to, lingered too long waiting for a shepherd's flock to cross their path. But they had their prize now: food enough to feed their tribe. Now they had but to keep it, and make their way back to the rest of their kin.

Kai saw his companions' eyes track restlessly over the horizon – no doubt searching for what had given him pause. At last one of them, a man called Comhnall, came forward and asked: 'Which god is whispering in your ear today?'

'I do not know,' Kai answered, 'but I would do well to listen to them.'

'I suppose you shall wait until the Novantae come back,' the other man said shortly. 'They shall be raising a war party to chase us, you know.'

'I know it. But there is danger here too.'

'None that I or any of the others can see.'

Kai ignored him. He leaned forward and laid his lips upon the forehead of his horse, asking for her counsel. It was an old Sarmatian saying that a horse had a third of the life of a man but thrice his wisdom. That when they started and stared at things unseen it was the spirits of the Otherlands that they saw; that when their ears twitched it was to listen to those fey creatures speaking their secrets. Yet for all their wisdom a horse could not speak – one had to read the scratch of a hoof against the ground, a gentle toss of the head, the way they sometimes looked towards a river and sighed like a woman longing for her lover.

His horse gave no such sign that he could see. Perhaps there truly was no danger there. Or perhaps it was that she did not know how to read the omens in this country – she was as much a stranger there as Kai was.

At last, Kai said: 'We must go along the river.'

A murmuring of dissent from the others. One of them, wounded by a cut across the arm, hunched miserably in his saddle, his eyes closed against the pain.

There were two paths that would lead them back to the rest of their kin. A long, open path along the river, where any scout of the Novantae might see them from a league away and cut them off at the shallow ford. Or there was the shorter way through the forest, a way they had gone many times before. A quick and hidden path, it seemed, and yet it was from those rustling leaves that Kai was certain he could hear the omen speak of death.

Comhnall spat upon the ground. 'Why?' he said.

'I do not like the look of the forest.'

'Do your people not have trees, back in Sarmatia? Why do they frighten you so?'

'I cannot say,' Kai said reluctantly. 'But I have ignored omens before, and I have always regretted it.'

'The path through the forest is the shorter,' said Comhnall. 'If we go through the open country, we shall have a Novantae warband upon us before the day is out.' He levelled his spear at Kai's great Sarmatian warhorse, taller and stronger than those the others rode. 'And *you* might be able to run in open country. But we cannot. The forest shall protect us.'

'Comhnall...'

'No,' the Votadini warrior said, shaking his head. 'You are no captain to command us. You are not even...'

The words died before they could be fully spoken, but Kai knew them well enough – he was not truly one of their tribe. Copper-skinned where they were fair, his skin marked with twisting tattoos of dragons and antelope that held no meaning here, there was no mistaking him for one of the Votadini, nor his warhorse for one of their shaggy-haired ponies. Five years he had spent amongst the Votadini, after he had crossed the Wall and left the Romans and the rest of his own kin behind, but for all their claims to have taken him in, and for all that he had fought for the tribe with horse and spear, he was still not one of them. Perhaps he never would be.

He looked around the other warriors of the raiding party, searching for allies. He found only the carefully blank gazes of men who had already made up their minds. One, a young lad, Oisean, barely old enough to hold a spear steady, seemed as though he was about to speak, but at the last moment his head dipped down, and the boy held his tongue.

'So be it,' Kai said. 'Let us hope the god speaks false to me.'

A bitter laugh then from Comhnall. 'A good hope indeed. For when have the gods ever spoken in our favour, since you came amongst our people?'

At the edge of the forest, there was only silence. No sound of singing birds, no shifting of wolf or boar or deer through the forest, and even the trees themselves seemed to hold their breath, as if in waiting.

Kai looked once more to Comhnall, a silent question in his stare.

'The Novantae could not have come so far,' Comhnall said, in the manner of a man trying to convince himself. 'The Selgovae avoid this place. And the Romans fear the woods even more than you do. There is no one here.'

'Tell that to the birds,' Kai answered.

They moved slowly through the trees, picking a path through old game trails where the deer had wandered for centuries. By some unspoken agreement, they kept the edge of the forest close, like a sailor keeping in view of the shore, for they were afraid to lose sight of open ground.

The sun fell low, the reddish light cutting through the trees, sharp and blinding. Still no birds sang, and even the goats – trussed up, slung across horses, surrounded by men who stank of blood – fell silent, in the way that animals do when they know that a predator is close by.

Then Comhnall, the first man in the line, tugged on the

reins of his horse and went utterly still in the saddle. Kai tried to find the danger that his companion must have seen, and his eyes played tricks on him – rainwater pooling on a broad leaf became the shining blade of a spear for a moment; a ringed pattern of lichen upon the bark of a tree seemed to be two wide eyes staring back at him. But when he blinked and cleared his vision, he saw no sign of ill omen there. Nothing but the empty, silent forest.

Kai stirred his horse forward to the front of the line. 'What do you see?' he said.

Comhnall made no answer. He levelled his spear towards the ground, the blade trembling as it pointed the way, and Kai saw then what filled that man with fear.

The ground in the clearing had been torn open. Black soil exposed to the sky, like old blood congealed upon a festering wound. He could see the marks of the hands and blades that had hacked the earth apart, as though something great and terrible had clawed its way out of the soil – some monster tearing itself out of its own grave.

'A scavenger?' said Kai. 'Perhaps a man was buried here too shallowly?'

'No animal did this,' Comhnall replied, his voice strangely flat. 'And this is like no grave I have ever seen.'

It was true – there was no mark of a cairn, and amongst the tribes of the north a forest was thought an evil place to lay the dead. The fell spirits gathered in the trees at night, or so it was said, and a dead man left buried there would not remain so for long.

Kai reached out and laid his hand upon the other man's arm, but Comhnall gave no reaction to the touch. 'We must go now,' Kai said.

Comhnall nodded, his eyes dull as one waking from the dreaming. 'Yes. But it will not matter.' And he reached back and patted Kai gently upon the hand. 'I am sorry I did not listen to you,' he said, a terrible kind of peace in his voice.

It was a peace that Kai did not share as they went further into the woods. There was only a maddening sense of fear, rising like a river in flood. He tried to tell himself that he was being foolish – Comhnall had been right to say that the other tribes avoided this place, and the warriors he had with him were brave and battle-tested. And though it was said the gods always spoke true, they were creatures of all times and of none. It might be that they had seen a massacre in that place that would not come to pass for a hundred years, that they came screaming warnings to him about a killing yet to come.

All of that was true. Yet, in the end, none of it mattered.

They came from behind the trees and rising up from the ground – no artful ambush from many sides, but a sudden rush of men, charging in a wordless silence that was more frightening than any war song. Ghosts rising from the bracken, the low sun bright upon their spears, glinting upon the arrowheads drawn back to be loosed, and then the arrows were whispering through the trees, the air alive about him, a living, biting thing.

Already one of the Votadini was struck and falling screaming from his saddle, but Kai's fear was gone at once. For fear was born of choice, and there was only one left to Kai – he levelled his spear and called for his companions to charge.

The ground was uncertain beneath them, the trees clustered

thick and their branches reaching down like grasping hands that threatened to pluck him from the saddle. But Kai had trained these horsemen of the Votadini well, given them that faith in the weight of horse and rider, the long reach of the spear. And so the horses strode forward, the spears tipped down to form a second forest of ash and iron.

The raiders should have parted before them – it was a law of battle, as immutable as the principles of nature. The sun rose and fell each day, spring followed winter, and men of the northlands could not stand firm against the charge of the cavalry. But those warriors swept forward silently, close enough for Kai to see blank and empty eyes, arms blackened with earth from where they had dug something from the broken ground. As if the dead rose before him, fearless and terrible in search of their revenge.

Kai saw a tattooed man run forward, his hair stiff with lime and his beard neatly trimmed, a warrior who had made himself beautiful for his own death. He went to that death gratefully – arms open in an embrace even as he threw himself upon Kai's spear, a smile across his face that trembled only briefly as the spear ran him through.

The Votadini saw it too. A shiver of fear passed through them, and the horses were faltering, stumbling, twisting away, the charge breaking apart even as the raiders rolled over them like a wave, leaping up to drag the Votadini from the saddles, swarming underneath to gut and hamstring the horses. Some of them were crushed beneath the hooves, others spitted upon the spears. But not enough.

Only Kai's horse kept him alive, fighting and biting and stamping away – old as she was, she had known many battles, raised to be a killer of men. And, like the men she faced, she was not afraid to die.

'Forward! Push through, push through!' Kai screamed, as he put his horse to flight and hoped that the others might follow.

A stumbling retreat as he made for the trees – the stink of horse sweat in the air, the screams of the dying sounding in his ears as he waited for the cold feel of iron against his skin, as he fought his way towards the light that flowed through the trees, that led the way out to open country beyond.

And Kai was almost there, so close as to almost be able to reach out and touch that place of safety, when the spear struck home.

His horse should have seen the danger, but she was half blinded, blood pouring from a cut above her eye, and she did not see the man in time. A warrior who came from Kai's left, so close that Kai could have leaned forward and touched his cheek, a man who seemed to move so slowly and yet Kai was slower still, lifting and swinging his sword with all the clumsiness of a man in the frozen moment of a dream.

Yet all at once, the world spun back into motion. The spear quick and biting, a tremor running through Kai, a hot flow that poured down his legs like a river in flood. A wound that he could not yet feel, and Kai felt a beautiful calm descend upon him. Not a question of whether he would live or die, not now – only the hope that he might lead some of his people to safety. That the giving of his life might mean something.

He brought the sword down upon the man who had killed him, watching the raider roll and break beneath the hooves. And he was out, then, out and free. The light bright and blinding against his eyes as he broke once more into the open country, leaving the forest behind as a waking man escapes a nightmare.

Kai let the horse gallop for a moment, let her taste of life and freedom – let himself taste of it too, that joy that every Sarmatian knew in a ride across open country. He was grateful to feel it, one last time. For still he could feel the blood running down his body, so much of it that he knew his wound must be a mortal one.

It took all the courage he had to look down and see where he was wounded – not at the belly or the back, nor the secret place inside the thigh where the lifeblood flowed like a river. He ran his hands over his skin, waiting for the fingers to catch upon an open cut, to feel the press and flow of the blood. He could find nothing. Then he lifted his gaze higher, and he saw at last where the blood was coming from.

The goat he had taken in the raid, still trussed across the peak of his saddle. He saw the blood trickling from its mouth, the blank eyes that stared sightlessly up at the sky, the crimson wave that marked the wool like dye. It had taken the spear for him, the way heroes gave their lives for those that they loved.

A moment of merry, mad laughter, to know that he would live, spared by a goat. Until Kai looked back over his shoulder, and felt the laughter die upon his lips as quickly as it had come.

He had heard hoofbeats behind him, and had hoped to see many of his companions there. But it was only the echo of his own, ringing like mockery from the cliffs. Of the dozen men he had led, only he remained.

And those men in the forest – Kai wanted to believe that

they had been bandits or raiders, some cult of the Selgovae driven death-mad by the prophecy of a dream-reader. But in his heart, he knew who they were. An enemy he had thought destroyed five years before.

The Painted People.

3

It was dusk by the time that Kai returned to the Votadini.

A frighteningly slow journey, on an exhausted horse that shook and trembled and sweated as the battle fever left it. For all he knew, the deepening shadows of dusk might have been teeming with the Painted People, and each turn of the wind threatened to bring with it the sound of war cries, bowstrings, arcing spears, the thunder of hooves. But on the long path back home, through the hills and towards the western shoreline, there was nothing but the wind to be heard. Until at last, with the sun almost fully fallen from the sky, Kai heard something new.

First, there was the sound of the sea, the whisper and crash of the waves breaking over and over again. And then a moment later, mingling with the call of the water and the cry of the gulls, he heard music.

The Votadini had hidden their camp well, concealed in a sheltered inlet. The cookfires smouldered gently, and what smoke they offered was carried away by the endless wind to be hidden in the mist of the sea. And so it was that Kai heard them before he saw them – the voices of the Votadini, raised in song. The restless chants of death and rebirth, the half-forgotten hymns of their gods. Old music, old as the hills and the heather, all sung in a language only half familiar, in a tongue that was not his own.

But there were other songs there that he knew all too well, Sarmatian songs that he had first heard upon the eastern steppe. There were bright lays of reckless heroism ringing in the air – a dying king's sword cast into water, a tree of golden apples that might change a woman into a man, a quest to a city below the sea. He heard too the sweet sad songs with which the Sarmatians remembered their dead, the music that spoke of the darkness and dust and the half-life that lay beyond the grave. He had taught the Votadini those songs over the long years of exile, so that when he closed his eyes about the fires at night, he might, just for a moment, imagine himself back upon the steppe of the east. That he might, if only in dreams, find his way home once more.

And then, as though some spell had taken him back to the beautiful steppe, from the darkness a voice called to him in the tongue of the Sarmatians – a woman's voice, offering Kai the first half of a proverb: 'Though our lives be short...'

'Let our fame be great,' Kai answered, finishing the saying. And from the shadows, a rider came forward to welcome him home.

Under the light of the moon she had a face that might have been a mirror to his own – sharp high cheekbones, thick black hair close-cropped to her scalp, and cold grey eyes. A smile upon her lips, quick and shy and oddly crooked, as though it were a gesture half practised, learned through mimicry. Even in that half-light, it would have taken a stranger but a moment to see the resemblance between Kai and Laimei, to know them for brother and sister.

'I should have run you through,' she said, tapping the spear in her hand, 'to answer the challenge so slowly.' Laimei's eyes darted across the horse that nodded with weariness, the gutted goat on Kai's saddle. Her gaze at last came to rest upon Kai's spear, the blade darkened and bloody. 'The others?' she said.

Silent, Kai shook his head.

'Not like you to walk into an ambush,' she said.

'I heard the warning of a god,' he said, 'but I could not make the others listen.'

'It was the Novantae, come in search of their herd?'

'No,' said Kai. 'They came on us in the woods in the Dùin valley, outside of Novantae lands.'

'Who were they?'

Kai did not answer for a time. In his heart, he knew the truth of what he had seen, amongst the empty eyes and twisting tattoos, in the careless way those men had fought and died. Yet even so, it seemed ill luck to speak it aloud. He could only bring himself to speak in a riddle, and let her voice the true answer.

'Men of many tribes, and none,' he said at last. 'Of those who belong in the north, but who came once to the south. Men whom we have killed many times, but who will always rise again to fight once more.'

'The Painted People,' she said, without hesitation, for she had always been so much braver than him.

'It is so,' Kai answered. 'I had hoped never to see them again, but it is so.'

As he spoke those words, he thought to see a familiar look on her face – a wolfish smile, joy at the thought of a battle soon to come against a fearful adversary. For she had been a great hero amongst the Sarmatians, and she had earned herself the fearsome war name of 'the Cruel Spear'. She lived for battle, and had always hurried towards death with a champion's careless indifference.

But there was no smile upon her face now, none of the champion's joy in anticipation of a battle soon to come. Only a sudden stillness to her, a dimming of the light in her eyes, her breath held a moment too long. If he had not known her so well, he would have thought her afraid.

'Come,' she said abruptly, turning her horse back towards the sound of the songs and the sea. 'You must bring this news to Mor.' And together, they rode down to the beach where the Votadini had made their home.

For all the music that filled the air, it was no joyful encampment that they came to. A site chosen for concealment and not comfort – boggy ground with only a distant and brackish stream for fresh water, a bank of earth that hid the Votadini from sight but did little to protect them from the wind and the rain that came from the west, and all about them the men and women moved with the hurried, restless look of a people far from their home.

For Kai and Laimei, raised as nomads upon the steppe far to the east, a wanderer's life was all that they had known. They would think nothing of passing a year without sleeping in the same place twice, and they would feel their gods and their ancestors guiding them from the stars above in every place that they went to. But for the Votadini, this way of life was not by choice. Their people bonded with the land, generation after generation. The favour of the gods they earned through a long, careful courtship with one particular river, a forest whose trees became as family, a mountain that watched the Votadini for a century before the spirit within chose to speak its secrets. Five years before, they had been driven from their homes by the Romans, and so now they travelled in terrible silence, lost and unguided, a people whose gods no longer spoke to them.

In those five years, the Votadini had tried many times to make a new home. First they had gone to the high hillsides of the inland country, raising goats on the bleak mountainsides until blight took the herd and the bitter winter drove them down. They had spent some time by a great loch, until a Selgovae war party slew half their number and drove them away. Now to the coast they went, though they knew no art of ship or sea. They went there without hope, like a starving animal that wanders away from the herd, seeking its own private place to die.

And yet here they still stood – the proud Votadini. Children played freely, running from campfire to campfire with branches in their hands, pretending to be warriors. The women gathered close in kinship, tending the herds and the cooking fires, laughing and singing together. Only the men seemed truly defeated, sitting sullenly with dull spears in their hands and pondering their shame.

At the sight of those people, Kai pulled at the reins of his horse, bringing it to a stop. 'I do not know how to face them,' he whispered. 'I return alone. It is a shameful thing.'

A hiss of irritation from Laimei. 'We shall face them together,' she said simply. 'And you did what was needful.'

'And what was that?'

She nodded to the dead goat on his saddle. 'You brought back food,' she said, with a champion's coldness, 'and fewer mouths to feed.'

Kai made no answer. He could see that it was too late to turn aside, to try to slip into the camp unnoticed. Already they were rising and gathering from the fires, walking forward with shuffling steps. The kin of those that Kai had left behind, had left to die.

Comhnall's wife was there, looking upon Kai's face and receiving a silent answer to her unspoken question. She might have been a carved statue of grief then, and a part of Kai could not believe she would ever move again. Another man laughed at first to see Kai return alone, as though the Sarmatian had told a particularly fine joke, until that laughter twisted into weeping, into a keening cry that echoed from the cliffs around them, the stone repeating that cry back to him in hollow mockery. And there were others who merely looked at Kai and nodded once, eyes dull, and gave no more sign of grief than that. They were a people grown used to loss by now.

Laimei went amongst them then, slipping from the saddle to offer some champion's blessing to the broken and the grieving. And so Kai went alone through the camp of the Votadini, past sputtering cookfires and people huddled together against the cold and the dark. He made his way down to the beach itself, where a single figure waited for him – a shadow in the darkness, leaning back from a dying fire.

'May I swallow your evil days, Mor,' said Kai, offering the old Sarmatian greeting.

'And I yours.' A shadowed hand swept towards the fire. 'Sit, and tell your story, and we shall share what little bounty we have.'

When Kai sat down, he saw there was little indeed for the chieftain to gift to him – a few mouthfuls of a hare stew, a single gulp of heather beer. But even so, Kai felt some strength returning, nourished more by Mor's presence than by the meagre fare.

'A poor feast for a chieftain to offer a champion,' Mor said, 'but it must do well enough.'

'I do not feel a champion today,' Kai answered.

'Indeed. The spirits of the dead walk with you.'

Kai shivered. 'Do you see them around me?' he asked.

A rasping laugh answered him. 'Oh no, no, I do not have that art. But I know they are there, nonetheless. Come, tell me of how they died, so that they may rest a little easier.'

And so Kai told him of the dead, and of the living too. Of the whispering god that had tried to warn him, of the men in the forest who did not fear to die.

The chieftain leaned forward as Kai spoke, letting the light of the fire play upon his face – a face marked with laughter and not with age, though Kai knew the man must have passed more than fifty summers. Still he had his red hair, lined a little with silver here and there, as when the fire of a forge burns so hot as to turn almost white. Some of the Votadini whispered of witchcraft that spared him the cruelty of ageing, but Kai thought it his spirit alone that kept Mor young: a restless spirit that had too much to do upon the earth to age so soon, who would need two lifetimes to accomplish all that he wished for. Some chieftains held their place through brute strength and a steady spear, others through omen and heritage. For this man, Mor of the Votadini, it was the sense of luck and the joy of life that earned his place as their leader, undiminished by the hard years of exile.

Kai told him everything – almost everything. For when he had finished at last, and Mor had stared for some time into the fire, the chieftain said: 'And what is it that you are afraid to speak of?'

'I can hide nothing from you, it seems.'

'It was once said that it was my gift,' Mor said, 'to see the hearts of men.'

'No.'

'No?'

'Your gift,' said Kai, 'is that you are gentle with the secrets you find there.'

Mor clapped his hands, threw back his head, and laughed. 'Oh, that is kind of you to say. And it is true, I hope.' He leaned forward once more. 'So tell me this secret of yours and I promise I shall handle it kindly.'

Kai looked down at his hands – the blood and dirt scored deep into the lines, marking him like tattoos. 'It was not the Novantae who we fought in the forest,' he said. 'Nor was it the Selgovae. It was the Painted People.'

The smile dimmed on Mor's face. 'I had hoped that we had seen the last of them,' he said. 'But I knew, in my heart, that it was not so.' He cast a glance around the encampment at the hollow cheekbones of the children, the empty places around the campfires where ghosts kept the living company, the fear with which the sentries looked out upon the darkness. All of the signs of a dying, hunted people.

'What shall we do?' Kai asked.

Mor fed twigs to the dying fire for a time and did not answer, his eyes tracing over the leaping flames. At last, he said: 'We cannot run from them – we can barely stay away from the other tribes of the northlands. And so we must fight them. And we cannot fight them alone.'

'You cannot mean—'

'Not the Romans, Kai. I shall not go to them unless I have to.' Mor cast the last piece of wood into the fire. 'We shall go to the Novantae, the Selgovae. To any other tribe of the northlands who will stand with us against the Painted People.'

Kai shook his head. 'We raid their cattle; they hunt us like wolves. There can be no friendship between us.'

'How long did you feud with your sister?' Mor asked quietly.

Kai turned his head and looked back to the camp of the Votadini. He could see her shadow there, pacing back and forth, restless as a hound for the hunt. 'Ten years,' he said.

And it was true – it had been a feud marked by the blood of their father, that had festered and grown for nearly a decade, and such things were rarely ended amongst his people except with a killing. Yet they had found a miracle of forgiveness, even a wary kind of love, in that exile north of the Wall.

'You hated each other, and now you fight side by side once more,' the chieftain said. 'So it shall be with the Novantae, and the others.'

'Perhaps,' said Kai. 'If they believe that they can win.'

'Why should they not? The Painted People are fearsome, but they have been defeated before. We broke them, in the battle beneath the Wall.'

Kai shook his head. 'There was something different to them, out in the forest. They did not fight like any man I have fought before.' And again, he looked out towards the shadow of his sister. 'They fought like she does.'

'You think something has changed?'

'I do.' A coldness danced across Kai's skin. 'There was something else I saw,' he said. 'In the woods where they

33

ambushed us, something had been dug from the ground. Do you know what that might be?'

And as Kai spoke those words, something changed in Mor.

Kai had heard a tale of the Votadini, told about the fire at night. Of a hero, who had travelled to the land of the Unseen Court to take a wife amongst the spirits who lived there. He was blessed with eternal life so as to be a fitting husband to his spirit wife, as long as he never let his feet touch the earth of the mortal realm. But one day that hero fell from his horse, and as his skin kissed earth, all of those years came upon him at once.

So it was, it seemed, with Mor. A trick of the fire and shadow, no doubt, but it was as though the lines of laughter spread like spiderwebs across his face, the fiery hair whitening beneath the light of the moon – and then he was himself once more, his head bright red and his skin unmarked. A decade of years came and went in a single beating of the heart.

'Do you know what was buried there?' Kai said again.

Mor made no answer at first. He leaned forward and blew upon the embers of the fire – they caught, flaring and sparking back into life once more, before fading into the darkness. 'I may know,' he said at last. 'But I cannot speak of it yet.'

'Why?'

'Because if it is true,' Mor said softly, 'there is no hope left for us. And still, I want to believe that there is hope. Do not take it away from me – not yet.'

In the distance, the songs fell silent. It seemed the Votadini could sing no longer – perhaps they too found their hopes fading with the dying of the fires.

Mor's hand closed about Kai's, lifting him to his feet. And back at the camp of the Votadini, the others were rising too – grey-faced with grief, clutching their empty stomachs, yet still they rose together. For always after the song came the dancing. No matter how hard the day had been, the Votadini always ended it in a dance.

As he went back to join them, Kai tried to forget himself in those now familiar steps of a dying people – in the touch of a hand, the stamp of a foot, a whirling turn through a circle of his companions. But at every pause in the dancing he found his gaze drawn to the south.

For somewhere distant, out there in the night, was the great Wall of stone he had abandoned five years before. And somewhere south of that Wall, the friend and the lover he had left behind – Lucius and Arite. He could only hope that they were well, and fear that they were not.

Another hand clutching at his – Laimei was there, always so sure of her movements on the battlefield, yet so clumsy and hesitant in the dance, seeking him to help guide her. And he rejoined the Votadini at her side and sought to leave his grief behind him, to let himself be held close by his people and forget the past in those endless, looping steps of the dance.

He told himself that the danger was here, in the northlands. He told himself that the battle would be won or lost here, and that it could not touch those friends he had lost, south of the Wall.

He could not know how wrong he was.

4

It was a lonely duty, to stand guard upon the Wall at night.

That unbroken line of stone stretched from one sea to another, east to west, a pale garrotte cutting across the land. Upon it, countless sentries stared north, ever watchful over that edge of an Empire, that border between one world and another. In the past, the Painted People had come from the northlands in great numbers – burning, pillaging, killing. Yet for five years there had been no more to see than the occasional loping shadow of a wolf, or the sudden white flash of an owl. Upon those high ramparts, the wind howled and echoed as though the air itself sought to pluck the sentries from the Wall and dash them against the ground, and so the sentries did little more than huddle in their cloaks and stamp their feet, glancing to the east from time to time to pray for the coming of the dawn.

That night, two men looked out from the western tower of Cilurnum, the Fort of the River and Pool. They were men who might have been brothers to Kai and Laimei, Sarmatian warriors in service to Rome, bow-legged from a life in the saddle and cursing the cold west wind. They did not speak, and the only sounds were that bitter wind and the rushing whisper of the river that ran beneath them. Their silence was a courtesy, allowing each man the privacy of his dreams. For if they half closed their eyes and looked upon the shadowed landscape, they could, for a moment, imagine that they looked upon their homes, the steppe of the east. The place that they longed for, and knew they would never see again.

But that night, the silence was broken.

It was not the howl of a wolf or the crack of distant thunder that shook the Sarmatians from their idle dreaming. It was the sound of hooves beating upon the heather – a lone rider, coming in from the darkness.

In the deepest part of the night the veil between worlds was said to draw thin, and for a moment it seemed that rider might be a phantom from the Otherlands, bearing some fearsome message from the dead. But soon enough the Sarmatians could see him – not a ghost but a man upon a Roman horse that galloped towards the Wall, heedless of the darkness and uncertain ground.

The rider did not slow as he rode towards the fort, did not answer the challenges that rang out from above him. He rode until he was in the shadow of the Wall, a trembling hand reaching out to touch the stones as though he could not believe them to truly be there. And that rider was speaking to them then, in a hoarse whisper – it was not a watchword of Rome, one of the passphrases with which soldiers of the Emperor greeted one another. He simply said: 'Please.'

The Sarmatians on the Wall gave no answer. Silent, one

of them lit a torch from the brazier beside him, and cast it down. The fire flickered and hissed in the softly falling rain, but it offered enough light for them to see, at the bottom of the Wall, something from their nightmares waiting there for them.

The rider was almost naked, his skin ghost pale. His thighs were lashed to the saddle with leather thongs, a Roman helmet tied mockingly onto his head. The rest of the arms and armour had been stripped away – rich prizes in iron and trophies of victory for whoever had done this to him. He was bowed forward, exhausted, clinging to the neck of his horse in a weary, loving embrace. And in the light of torch, they could see the flanks of the horse painted crimson in blood, the sign of some terrible wound that they could not yet see.

The wounded man placed trembling hands against the neck of his horse and began, slowly, to lift himself tall in the saddle. The men high on the Wall saw his face first, saw where his lips and tongue had been chewed to pieces in his pain. They saw a scattering of blood upon the chest and the imploring hands that he lifted up towards the Wall, yet still they could not see his true wound.

It was only when the man leaned back until he was almost lying flat upon the horse, when he laid his hands upon his thighs and encircled his terrible injury, that the Sarmatians saw what had been done to him.

'Please,' he said. 'Help me.'

The man did not live beyond the changing of the guard. Little did he speak through his ruined lips, his mind broken by the pain he had suffered. But still, it was a clear message he brought back from the north – one part written in ruined flesh, the rest spoken in a few desperate, feverish words.

And now a Sarmatian messenger took those words south, travelling down the iron roads. He passed through the hills and the heather that the Brigantes called home, where hawks dived for the hares that scattered and ran across the open moorland, and where shepherds guided their herds over the hillsides and dreamed of the different lives that they might have lived. He went further, leaving scattered farms and steadings in his wake, riding past the fields where hard-faced men and women scratched a living from the soil, until at last he came to a place where one river met another.

Once it had been an empty, sacred place, where the gods of the rivers might commune together. Now it was a great Roman fortress that ruled the northlands, a place called Eboracum.

In many far-flung corners of the Empire, such outposts were a poor sight indeed – the Legions shambling and filthy, stinking of wine, living only to loot and rape their way through the province they were ordered to protect. But not in Eboracum. The legionaries stood upon the ramparts with the proud look of soldiers, not the wolfish manner of brigands. The merchants bartered openly in the streets, rather than scuttling about in fear of one gang or another. And outside the fort, upon the parade ground, there were Sarmatian horsemen moving in the endless dance of drill and practice.

The messenger came within those walls of stone, to the

principia at the heart of the fort. His journey ended there, with him standing to attention before the man who kept the fragile peace, here at the edge of the world: Lucius Artorius Castus, Legate of the North.

He did not seem a fearsome warleader, not at first. For though he had the reddish-gold hair that was said to be the mark of the Roman princes of old, and though his face was marked with the scars of many battles, his eyes were lined with laughter and sorrow both, and there was a gentle cast to his face that did not speak of tyranny. One might have thought Lucius some poet or philosopher, better suited to a life spent debating in the Forum than fighting upon the battlefield, until he lifted his head and looked closely upon the messenger – his eyes were patient and attentive, but they were cold too, and it was as though they somehow belonged to a man from another place, another time. A killer's eyes which had found their way, through spell or by curse, into the face of a poet.

'Where was the man from?' was all that Lucius said, when the messenger had given his report.

'From Trimontium, sir. Our northernmost outpost beyond the Wall.'

Lucius laid his hands upon the map before him, a single tap of a finger marking the place bearing that name. 'Our scouts have confirmed it?'

'Yes, sir. It is destroyed. No trace of the garrison.'

A sudden curling of Lucius's fingers upon the map, as though he recoiled in pain from that place. 'I said to the Governor that we should leave those old forts to the weeds and the wolves,' he said. 'Those men should never have been there.' The messenger before him shifted on his feet, uncertain.

Lucius gave a weary smile. 'No answer is expected to that, do not worry. I shall not make you speak any treason today.'

'Thank you, sir.'

Lucius said nothing for a time. It was a familiar story that this messenger had brought him, the oldest story of border country – long seasons of uncertain peace, where the local tribes gathered in the shadows at night and whispered their hate like a prayer, and then a fort burned or a patrol ambushed. The old wounds of the feud breaking open, the blood running free once more.

But there was something in this story that was different.

'You are certain of his wound?' Lucius asked. 'That it was not taken in battle?'

'No, sir. No other marks of war upon him. They gelded him like a troublesome stallion, and sent him to us.'

'And he could not say who had done it to him?'

'No, sir.'

And there it was. For all the tortures the local tribes might put a Roman captive to, Lucius had never heard of such a thing as that. For each of them was particular in their cruelties, just as the Romans were. The Damnonii chose to offer their captives to fire, the Brigantes raised them on stakes, the Iceni hanged them from the tall yew trees. And a memory came unbidden then, of when Lucius had seen such wounds before. Far to the east, upon the steppe. A cruel death given at the hands of a great champion of the Sarmatians.

Lucius looked once more at the messenger who stood before him. 'I think that there is something that you keep from me,' he said.

The Sarmatian started, as though struck. 'There is,' he answered at last.

'Why is that?'

'I am afraid to speak it, sir.'

Death it would have been, to speak to any other Roman commander that way. A legate's duty, to execute a man at the slightest hint of cowardice or a lie. Such was the way the Romans held their discipline, such was the way in which they had conquered half the world. And yet Lucius, to his cost, had won the loyalty of these men with love, a love he now saw reflected in the Sarmatian's eyes.

And so Lucius did not call to his guards to shackle the messenger in iron, to take him to be crucified before the gates of the fort as a warning to others. He simply smiled wearily, patiently, and leaned forward. 'What is your name?' he said.

'Tasius, sir.'

'You bear the Hand of Fire?'

Tasius rested his glove upon his cuirass – an insignia carved there, five fingers of fire reaching up into the sky. 'Yes sir,' he said. 'I fought with you at the Battle of the Burning Wall, five years ago. It is my honour to wear the mark that I have earned.'

'And why is it that you keep a secret from me?'

'It shall wound you to hear it, sir.' Tasius hesitated. 'And it is spoken, amongst our people, that you are much wounded already.'

'I am a warrior as you are,' Lucius said. 'And so I would rather take the quick wound than the slow – wouldn't you?'

'Yes, sir.' Tasius licked his dry lips, and said: 'A last report came back from the fort, before it was burned. And it said they had seen signs of the Votadini nearby.'

Lucius made no answer for a time. The name of that tribe

hung in the air – a living, evil thing. For the Votadini had fought with him against the Painted People, five years before. And in return, at Rome's command, Lucius had burned their lands and driven them from their home. And though it had been done to save his Sarmatians, of all the evil Lucius had done in war, he could think of nothing more shameful than that.

Little wonder that Kai and Laimei should have deserted him five years before, rather than take part in that act. Little wonder too that they might return now for revenge.

'There has been no sign of the Painted People?' said Lucius, almost hopeful as he spoke.

'No sir,' Tasius answered. 'Not for many years.'

No longer did Tasius stand before him to attention in the manner of the Roman army. For a moment, as the Sarmatian shifted his weight and hooked his thumbs through his sword belt, all sense of rank disappeared. They were brothers of the steppe once more, as though they were still in that place that made all men equal. 'If it comes to it,' he said, 'you need have no fear for the loyalty of the Sarmatians. We have no care for Kai – it would be our delight to hunt the deserter. And our pleasure to test ourselves against the Cruel Spear.' Tasius's head fell then, and he stared at the ground. 'But I fear it shall not please you. I know you wish to keep the peace, sir. But I fear it is already broken.'

And then Tasius seemed to remember himself once more – snapping back to attention and offering a salute that, even after five years in service to Rome, still seemed clumsy, unnatural. Like a child aping his father with a gesture that was not his own.

'Thank you, Tasius,' Lucius said. 'You shall be well rewarded.'

'Thank you, sir.' And in Tasius's eyes, a silent question.

Lucius answered it: 'If we go north, Tasius, you shall come with me.' He sighed heavily. 'But there is someone I must speak to first.'

Tasius wrinkled his nose in disgust. 'The Governor, sir? He is a coward and a fool.'

'Oh no,' Lucius answered, almost laughing at the other man's contempt. 'I go to see someone much wiser than that.'

'Arite?'

'Just so.'

And at that, Tasius nodded. 'A good thing, sir,' he said, offering his clumsy salute once more. 'I am glad that you go to see her.'

'Is that so?' said Lucius.

'Of course.' And Tasius was smiling then. 'It is always said amongst our people that it is bad luck to go to war, unless a woman thinks it wise.'

Out into the fort Lucius went, bodyguards trailing him like shadows cast by firelight. He made his way through the streets of Eboracum, answering the salutes of legionaries and auxiliaries, until he passed through the gates and over the river, and entered the *vicus*.

For there, on the other side of the water, lay the sprawling, chaotic township that sprang up in the wake of every Roman outpost. It was a fickle, changeable thing that moulded itself to the desires of the fort from which it grew. In Vindolanda, the men longed for nothing but strong drink, and so the ripe sharp scent of wine could be smelled a mile away. In Coria, for reasons that none could say, the soldiers were vain, and so perfume shops and jewellers clung close to the walls of the fort, vying for the silver of the Legion – even the poorest girl of Coria wore shining glass beads at her wrists and twisted necklaces of gold around her neck, gifts from one of her lovers. Here, in Eboracum, it seemed the men longed for women, and for music. From every corner came the syncopated beating of a drum, or the plucked strings of a harp. Within every alleyway lurked an exhausted woman, the kohl thick-painted around tired eyes and a tunic slipped from a shoulder as she waited to ply her trade.

Lucius did not go chasing the sound of music through the streets of the *vicus*, and nor did he head to one of the darkened alleys where a down-on-his-luck soldier might find the flesh he sought for a scattering of silver. Instead, Lucius made his way to the edge of the *vicus*, to a house upon the banks of the river that looked out into the open country. The kindest home he might offer to a Sarmatian woman who came from a land without cities or towns, walls of stone or monuments to the gods. A place where she might look upon the meadowlands, half close her eyes, and imagine that she was free.

Arite was there when he arrived, looking out towards the golden sun as it sank towards the horizon. The sunlight fell upon white scars on her hands and cheeks, old wounds of battle that she wore proudly as trophies. She was one of the fairer Sarmatians, braids of gold and silver hair falling about her shoulders – a little more silver there than had been visible before, or so Lucius thought; more than had been earned by the passage of the years he had known her.

She glanced back over her shoulder – something must have given away his thoughts, for she said: 'Grief makes old men of us all. That is our saying upon the steppe. You look old too, you know.'

'You do not, Arite,' he answered, 'save for that silver in your hair.' And it was true, no idle flattery. Arite still moved with the grace and strength of a young warrior new to the warband.

She waved a hand in the air, as though parrying the compliment, and said: 'What do your soldiers say, when you tell them that you come here?'

'The Romans think you a witch, a seer, or a dream-reader. The stories change depending on who I speak to, and how much wine they have had. The Sarmatians think you are my lover.' He smiled at her then and said: 'A rare thing, for both our peoples to be wrong.'

'Not so rare, I think. For men to be fools, and not see the truth of things.' She hesitated, tucked a braid behind one ear. 'And I think that I cannot blame them. For I myself do not know why you come here.'

'I value your counsel,' said Lucius.

'Oh, I have no doubt of that. But I think I remind you of much that you wish to forget.'

A blur of motion from the corner of his eye – that was all Lucius saw at first, and a lifetime upon the battlefield had him reaching for the sword at his side. But it was only a child dashing from the house, long dark hair trailing behind the boy like a banner. And in his hand was a branch and not a blade, a war cry singing from his lips as he struck down low, almost at Lucius's ankles.

A clucking of Arite's tongue as she strode forward, hands reaching towards the boy. But rather than taking the branch from him and cursing him for startling a guest, she caught the child by the wrist and patiently corrected the swing of the cut – he had only half turned his wrist, and a shield would have turned the blade aside.

'A little young you are, Akkas,' Lucius said, 'to be swinging a sword around. Even a sword of wood, like that one.'

Akkas grinned at him, gap-toothed. 'No!' he cried out, before he charged out to the riverbank, practising that same cut over and over and over again.

'The boy is right,' Arite said. 'It is never too young to teach the killing art. Sarmatians ride before they can walk, know how to kill before they know anything else.'

'He shall be a warrior, then? Like his father?'

'And his mother,' Arite said absently.

'It is what you want for him?'

'What else is there?'

A silence came then. Lucius had buried all his children many years before, lost to the Antonine plague, and he knew that Arite had buried all of hers back upon the steppe – they had been lost to famine and fever and to Roman spears alike, all save this one, a child born against all the odds. It should have been a joy to look upon him, and yet for Lucius there was always an ache about the heart. For the child looked so much like his father. So much like Kai.

'This is no idle visit, I think,' said Arite. 'You have a grave look about you. The kind you always wear before a battle.'

'Our forts north of the Wall are burned, our soldiers killed.' Lucius hesitated, and then he said: 'And there are rumours that speak of the Votadini returning to their old lands.'

A shiver passed through her. 'Only rumours?'

'For now. Yet somehow I believe them.' Lucius looked down at his hands. 'I had hoped that the peace might hold, and that they would never come back. A foolish hope, it seems.'

She laughed then, a harsh and bitter sound. 'Peace, you call it? Burning their lands and driving them north. A Roman kind of peace, that is. It would be no surprise for them to come looking for revenge, only that it took them so long to do it.'

'You think it is them, then?'

'How can I say?' she answered. 'If I knew Kai's heart better, he would still be here, would he not?'

Lucius made no answer. In silence, together they watched Akkas practising the looping strokes of the sword – silhouetted now, where he stood on the bank with the falling sun behind him, like one of the shadow puppets Lucius had seen in the marketplaces of Rome, where lantern and cloth made men into giants and heroes. No doubt that was what Akkas thought himself to be, there beside the water, for in the old stories it was always beside river and sea that the heroes did their bravest deeds. It was always beside the river and sea that they met their deaths.

'I wonder if you want to believe it is Kai and the Votadini,' Arite said at last. 'Then you might have cause to go north of the Wall and speak with him once more.'

'If I were to go there,' Lucius answered, 'I would have to hunt him, and kill him.'

'It would be over, at least,' she said. 'You might be free of him.'

'And you?'

She tilted her head to the side, fixed him with a steady swordsman's gaze – a reminder of the warrior she had once been. 'Unlike you,' she said. 'I am free of Kai already.' She sighed. 'Do you ask for my counsel on what to do? Or for my forgiveness, if you go north to kill him?'

'Both, perhaps.'

She did not speak again for a time. He watched her trace the pattern of an old sword scar between thumb and forefinger, as though seeking wisdom from the wound.

'You are no coward,' she said at last. 'You shall do what you must.'

'I do not wish him dead.'

She shook her head. 'Still, it seems, you have not learned to think as a Sarmatian. No braver death than in battle – Kai shall thank you for a good death, if you are the one who gives it to him. It shall not change what he thinks of you. That Kai loves you, I have no doubt. It shall be true even as you open his throat.'

'That Kai loves you, I know *that* for certain.'

'Perhaps,' she allowed, a bitterness in her voice. 'Though would he not have stayed, if that were so?'

The silence returned. Many times before had they sat beside that riverbank, watching Akkas play. Sometimes speaking, many times saying nothing at all, merely tending their wounds of the heart in their own private ways. But it was there on that day, at last, that Lucius found the courage to ask a question that he never had before.

'Do you hate him?' said Lucius. 'For going across the Wall, and leaving you behind?'

Arite thought on this for a time. 'I do,' she said. 'Not that he went, but that he did not have the courage to tell me why. I do hate him for that. And you?'

'Yes,' Lucius whispered, the word spoken like a confession.

'And so you do not trust the rumours of the Votadini. Because you *want* them to be true.'

'Yes,' Lucius said once more.

'I do not think I can ever forgive him for abandoning us.' She hesitated. 'Could you?'

But there was no time for an answer – the boy charged back from the riverbank and hurled himself into Arite's arms, and she, laughing, held him up towards the sky.

There should have been joy in seeing them together, Arite and Akkas. The child was a miracle against all hope, a memory of love made flesh. And yet Lucius thought he saw something more of duty than of love in the way she tended to the child. For all the kindness that Arite showed the boy, she reminded Lucius of a sentry standing at his post, stamping his feet against the cold, waiting impatiently for the changing of the guard. There was something she had lost, some part of her that Kai had taken with him when he had gone north. Just as he had taken something from Lucius.

Many times, Lucius had imagined the fate of the friend he had lost – a thousand lives given to Kai, in thought and in dreams. In his mind he had seen Kai herding sheep across the rolling hillsides and singing the old travelling songs of the Sarmatians, or standing triumphant on a bloody battlefield as a victorious champion with the sunlight shining.

In his vindictive, lonely moments, Lucius had seen Kai in a rain-sodden bothy, coughing bloody phlegm as a fever took him, or cut down in a feud over a woman. And as Lucius made his way back towards the fort in the deepening twilight, there was a longing then, such as he had not felt in many years – a longing to see Kai but once more, no matter what the cost.

A dangerous wish, he knew, the kind that the spiteful gods enjoyed and always sought to fulfil. For Lucius knew it would be death to one of them, if he and Kai were to meet again.

5

Upon the bank of a river, three riders sat upon their horses – Kai, Laimei, and Mor, the green truce leaves of holly and yew dulling the brightness of their spears.

Bonfires were lit beside them, the flames reflecting in the water as though it ran with liquid gold. Those fires were a gesture of trust, for the three of them to stand unguarded in that place and give that signal of light – a peace offering to the Novantae who might be watching from the other side of the water.

'Meet when the moon is high,' their message to the Novantae had said, but each man's eye saw such things differently. This was not to be a Roman meeting, where time might be measured in the running of sand through an hourglass or the gentle trickling of a water clock. And so Kai had no way of knowing whether the Novantae were late, or did not mean to come at all.

All that they could do was wait, and hope, and that was easier done by some than others. Laimei's horse tossed its head restlessly, pawed at the soft earth of the bank with one insistent hoof. And as if giving an answer to that gesture,

Laimei said: 'We shall be waiting all night. They will not come.'

'They will,' Mor said, as he traced a finger across the truce leaves on his spear.

'We raid their herds and drink of their rivers. They shall make no peace with us.'

'Peace?' Mor shrugged. 'Perhaps not. But they shall come and speak, at the very least. You do not know the Novantae as I do.'

She shook her head and spat upon the ground. One of Laimei's black moods was upon her, while Mor sat calm and even cheerful upon his shaggy-haired pony. Perhaps, Kai thought, that was why he had chosen her to stand there beside him – her darkness might make his light shine that much brighter.

The chieftain caught Kai studying him, and grinned in response. 'What is it you think of, Kai of the River Dragon?' he said.

'I wonder what my purpose is here,' Kai answered. He nodded towards his sister. 'She is the bloody spear you show the Novantae, and you are the hand of peace. What am I?'

'Perhaps something in between, or nothing at all,' Mor said. 'For I know that you have the touch of the gods upon you. Others may see it too, I think.'

'I would not call myself so lucky as that.'

'Oh, it is not a thing of fortune,' Mor said. 'Quite the opposite. The gods use you to turn the world, and it is a hard thing, to be their lever.' The chieftain's bright eyes dimmed for a moment. 'I knew that from the first moment I saw you.'

'The first time that I saw *you*,' Kai said, 'you rode a chariot – do you remember? An ancient thing, half rotted and worn nearly to splinters, that seemed likely to fall apart even as you rode it. Even so, it was a glorious thing to see.'

Laughter in the darkness. 'Yes,' Mor said, 'I remember. A relic of an older time, like me.'

'What happened to it?'

'Burned, the night we left our homelands behind,' Mor said, and he sighed wistfully to himself. 'A poor kingdom of heather and rain I had, but I did truly feel like a king when I rode in that chariot, or a hero from the Dawntime. I wish that we had not burned it.'

'Aye. But wishes are useless things.'

'No,' Mor answered at once. 'They tell the gods how we want to reshape the world. And sometimes the gods listen.' He looked down at the river, tracing patterns in the water with the tip of his spear. 'I have lost the lands of our ancestors,' he said. 'I may have doomed my people. But no, I do not wish that I had acted differently.' The spear swam up out of the water, and Mor fixed Kai with a testing gaze. 'And what of you? What do you wish for?'

A clutching feeling about the heart to hear those words spoken. A dozen forbidden wishes springing to Kai's lips, aching to be given voice. But there was no time to speak them. For then there was a soft rattle of metal and horn as Laimei shifted in the saddle, pointed her spear towards the darkness.

'Enough of this,' she said. 'They are here.' And as she spoke, from the darkness, three shadows came forward to greet them.

The first was Eacharn, chieftain of the Novantae – a squat, heavyset man, his grey hair falling about his shoulders like rain silvered by the moonlight and a chieftain's torc around his neck. The second rider was his son, sitting restless upon his horse with all the impatience of youth, and the third was a tall, proud-looking man, his arms so crisscrossed with scars and tattoos that, in the light of the fires, Kai could not tell where one began and the other ended. That scarred man stared at Laimei balefully, like a wild wolf who sees a leader from another pack.

A father, a son, and a champion – it was as though it were one of the stories that the bards liked to tell, where great heroes fought echoes of themselves. But those three had not come to the river alone.

For in the darkness beyond those three, the shadows teemed – the warband of the Novantae gathered there in great numbers, greater by far than the Votadini. Only the shallow river separated them, and the fragile custom of the truce.

Mor spoke first. 'My greetings to you,' he said, 'Eacharn of the Novantae.'

'I told you before,' the chieftain answered, 'that I would kill you if I saw you again, truce or no truce.'

'And yet you are here.' Mor tilted his head to the side. 'And you may speak my name in full – I am Mor of the Votadini. Our spears have been set against each other many times, yet we may still hold to the old courtesies.'

'Mor of the Votadini?' Eacharn snorted. 'Do you still have the right to that name? What are a people without a land to call their own? No more than a tick upon the head of a horse, sucking blood.'

And as those words echoed back into the darkness, a rattle of spears answered them. Mor stilled them at once with a lazy wave of his hand.

'You are angry at my people,' Mor said, 'for we take your

cattle and darken our spears with your blood. Yet the cattle raid has never been a thing of hate or shame. Not for those who raid, nor those who lose the cattle, if it is honestly won. We make our home, such as it is, in the marshes and the beaches and on the bare stones of the hills, in the places that are of no use to the Novantae. Our people may be enemies, but we do not need to hate one another. And I think there is another enemy that may concern us more. One that hunts men, not animals. One that hates us, and that we may hate together. The Painted People.'

This time, from behind Eacharn, it was Mor's words that drew an answer from those in the shadows. A whispering, echoing sound – the soft cries of grief that echo around funeral fires. And Mor nodded, as though in answer to those wordless cries. 'They have hunted your people too, it seems,' he said.

Eacharn glanced to his side, at the young man who looked so akin to him. 'They have,' he said. 'My first-born son led the warband against them before the last full moon. None of them returned.'

'Then we have a common enemy,' said Mor. 'They are strong. Too strong to face alone. But such a thing should be enough to end our feuding.'

A soft, echoing laugh answered him. 'Even when the Romans came, our tribes could not put aside their hatreds. We betrayed one another to them for the gifts of gold and silver. Why should it be any different now?'

'The Painted People were not always called that,' said Mor. 'Once, they were many different tribes – the Damnonii, the Venicones, the Taexali, and others whose names I do not know. They hated each other too, not so long ago. If they can stand together, why should we not do the same?'

At those words, Kai saw the champion of the Novantae lift his head at the promise of a glorious battle. But at once, the chieftain shook his head. 'It is a beautiful vision you have,' Eacharn said, 'one fit for the bards to sing of. Yet it is no use. You stood with the Romans to face them five years ago, and what did that bring you? Hunting other men's goats in land that is not yours.'

Mor made no answer for a time. He looked away, turning his face towards the caressing wind that blew from the west, one hand idly looping through the golden mane of his horse. He might have been a carefree wanderer, a bard in the wilderness seeking the whisper of a spirit that might gift him a song if he were proved worthy. Not a chieftain of a dying tribe, bargaining for the future of his people.

'I never thought,' Mor said at last, 'that the chieftain of the Novantae would not choose bravery. For what could be braver than trusting the open hand I offer you? What could be braver than facing an enemy who they say cannot be beaten?'

And Eacharn did smile then, cold and bitter. 'Oh,' he said, 'you speak like a horse trader with a lame stallion to sell. For all your trickster's words, I know what you hide from your companions. But you cannot hide it from me.'

'We must fight,' Mor said, 'or we shall die. And better to die together, with a chance of victory, than to die alone. Those are the paths that we may take.'

'No,' said Eacharn. 'There is another path for us.'

A voice from the darkness – a high, wailing sound that seemed to close Kai's throat like a ghostly, grasping hand.

He could not place the sound at first, and for all he knew it might have been the cry of some fell spirit that hunted in the darkness, one of those unseen monsters whose voice could stop a man's heart and steal his soul.

But then the sound came again – the cry of a baby, cold or hungry, that called out from the shadows beyond where the Novantae gathered. Hearing that sound, Eacharn's skin went pale, as white as the high moon that hung above them.

'You bring your warriors into the warband young, it seems,' Mor said softly.

'I shall not speak of this with you,' Eacharn whispered. And he reached forward and laid his spear fully into the river, let the running water begin to unwind and steal the truce leaves from the haft and the blade. 'We shall not set our spears against you, Mor, or hunt you in whatever cave or marsh you have chosen to call your home. But we shall not fight beside you.'

'I shall speak to the others. The Selgovae, the Epidii. Perhaps they shall see this dream, as I do. Perhaps they shall be braver.'

'No,' Eacharn answered, 'they shall not.' He shook his head. 'Go now, while this truce still holds. Before the war fever comes upon us, and these bright spears are darkened in your blood.'

Mor offered a bow from his saddle, plucked a truce leaf from his spear and cast it into the river below. And without another word, he turned away and rode back into the shadows. Laimei followed him, after one last contemptuous glare at the champion of the Novantae.

Kai should have gone with them, for he could feel the truce as though he held it in his hands, as delicate as a rotten twist of silk. But there was something else there too – once more the cold touch of a god upon his shoulder, telling him to linger in that place a moment longer.

The champion of the Novantae spoke then. 'You insult us,' he said, his voice hoarse and thick from long disuse, a man more used to trading strokes of the spear than words. 'You think we shall turn our backs to you first, on our own land? Go now, or die.'

'I mean no insult.' Kai dipped his head towards Eacharn and laid his hand upon his heart – an old gesture from the steppe, but perhaps it might still hold some meaning here on the other side of the world. 'There are things that a chieftain may not say to another chieftain,' he said. 'Words that a man of the Novantae will never speak to a man of the Votadini. But I am a Sarmatian. Their ancestors are not my ancestors. This land is not my land.' He hesitated. 'I think that there are words you long to speak, and you may speak them to me.'

The champion bristled, tossed his spear in the air to rest the haft in the palm of his hand, ready to throw. But he was stilled by a single word from his chieftain.

'Why?' said Eacharn.

'Because there are children in the shadows behind you.'

A shiver passed through Eacharn then, and it was as though he shook some mantle of kingship from his shoulders. It was a man before Kai then, and not a chieftain – a man who seemed lost and afraid, out there in the darkness.

Kai spoke again: 'I think that I know the path that you mean to choose.'

'What path is that?'

'The same one that my ancestors took,' Kai answered, 'or so the old stories say. They were the giant-slayers and god-killers. When they faced an enemy they could not defeat, they dug their own graves and threw themselves into them.'

A smile, then, from Eacharn. 'Better to choose where to dig one's own grave, yes?'

'Better to not have to choose at all.' Kai hesitated. 'It is not your warband out there behind you, is it? It is your whole tribe.'

'Yes,' said Eacharn. 'A shameful thing that I could not speak to Mor. For we are to become a placeless people, just as you are. We are to abandon the lands of our ancestors.'

'Where shall you go?'

'What does that matter to you?'

'Perhaps I may make certain our paths do not cross,' said Kai.

'Aye. There is wisdom in that.' Eacharn hesitated. 'We go south,' he said at last.

'There is no safe ground there. The Romans have made sure of that.'

'We shall go beyond the Wall.'

A moment of silence, and Kai found he could not look on Eacharn any longer. He turned his gaze to the river, still shining in the light of the fires – useless, even if it had been liquid gold, for what use was gold to doomed men?

'The Romans shall destroy you,' Kai said at last.

'I would rather face the Romans than what comes for us from the north,' Eacharn said. 'It is a better death they shall give us, than that we shall receive from the Painted People. That is the grave I choose to dig.'

'Why?'

'Nothing may stop them now,' Eacharn said. 'Because they have the Burning Cauldron.'

'What is that?' Kai asked.

The wind blew and caught Eacharn's cloak – some breath of a fey spirit, marking an omen. 'Ask Mor,' the chieftain said. 'He can tell you better than any man.' And Eacharn nodded towards Mor and Laimei – shadowy figures now, like those seen in dreams. 'Now go,' he said, 'and join the others. Do me that last courtesy.' Out into the darkness Eacharn stared, at the land he had been born in, a child raised to be a king. Perhaps it was the spirits of his ancestors he saw out there, silent shades who mouthed their grief and their shame at what he was about to do. 'I would like,' he said at last, 'for one more time, to feel like a king of these lands.'

One more truce leaf cast into the air, an offering, a gift, and a farewell, as the wind caught it up and held it suspended. And then Kai was away, spear thrust high in the air – a warrior's salute to the brave and the dead.

6

B elow Lucius's feet, the cold stone of the Wall. Before him,
shadowed by night, were the wild lands that lay beyond
the reaches of the Empire. As he looked out upon that view he
shivered with more than just the cold. He drew his cloak close
about himself, the softness of the wolf fur brushing against
his cheeks.

He had come to Cilurnum that morning. The Prefect of the
fort had greeted him with a crisp salute, offered him wine,
food, even women if he so desired, all that might be mustered
out here at the edge of the world. Lucius had merely asked
for the indulgence of an old soldier, to stand a watch upon
the Wall. The Prefect gaped in disbelief, but Lucius had held
firm in his desire.

Out before him now lay the darkness of the land beyond
the Wall, the shadows of the bracken moving gently in the
breeze like exhausted dancers at the end of the night. It was
a place that he had not seen for almost five years and yet,
even shrouded in darkness as it was, he could have described
every part of it. Gouge the eyes from his head, and he might

still speak of the curve of the hillside to the east, shaped like a woman's back. Or the way a copse of trees all tilted down towards the ground, bowed over by the wind like actors answering applause.

That wind blew hard from the north now. A swift-footed messenger from another world, the Sarmatians called it, and when it blew strong they sang as if in answer to it, seeking to drown out the evil whispers that it brought with it. But Lucius, standing his watch like the lowliest auxiliary, kept silent and listened. Perhaps somewhere on the wind, amidst the curses hurled down from the Novantae and the Selgovae and the Votadini towards the Romans on the Wall, was some message from Kai. Some whispered word, carried on the air, that might prevent the war to come.

Footsteps close by, the regular tap as the butt of a spear struck the ground, the slow, even tread of a sentry making his rounds. When Lucius turned to face that sentry he saw that it was Tasius who approached him, the Sarmatian who had come south bearing ill-fated news from the Wall.

'Do you know the watchword for the night, sir?' Tasius asked as he approached.

'I am afraid the Prefect forgot to tell it to me.'

'I should spear you through, in that case.' Tasius grinned at Lucius. 'Or should I spear the Prefect for forgetting to tell you?'

'You would kill your commander for me, if I asked you?'

Tasius shrugged. 'You are a legate and he is a prefect. Nothing matters more than rank for the Romans – this much I have learned. I shall do as you ask me to.'

'I think something more than rank matters to you.'

'Aye sir, it is so.' Tasius looked towards the north, squinting into the cold wind. 'May I ask why you stand a watch tonight, sir?'

Lucius blew upon his fingers, but it did not chase the numbness from them – there was only a fleeting sense of heat rolling across them before they were unfeeling once more. 'Soon,' he said, 'I will ask you and your companions to go to the north once more. To fight and die. And I shall not ask any of you to do what I would not do myself.'

Tasius grinned. 'Not even freezing upon the Wall for no good reason?'

'Not even that.'

'Have no fear, sir,' said Tasius. 'We shall follow wherever you lead us.'

A shiver then, and not from the cold. For of the five hundred men that Lucius had once commanded in that fort, scarce a hundred still lived – the rest were buried not a bowshot from where he stood. And how few of those hundred would live to see the end of their service to Rome? Time and time again, he had led the Sarmatians to death, and yet still they loved him for it.

'How fare the Sarmatians here?' Lucius said. 'Speak freely.'

Tasius scratched at his jaw, and thought for a time. 'They are good enough,' he said at last. 'A little soft. Save for a few cattle raids and border feuds, they have had little enough to keep them sharp. Yet the old ways still hold, for now. They practise and train – there is great competition to have the honour of serving in the Dance of the Horses each year.' He tapped the insignia upon his armour, the Hand of Fire grasping at the sky. 'There are few of us left who have fought in a true battle, but enough to teach the others what we know.' He looked out over the Wall, towards the north. 'They shall not fail you, on the hunt. They long for such a thing, more than anything.'

'And you?'

Tasius smiled wistfully. 'I long for the eastern steppe, and the wife that I left behind. To fight is a duty and not a love for me now. A proud duty, but even so...'

The words trailed off to silence, and there was an ache about the heart to hear them spoken. It might have been Kai speaking then, of that longing to go home, to the east and the steppe. For that had been the bargain made with the Sarmatians – twenty-five years they would give to Rome, and then they could go home once more. The promise Lucius had made, and that Rome had broken. Some scattering of Sarmatians might live long enough to earn their freedom. But they would never be allowed see their homes again.

With that thought in his mind, Lucius took one last look over the Wall, listened once more for a message carried upon the wind. And at last, there in the deepest part of the night, he was given such a message.

It was not a whisper carried on the wind, or the soft music of a distant player. It was a hiss like a snake, a shadow tearing through the air – that was all the warning Lucius had. A gasp of pain, a coppery smell in the air, and Tasius was stumbling beside him, clutching at Lucius but not uttering a word, his cheek carved open by an arrow, his mouth ripped into a crooked, bloody smile.

Another whispering volley of arrows flew past, and with them came something more terrible still – the haunting high singing and drumming of a tribe of the north, marching to war.

The raiders came from the darkness below. A surging flood

of shadows, a thing from the nightmares of every man who stood upon the Wall, and Lucius felt as much as heard the heavy ring of a ram striking the gate.

A nightmare it might have been, but a nightmare that the Sarmatians had prepared for, over and over again. Their horns blew the alarm, javelins and stones fell in an avalanche of iron and stone, the heavy *thrum* of the ballista sounded out like the beating of a giant's heart. Lucius heard a Sarmatian war cry roar from the ramparts, his name spoken like a curse, over and over again.

Lucius! Death! Lucius! Death!

And with his own name ringing in his ears, as though he were some god of war worth praying to, Lucius looked down and saw the raiders clearly.

He saw a man, ashen-faced and weeping with grief, beating an iron sword to splinters against the stones of the Wall, the way that some of the heroes of old were said to have lost their minds at the last and fought a hopeless battle against a mountain or the sea. He saw no ladders or ropes that those raiders might use to scale the Wall, only the little tree they used for a ram – already splintered with the striking, it would break long before the ironclad door that they sought to destroy.

A different kind of fear took hold of Lucius then, to see such a reckless, hopeless attack. For the tribes of the north were not fools or savages. They knew well enough how to storm the Wall if they had to. It was not an act of hate or war that he was witnessing, but one of utter madness. He stood there, his sword useless in his hands, and watched the slaughter, waiting for the tribesmen to turn and break and run as they surely would. For that was a law of war that he had never seen broken, no matter how blood-mad the warriors were or how desperate their cause. In the end, they always ran when the cause was hopeless.

But these warriors did not. Even when there were only a handful still standing, they fought on. Even when only one remained, he did not run. Lucius watched a grey-haired man, who should have spent his twilight years trading stories about the fireside, hopelessly trying to lift the ram one last time before a flurry of arrows struck him to the ground.

And at last, there was only stillness beneath the Wall.

When the northern gate swung open, a sea of darkness lay beyond.

The Prefect, his voice cracking, called the order to advance at once, but the Sarmatians did not move. They merely looked at Lucius.

'Not yet,' he said.

They waited for a volley of arrows or the charge of a screaming warband, for some trick or purpose to be revealed in the senseless slaughter. There was nothing but the wind, and the choking whispers of the dying.

'Forward,' Lucius said at last.

All about them, the charnel smell rose thick in the air – the hot, coppery scent of blood, the rankness of flesh cut open. On the ground, fallen warriors began to move once more, as in those folk tales where the dead rise and hunt the living.

But these figures, pierced and broken, could not stand. They could only lift bloody, trembling hands up to the sky, whisper to those who approached them. And though the dying spoke in an unfamiliar tongue, the Sarmatians knew what they asked for. Silently, the Sarmatians dropped down from the saddles, and when the clouds parted above them the light of the moon fell bright upon their blades.

Death in battle was rarely quick. Lucius had seen men with guts unspooled upon the ground and heads half staved in who would cling to life, days spent in hopeless agony. It was with a warrior's mercy that the Sarmatians moved through the battlefield and slit the throats of the wounded, a mercy they would have cried for themselves had their positions been reversed. Yet even so, they hesitated as they knelt beside the dying, and Lucius soon saw why.

There were women there, and children too.

The women bore no weapons of war save for, here and there, a stone in their hand, or a little knife better suited for cutting cheese than for cutting flesh. Some still carried the wicker baskets with which they gathered kindling, which still bore twists of herbs to give taste to a stew. The children carried nothing but the whistles and switches with which they had once guided herds of sheep and goats across the rolling fells.

The Prefect, white-faced and trembling, came up next to Lucius. 'Who are they?' he said.

Lucius knelt next to one of the warriors, the one most richly dressed with a fine torc of gold about his neck, a beautiful iron sword still clutched tight in his grey hand. 'The Novantae, I think, by the markings upon this man.' He nodded towards a banner, broken in half beneath the young man who had carried it – little more than a boy in truth, a child whose face was a mirror of his chieftain's. 'They favour the bear as their symbol, when they go to war.'

'They are far from their lands,' said the Prefect. 'They must have been desperate indeed, to come and fight with us in this way.'

'They were desperate,' Lucius answered. 'But they did not come to fight.' He levelled a finger to where two bodies lay, and for all the evil Lucius had seen done in war, still his hand was trembling – he pointed to a mother and babe that lay in one another's arms, stitched together by an arrow. 'Their whole tribe is here,' he said. 'Every one of them who could walk or ride or crawl, and even those who could not. You shall not tell me that woman came to fight with a child in her arms.'

'Then what?' said the Prefect.

'They came here to die.' And Lucius looked to the north, to the darkness beyond the Wall. 'For there is something out there that frightens them more than us.'

7

The sun was low as Kai led his sister into the valley of Dùin, and through the scattered clouds it painted the sky above a bloody red. Just the two of them rode together, for they were no hunting party or warband that might rely on strength in numbers, but scouts who would have to count upon the fickle favour of the gods to keep them safe. And perhaps they would have ghosts to guide them too, for it was a familiar path that Kai followed – back to the forest where he had been ambushed by the Painted People, back to the place of the dead.

For that had been Mor's command, after the truce with the Novantae. The warriors of the Votadini had scattered across the land, pairs of riders wandering and searching, following the signs of disaster like carrion crows. Seeking the burned-out shieling, the fresh earth of a shallow grave, the marks of a warband on the move where they were written into the earth, in gouged earth and trophies of the dead hung from the trees. Seeking the Painted People.

'What is the Burning Cauldron?' Kai had asked his chieftain

when that command was given, remembering the last words of the Novantae chieftain.

'Find the Painted People for me,' Mor had answered, 'and I shall tell you.'

And so Kai had chosen to go back to the one place that he knew the Painted People had been – back to the forest of Dùin.

It did not look such a forbidding place now, just a ragged line of low trees with nothing to be heard save for the gentle music of the river that ran close by. But when Kai looked upon the yew and the ash, he could almost see once again the Painted People rising silent amongst the trees, killing spears in hand. When he listened to the passage of the swift-running water, he could hear once more the screams of the men who had died beside it.

As Laimei looked upon the forest, she simply nodded once, as though the woods were some worthy swordsman that she faced upon the battlefield – an enemy fearsome enough to honour those who faced it.

'An evil-looking place,' she muttered. For she and Kai came from a place of open plains ringed by the mountains, the trees to be found rarely in scattered copses. And while their people thought a single tree to be a sacred bridge between the heavens and the earth and the underworld, gathered together they spoke of nothing but disaster – a trap for man and horse alike.

Laimei shifted in her saddle. 'Do you truly think they shall return to this forest?' she said.

'They dug the evil out from there,' Kai answered. 'Perhaps they shall return to it. Perhaps this place is sacred to them.'

'A fool's hope. But we have nothing better.' She cast her eyes towards the low sun. 'We wait until it is fully dark. Then we may go chasing ghosts in that forest.'

'You think us fools to be here?'

'Yes,' said Laimei. 'I always wanted to die beneath the sun and the open sky. But as always, it seems, I shall not get what I want.'

'I might almost think you afraid,' said Kai, 'if I did not know you better.'

'You know me little enough even after all these years,' she said, not taking her eyes from the trees. 'For I am afraid now.'

It was true – he did not truly know his sister. That was what Kai thought to himself as they tethered their horses to spears thrust into the ground, as they daubed their skin with wet earth from the bank of the river and waited for the sun to fall from the sky. Long ago, during the ten years they had spent in a feud, her heart had been simple enough to know. He had failed to be brave, and she had hated him for it, as she hated anything that she might call cowardice. But in the five years north of the Wall, spending every day together and each night beside the same fire, he could never know what she would think or do or say. Her love, if that was what it could be called, had always been more mysterious than her hate.

And she proved that with her next words: 'Why do you not take a wife of the Votadini?'

'What?' he said.

He must have looked startled, for she laughed at him – a short bark of sound, like a wolfhound delighted by his master's trickery. 'It would do you good to have a woman,' she

73

said. 'You never learned to be alone, as I have.' She hesitated. 'Do you still think of her?' she said at last. 'Of Arite?'

'Yes, I do,' Kai said. For though there had been a few he had turned to in those years of exile – a woman who had led him into the bracken after the Beltane festival, and even Mor himself had shared his blankets once or twice in a strangely solemn kind of lovemaking – they had always been for but a single night. And once more, in his mind's eye, he saw the twining braids of silver and gold hair, the proud and fearless eyes staring back into his. 'I brought her much sorrow with my love.'

'I expect you brought her much sorrow with your leaving,' Laimei answered bluntly.

'No doubt that is also true.'

She fidgeted with the handle of her knife. 'So, why did you leave?'

'You have never asked me that before. Why now?'

She shrugged. 'It has been five years, and your heart has not healed. I only wonder why, if it grieves you so, you left her behind. A mystery. Solve it for me.'

Kai did not speak for a long time. He watched the passage of the sun, hoping to see it dip below the horizon and for the shadows to come, so that he would not have to answer. But as was always the way at the end of the day, the sun hung stubbornly in the sky, as though it waited for him to speak.

And so eventually, Kai said: 'I made a promise to a dying man.'

'To Bahadur?'

'Yes,' said Kai. And once more, the taste of earth and blood was in his mouth. Arite's husband lay at his feet, crushed and broken by a fallen horse. And he could hear once more the words, rising with terrible clarity, from the man who had once been his friend. 'Promise me,' Bahadur had said, and Kai had known all too well what promise he meant.

Laimei made no answer at first. Kai thought she might laugh at him and call him a fool, but instead she was silent, her eyes distant. Perhaps she was trying to see the world as he did, something that she had never had to do before – a champion had no need to imagine the mind of another, lesser warrior. Always, she had judged others by some code of her own that held no exception, for action and thought were as one to her, doubt an unknown thing.

At last she nodded, satisfied. 'When you rode north of the Wall to join us,' she said, 'I knew there was something different about you. I knew that you had learned to keep your promises.'

'You think that I was right to leave her?' Kai asked.

'No,' she said flatly. 'You are a fool, and so was Bahadur. But a promise is a promise.' She shook her head. 'Even so, I will never understand how you could give such a thing up. It seems a poor enough trade, that you should trade Lucius and Arite's company for mine.'

There was a strange tone to her voice that Kai had not heard before, as though she spoke a language that was not her own. Perhaps it might even have been regret.

And so Kai found himself asking a question he had never dared to ask before. 'I might well ask you,' he said, 'that very same question – why it is you take no man or woman yourself?'

She made no answer for a time. He saw her eyes go to the sun – perhaps she thought as he had, hoping to be saved by the coming of the night. 'Of that, I am afraid.'

'Laimei...'

But she spoke hurriedly then, almost tripping over the words: 'I am afraid that I do not crave love the way that you do – the way that all others seem to do. I am afraid of what that might mean I am.'

'You never had such doubts before,' he said.

She nodded slowly. 'I know now why the champions die young in all our stories. We grow weak as we age, weak of mind and heart. I want to become something other than I am. And I do not know how to do that.'

And to that, Kai could not think of a single word he might say.

All his life he had looked to his sister to guide him. When they had been children without a mother she had raised him herself, and even in the long years of their feud, he had followed her like a traveller following the north star homewards. Never once had he thought that she might turn to him for guidance – in that moment, when she needed him most, he found that he had nothing to offer her.

And so Kai could do nothing but give a coward's glance towards the sun. He saw, with relief, that it had fallen below the horizon at last.

She smiled to see him struck silent, a bitter little twist of the mouth. 'Come,' she said. 'It does not matter. It is dark enough now. Let us be gone.'

When at last they came to the edge of the forest, a shiver of fear ran across Kai's skin. He felt naked without a lance in his hand or the weight of cuirass upon his shoulders, helpless with no horse beneath him. With his sister beside him, he felt the mad, foolish urge to clasp her hand for comfort, the way they had sought to make each other brave when they were children.

And then, as if in answer to that unspoken wish, he felt her fingers close about his. 'Come,' she said, her voice impatient, 'stay close to me.' And he did not know if she spoke as his war captain, or as his sister. Perhaps she too felt those half-memories of games played long ago, as they wandered into the night and chased the spirits of the dead amongst the trees.

They moved through the forest, and it seemed to fight against them like a living thing – thorns like spear-points, brambles slicing and cutting like the blade of a sword, branches that sought to wrap around an ankle and wrestle them to the ground. Their journey was slow, maddeningly slow. A few steps forward, then suddenly holding still to listen for the sound of a footfall in the undergrowth, the whistle of a sentry, an arrow nocking to a bow.

And at last, they did hear something. No sound of war or danger, nothing that spoke of death soon to come, yet even so, it was more frightening than that. For somewhere before them, deep within the forest, they could hear the beating of a drum.

One at first, but soon it was joined by another, and another, and another. This was no lone hunter, warding away the loneliness of the night with the music of his tribe. It was the sound of a festival, a ritual, or an execution.

Dim and distant through the trees, the light of a fire. And as they drew closer to the fire, there was movement in the forest, shifting and rustling from all around, as though some dragon from the old stories swept its scaled hide through the forest to shiver the branches of the trees and scatter the leaves to the wind. Yet for all that, Kai could see no one in the darkness, only the trees and their shadows, the dim and flickering light that he and his sister stumbled towards.

Then the fire flared high, shockingly bright. And as Kai cast up his hand to shield his eyes, he saw that they were not alone.

All about them, in front and behind, men stepped from the shadows of the trees. Spirits of the Otherlands they seemed at first, until they gave voice as one, songs rising up into the burning air in the countless tongues of the Painted People.

They were close, far too close, for Kai and Laimei had wandered amongst them unwittingly. Kai waited for one of those shadows to level a finger, to scream in triumph and mark them as intruders. But no sentry cried out. All eyes looked inwards to the fire where, silhouetted by the flames, a great figure stood.

A tall, thin man, made monstrous by that trick of the firelight. Almost a giant he seemed, yet a monster would have been less frightening to Kai than the man who stood there now. For the light shone on a face that Kai knew all too well – his cheeks were hollow, eyes black in the shadowy night, and with a cloak wrapped close about him he looked much like his namesake, a carrion crow watching over a legion of the dying and the dead. It was Corvus, king of the Painted People, who stood there before them.

The cloak fell to the earth, and Corvus stood there naked before his people. And as the flickering light danced across his skin, Kai saw then the terrible wound he bore below his belly, nothing but a scar where his manhood should have been. No ragged wound of war, but a mark of ritual, a single clean cut of the knife. And Kai understood then how Corvus had bought his life after the battle beneath the Wall, the sacrifice that he had made. Why the Painted People, who had once followed him as a warleader or a king, now worshipped him like a god.

Corvus lifted his hands to the sky, and as the Painted People chanted in response, there were words that Kai knew, repeated over and over again.

The Maimed King! The Maimed King!

A mad urge rising, to turn and run from that place. The Painted People would see him in an instant, pull him down like dogs bringing down a deer in the hunt, offer him some slow death by torture to appease their furious gods. But it took all the courage that he had to hold his ground, for to stay had a danger of its own. There was madness in the air, twisting about them like a living thing. Somehow, Kai feared that madness more than the tortures of knife and fire.

Once again in the darkness, he felt Laimei's hand clutching his. Her lips almost upon his ear, the hot breath against his skin as she whispered: 'Be brave.'

And so he held still, and watched as the prisoners were brought forward.

Men and women were dragged from the trees, blood already running down their arms from the ropes knotted about their wrists. A cold touch about Kai's heart as he saw children there too, blinking and terrified in the light of the fire. Upon the skin of the prisoners were the tattoos of many tribes – the Novantae, the Selgovae, and even the Votadini. The taste of bile in his mouth then, as amongst them Kai saw a man he knew. Comhnall, the warrior who had led them into that forest but a few days before.

One by one those prisoners came forward and knelt before the Maimed King. Lips moving, words spoken that Kai could not hear. He did not need to. He had seen such oaths before.

For those prisoners looked upon the wound of the Maimed
King, stared back to where their children lay weeping amidst
the twisted roots of the trees. And they said the words that
would save their lives, and the lives of those that they loved.
And Kai knew then that this was how the Painted People
had grown many thousands strong, why the Novantae would
rather die than face them and become yet more prizes claimed
in flesh.

One by one, those men and women gave themselves up to
the Painted People. The old marks of clan and kin cut away
from their skin, and the new, crudely marked tattoos gifting
them a new life. Until it came to Comhnall of the Votadini,
and it was his turn to kneel and offer up his oath.

Comhnall had no look of courage about him – by the light
of the fire, Kai could see the sweat that ran down his skin,
the head drooping down until the chin touched the chest. But
something gave him the terrible bravery to shake his head,
and when Comhnall spoke, in a rasping, wretched cry, it was
loud enough for Kai to hear it. A single word.

'No!'

There was no second chance given, no hesitation or mercy.
Only a wave of the hand from Corvus, a dismissive, kingly
gesture, and the Painted People swarmed upon Comhnall and
dragged him to the ground. Half-starved and wound-sick as
he was, still Comhnall's terror gave him strength – it took
three men to hold him down, as another man knelt between
his legs, the knife shining in his hand, and began to cut. The
screams rising high, and the Painted People screamed with
him as though they shared his pain.

But, still, the most terrible sight was yet to come. For what
Corvus now held in his hands almost stopped Kai's heart.

At once, there was silence from the Painted People, and for all the chanting that had come before, the screaming that Comhnall had made as he was given to their gods, the silence was more fearsome still. At first it seemed as though Corvus lifted high a circle of pure darkness, as though he held some stolen piece of the night sky itself. But the fire raged and the smoke rose, and as Kai blinked the tears from his eyes, at last he could see what Corvus truly held – a cauldron of black iron.

Old and battered, the carvings on its side worn down almost to nothing by the passage of time and by endless cradling hands. It should not have been such a fearsome thing to look upon – better suited to sitting above a cookfire in a shieling – yet Kai knew that he must be looking upon the Burning Cauldron, that this was the great and terrible evil that the Painted People had dug from the ground in that forest. And soon enough, he was to know why.

Corvus knelt down then, beside where Comhnall finally lay still. And the Maimed King took the bloody prize from the ground, the piece of Comhnall that they had cut away, and he cast it into that cauldron.

A roaring all about them as the Painted People surged forward, jostling past Kai and Laimei, their hands reaching up – imploring their king, and seeking a gift from him.

Corvus granted his blessing as he reached into the cauldron and took something in his hand. A single pinch, a scattering of grey ash cast into the crowd, but to the Painted People it could have been saffron or gold leaf, every fragment of it seemed so precious to them.

As if in answer, the fire soared ever higher – the tree leaves above were catching, crisping and falling about them, swirling in the air like fireflies. The Painted People danced, singing even as the embers rained and fell upon their skin, revellers celebrating the ending of the world.

Now was the time to go, to flee into the night like frightened children. Laimei was already slipping away into the forest, crouching and moving with a wolfish lope from shadow to shadow. But Kai found himself stumbling, moving in clumsy half-steps, aping the movements of the dancers by the fire. And he was almost out, almost free of the light and safe in the darkness, when a figure strode from the shadows towards him.

It was a man of the Painted People, coming forward with empty hands and open arms, wild-eyed with the ritual and with the love of all those around him, smiling as he drew Kai into a close embrace. A repulsive intimacy – Kai could smell the stink of meat and heather beer upon that man's breath, feel dried blood scraping against his skin. He twisted loose and pushed the man away, more fearful of that embrace than the edge of a knife or the point of a lance, as though that terrible madness of the Painted People might be gifted through touch alone.

In a single beat of the heart, that warrior of the Painted People knew Kai for what he was – an intruder upon the sacred. No fear in that man's eyes, only a great and terrible joy. For what a blessing it must have been, to have another victim to give to the dark god of death that lurked in the cauldron.

Kai could not move. He could feel the spirits of the Painted People about him, willing the death of the Sarmatians, the Romans, all those who dwelt south of the Wall. A longing so strong that he felt himself bound by it, so that even as the warrior of the Painted People began to fumble for the dagger in his belt, Kai still could not move. A sacrifice was demanded in that place, and it was to be him.

Then a shadow rose behind the warrior – the shadow of death. There would be a sacrifice that night, but it would not be Kai.

A hand reaching and pulling at the lime-streaked hair of the warrior, the knife sawing and working beneath the throat, the blood running black in the darkness, and that man of the Painted People fell to the ground, grasping towards Kai with bulging, imploring eyes. Behind him stood Laimei, staring down upon the man she had killed. Kai knew well the look upon her face – the tilt of the lips, the colour in her cheeks, the eyes shining bright in the distant light of the fire. Not the look of pleasure that some took in killing, but one of a terrible serenity. A fire within her quenched, some question of the soul answered in full.

But, as always, it lasted only for a moment. A shudder passed through her body, and then she moved like a dreamer waking, restless and impatient, the bloody knife twitching in her hand.

'We must go now,' Kai whispered. 'He will be missed.'

She nodded absently, her eyes drifting towards the Painted People, still dancing about the fire in tribute to some forgotten, bloody god of the cauldron. 'Who would notice another dead man amongst them?' she said.

The fire flared up once more, the light of it shining upon her face – only for a moment, but long enough for Kai to see her clearly, to see something that he wished he could unsee.

For it was not with fear that she gazed upon the Painted People. It was the way that Kai had once seen a man of the

Votadini look upon a finely crafted sword, the way he had seen Romans stare up at the golden eagle of the Legion, perhaps even the way Kai's own eyes had once shone when he looked upon Arite, many years before.

A look not of fear, but of longing.

8

'So, Lucius, once more you speak of ghosts and mysteries.' The Governor of Britannia traced a finger round the rim of his wine cup and smiled. 'One might think you had gone mad out here, at the edge of the world.'

Lucius made no answer for a time and swallowed down the killing words he longed to speak.

It had been days of hard riding south to bring him back here to his headquarters at Eboracum. More days wasted waiting for this man, Caerellius Priscus, to answer his messages and come to the north. Now, he knew, he would have to sit through these insults, feints, and political games, while the Governor decided what must be done – perhaps this wearying, shadowy game of politics was the only entertainment left to Caerellius now.

Lucius turned his gaze from his guest, and let his eyes rest upon the sword that hung upon the wall of his quarters – that long Roman cavalry sword with which he had killed the last king of the Sarmatians, far out to the east. 'If the Governor wishes for evidence,' Lucius answered at last, 'he may dig into

the grave we dug by the *vallum*. Bring a little of that fine
Etruscan perfume for your nose, for the dead will be quite
rotten by now. But you shall find the women and children of
the Novantae there. Infants too, just as I have said.'

Caerellius raised an eyebrow, gave a little twitch of the
lips – it amused him, no doubt, to see Lucius so provoked. But
even so, the Governor stole a glance towards the doorway,
where his guards waited, standing to attention. Not the
Sarmatians of the fort, but the bodyguards that Caerellius
had brought with him. The man was not a fool, and he knew
where the loyalty of the Sarmatians truly lay. It was one of the
only reasons that Lucius still lived.

Caerellius ceased toying with his wine and tossed it back
in a single gulp with a shiver of distaste – a man used to good
living, even the best wine they could offer at Eboracum was
no doubt like vinegar to him. 'Well,' he said. 'I think we can
dispose of the usual courtesies.'

'You were being courteous before?'

Caerellius sniffed. 'More than you deserved. Your messenger
made quite the impression. Charging into Londinium on a
half-dead horse, striding into the forum with your message
in his hand, speaking of death and disaster. Not the kind of
thing that I might ignore.'

Lucius brushed a hand across his lips, hoping there was
no hint of a smile to be found there. His instructions to the
messenger had indeed been quite specific.

'So,' the Governor said, 'what is it that you wish to do?'

'Take a force beyond the Wall,' Lucius answered at once.
'Several *alae* of the Sarmatians, and half of the Sixth Legion
at least. Find whoever has attacked our people, and destroy
them.'

'Rather bloodthirsty of you,' said Caerellius. 'I did not think you had the courage for such things.'

Again, Lucius had to hold his tongue. Five years before, it had been Caerellius's command that had sent Lucius north of the Wall, burning and despoiling the land of the Votadini, driving away the warriors who had once been their allies. Caerellius had needed a victory beyond the Wall, Lucius had needed a promise of safety for his Sarmatians, and that was the bloody bargain they had made.

'It was foolish to fight then,' Lucius said at last. 'It would be foolish not to fight now.'

'Careful, Lucius.' Caerellius placed the wine cup down, steepled his fingers beneath his chin. 'I could have you killed, for speaking so to me.'

Lucius glanced towards the bodyguards. 'You could. But you would not leave the fort alive. My Sarmatians would pin you open and leave you for the ravens to butcher while you were still alive. That is how they deal with those who betray them.'

A moment's silence. Then Caerellius clapped his hands once, like a child delighted by the trick of a street magician. 'Oh, I have missed you, Lucius. In Londinium they are all fools, braggarts, and lapdogs. Your insolence has its own particular charm.' He swung his legs from the couch and stood, picking stray pieces of straw from his tunic. 'You may take an *ala* of your Sarmatians to the north if you wish. But the Legion does not cross the Wall.'

'Why?'

'I shall not waste Roman lives undoing your mistakes.'

'*My* mistakes?'

'Yes,' Caerellius answered as he wandered, as if idly, to the edge of the room, laid a finger upon the sword that hung there. 'For if the Votadini have returned, then it is one of your Sarmatians who leads them. What was the name of that man who fled across the Wall the first chance that he got? Kai, wasn't it?'

Lucius would wonder, afterwards, if Caerellius knew how close to death he came at that moment. If he knew well enough to recognise the glassy cast across the eyes, or the particular stillness that came upon a man before the killing – those murderer's marks written upon the flesh. Perhaps he did not, for it must have been a long, long time since Caerellius had faced a man willing to kill him.

'Perhaps it is one of *your* mistakes that I go to undo,' Lucius said quietly. 'We do not know for certain that it is the Votadini. After all, we never found the corpse of your pet, Corvus.'

The politician's composure slipped from Caerellius, just for a moment. For Lucius alone knew that man's secret – that Caerellius had struck a bargain with Corvus five years before, hoping to see a war break out that he might turn to his advantage, the beginnings of a bloody road that might have led him all the way to Rome and the purple robes of an emperor. But the wave of the Painted People had broken against the Wall: a great price paid in Sarmatian blood and marked by fire. And so they both remained there, trapped at the far reaches of the Empire, forgotten and abandoned by Rome.

'This hate you nurture, it is quite unnecessary,' Caerellius said. 'Five years ago, I was a legate and you were a prefect. Now you are a legate, and I am a governor. We have both done well.' Then the Governor smiled – a patient, fatherly smile – and said: 'You will lead the Sarmatians north yourself?'

'Yes,' Lucius whispered. 'I will lead them north of the Wall. I shall do your bloody work for you.'

'Good, good. Then I will remain here, in Eboracum. To watch over your affairs while you are gone.'

Lucius hesitated. 'I do not think it necessary,' he said at last. 'Little enough for a governor to do here. You shall be missed in Londinium.'

'Oh, I think it quite necessary. And it shows how little you know of Londinium, of this island. How little there is to do. How little we matter.' Caerellius shook his head. 'What would it matter to Rome if this miserable island sank away into the ocean? They would miss the tin and the slaves, I suppose, but nothing more than that.'

'It would matter somewhat to the people of the island, I think,' Lucius answered drily.

A small, tight smile from Caerellius then, as though Lucius had told a particularly laboured joke. 'I know you must think me defeated, to still be trapped here with you. To never see Rome again. You might still show some little respect.'

Lucius said nothing for a time. Then: 'In truth, Caerellius, I do not think of you at all.'

Caerellius made no answer at first. Many times before, Lucius had faced men who sought to kill him. In that strange intimacy of the battlefield, they had been close enough to smell and to touch, locked shield to shield and staring into one another's eyes. There had always been a kind of kinship there, born of pain – always the sense that, in another time and another place, he might have been a brother to the man who sought to end his life. For all the battles that Lucius had fought, perhaps Caerellius was the only man who had ever truly hated him. The Governor looked at him now not with the blank eyes of a killer, but with the restless, relentless gaze of a man learning to hate.

'There is a Sarmatian woman and a boy, here in Eboracum,' Caerellius said at last, a dangerous calm to his voice. 'I hear you are quite fond of them both.'

'Caerellius...'

The Governor waved a hand. 'Your love affairs are no business of mine. It should not surprise me that you have found a Sarmatian to whore for you – only that it is a woman, and not a man. But I shall remain here. I shall guard your affairs, and I shall watch over *them*. Come back with a victory, and they will be safe.'

Before Lucius could answer him, Caerellius was gone – the pattering, restless footsteps of an ambitious man, followed by the heavy tread of his bodyguards. Lucius was alone then, save for the mementos he had gathered in his chambers, the useless relics of a lifetime spent at war.

He knew the stories that the Sarmatians told of him: an undefeated hero, a killer of kings. Once he had wanted to believe them. But now, as the grey grew in his hair and the cold crept into his bones, he knew that they were lies. No hero, but merely a merchant of death, trying to strike the best bargain that he could in blood. Now another such bargain lay before him.

And, as he laid his eyes once more upon his sword, he knew what had to be done.

In the night, in her dreams, Arite found herself once more upon the steppe.

Every night, since the battle beneath the Wall, when she closed her eyes she found herself there. Every dream, the same dream.

The wide, open plain stretched out to the horizon and beyond, as though the whole world were encompassed by that great Sea of Grass. But it was not the steppe of Sarmatia that she saw, that place of tall grass and blue wildflowers dancing with the wind, the rivers looping through the land and the open sky shining bright above her. For the steppe of her dreams was barren save for a scattering of trees that were leafless and twisted with age, and the ground was black earth beneath a sallow, yellow sky. The stink of smoke in the air, for those trees had fires burning beneath them, and shadowy figures hung from their branches. This was the steppe of the Otherlands, which mirrored land where the dead and the dreaming sometimes met.

For there were travellers on the plain, there to be met by chance or fate. And though some of those faces came and went from night to night, there was one that she always saw. A man who rode across the steppe on a horse of bone, with a cluster of shadows that circled and shifted about him.

Long since, Arite had given up trying to flee from that figure. From bitter experience, she knew that if she tried to run, then that deathly horse of his would always outpace her. And so she waited, her hand reaching down and stroking the mane of the dream horse beneath, a gesture that had always brought her comfort in the waking world. Even so, that hand trembled as the rider drew close.

For it was Bahadur who came towards her, the husband she had lost five years before. The shadows that surrounded him were the ghosts of children. Her children. Their children.

Five had she borne with the man on that horse, and five had she buried – killed by famine and fever, sword and spear. And that flock of lost children rushed forward and reached for her hands, desperate and imploring. But though she could see the mouths moving, see the trails of black tears that fell like ash down their cheeks, she could never hear them speak.

Always a quickening of fear to see Bahadur, for she never knew which aspect he would have – the man she had known in her youth, always quick with laughter and with song, or the broken man he had become afterwards, when he had taken wounds of the heart that would not heal. Wounds that she and Kai had given to him.

They sat there in silence, in that shifting landscape of the dream, each waiting for the other to speak. Each knowing that they never would. For that was the cruelty of the Otherlands – a place where one might see the lost dead, night after night, but never speak with them.

But something was different then, something wrong with the shape of the dream. For in that soundless place, she could hear something – the distant beating of hooves upon the steppe. And upon the horizon she saw a figure that, in five years of dreaming, she had never seen in that place. Kai.

In a moment the comfort of hate was upon her, and in her hand a spear, mind-forged. The warrior's joy of seeing an enemy before her, an enemy that she could kill.

Kai seemed undaunted – he rode towards her across the open plain, no weapon in hand or cuirass upon his shoulders. He reached out to her and called her name as he drew close enough to kill, close enough to touch.

But a hand was upon her shoulder – she thought at first it was Bahadur, jealous even in death, meaning to keep her from that meeting. But it was a hand from the waking world, not the dreaming. The hand of her child, Akkas.

She thought at first that he must have woken from some evil dream of his own and sought comfort with her in the darkness. But when she saw his glassy, fearful eyes, heard the too perfect silence of the night outside, her warrior's instinct spoke of hunters in the darkness. She knew at once, even before she heard the scrape of a footstep, that danger was close.

And so at once she put her hand to the woodcutter's axe she kept beside the bed, gave a tap of the hand to Akkas's shoulder. The child was ready in a moment, a knife in his hand, but even in the darkness she could see those fingers trembling. A child of warriors was still a child, after all.

The footsteps moved to the front of the house, and so she slid back into the darkness, towards a crudely cut window covered by a wooden shutter. But the beams of moonlight were eclipsed as another shadow moved past the shutter – no escape that way.

A calm settled upon her with the knowledge that she could not run. She weighed the axe in her hand and steadied her breath. She thought only of the words that would leave her lips when the door opened, and they would not be a war cry or one of the songs of the dead, the kind that her people favoured when facing impossible odds. When those killers outside threw open that door, she would speak to Akkas – her last words would be words of love.

Then, the last thing that she expected. A soft, hesitant rapping upon the door. A voice whispering the old Sarmatian saying: 'Though our lives be short...'

'Let our fame be great,' she answered. And when the door swung open, it was Lucius that she saw there.

Given the lateness of the hour, he might have been a lover come courting, were he not dressed for battle – no ceremonial armour to be worn for a senator's indulgence, but the simple iron mail and short crested helm that spoke of a war soon to come. And upon his hip, the sword that the Sarmatians worshipped as though it were another god, the sword of many names – Kingkiller, Hard Cut, White Hilt. And he did look like something from the old stories as he stood there in the rain, solemn as a hero, shoulders stooped beneath some unseen weight that bore heavily upon him.

'If you come to court me,' she said, 'this is a strange way to go about it.'

'I would have thought it a fitting way to woo a Sarmatian,' he answered.

Beyond him, on the bank of the river, she saw the shapes of countless horses and riders, still as statues as the rain fell upon them, shadows in the darkness. 'You have rather too much company with you,' she said. 'And that armour would prove a tiresome delay.'

He grinned at her, suddenly boyish – no longer the grim-faced warrior with the weight of the world upon him, but the gentle, dreaming man that perhaps he once had been. 'I wish it were so,' Lucius said, 'but it is not.'

'You go to bring death north of the Wall?'

The smile faded as quickly as it had come, and he was solemn once more. 'Aye,' he said. 'And I ask you to come with me – at least as far as the Wall.'

'Why?'

The Roman's mouth twisted in disgust. 'Caerellius has

threatened you,' he said. 'He thinks to use you as a hostage – a whip to drive me on.'

'Then we shall kill him,' she said matter-of-factly.

'No,' he answered. 'He shall pay the blood price some day, but it is not today. Will you come to Cilurnum? You shall be safe there, amongst the Sarmatians.'

All at once, Arite was afraid, more afraid than she had been when she thought death was at her door. She had done much forgetting in Eboracum, but there in the north she would see once more the place where Bahadur had died, the place where Kai had abandoned her. She would remember them both, and remember that sense of love too, most dangerous of all. It was waiting for her there, in the shadow of the Wall, silent and patient, like a champion upon the battlefield who cannot be defeated.

The words were upon her lips, waiting to be spoken. A coward's words, begging to stay behind. But another voice spoke first from behind her – soft and shy and full of wonder: 'We go north?' Akkas said.

'Yes, Akkas,' said Lucius, 'we go to the Wall. Will you join us?'

Akkas ran to Lucius then, calling and laughing and wild with joy. Those words that the boy had longed to hear for his whole life – *journey, north, the Wall*. For he was a child of nomads, with all that restless longing of their people to roam far and free, yet he had never seen beyond Eboracum. He was like a hawk tied by its jesses to a post, giving up hope of the sky, now let loose at last and given his chance to soar.

And Akkas was laughing then, running towards the river. It was like something from the stories that he loved to be told – the shadowy horsemen upon the bank, their champion standing before them, an uncertain journey into the night awaiting them. And Arite felt it too, that lightness of spirit that comes when a journey lies ahead, that strange, particular magic that comes upon the heart, the way a horse seems able to outpace fear and sadness both.

She remembered the dream, the horseman in the distance, Kai reaching to her with open arms. And she felt the pull of fate leading her northwards, like a lodestone. Calling her towards the Wall. Calling her home.

9

A hand upon Kai's shoulder, shaking him awake from the depths of some dream that he could not fully remember, a dream of chase and pursuit.

There was a terror at waking into the darkness, and for a moment he thought himself back in the forest once more – the hot smell of blood in the air and smoke from the fire forcing its way down his throat, the joyful, murderous shadows dancing amidst the flames.

When he saw that it was his sister who stood above him, Kai's fear diminished, but it did not fully disappear. For he remembered once again what he had seen upon her face, in the forest: the look of naked desire as she watched the ritual of the Painted People.

'It is time,' she said. 'Mor wishes to speak with us.'

Kai looked up at the blackness of the night sky. 'Mor sends us to rest, then drags us out again before dawn?' he asked. For it had been a slow, long, fearful journey back to the camp of the Votadini – their nerves worn thin, some silent agreement between Kai and his sister that it would be dangerous to spend another night apart from their clan, as they fled in terror from what lurked in the night behind them. They had stumbled into the campground on the beach exhausted, and when they had begun to speak Mor had sent them to rest. Now, but a few hours later, in the deepest part of the night, it seemed he had changed his mind.

'He says that whatever news we bring, it is best spoken in darkness.' Laimei shook her head. 'He has picked a fine time to be superstitious,' she said.

They picked their way around the embers of the campfires and through the sleeping Votadini, the people of the tribe lying still as the dead. Soon enough, they came to where Mor sat. The chieftain was staring out across the sea, the campfire beside him long since burned down to ashes, his eyes fixed upon an island a little way off the shore. In the night that island was a looming black shadow, but here and there Kai could see a few points of light – fishermen or pirates, exiles or holy men, lighting beacons in the darkness for other men to see.

'What do they call that island?' asked Kai. 'And why do you stare upon it? You think it may be another place for us to run to, if we have nowhere else to go?'

'My people call it the Island of Spears,' Mor answered. 'And no, we shall not go there. It frightens me to look upon it, and I am trying to understand why, what message the gods hold for me in this fear. Perhaps it is that I must not flee this country and take to the sea. That I am like those spellstruck heroes from the stories, who must always touch the earth of their homeland, or they shall die.'

'You have no need to go searching for ill omens,' Kai said. 'We have seen enough of those already.'

'Very well,' Mor said. 'Sit with me and tell me of them.' He sighed heavily. 'Though I think that, in my heart, I already know of what you will speak.'

'There were others,' Laimei said. 'Other riders of the Votadini that you sent all across the northlands. They have brought back warnings of their own?'

'They have brought back nothing,' Mor answered. 'None of the others I sent out have returned.' He reached down and ran his fingers through the ashes of the campfire beside him, letting it drift from his fingers like falling snow. 'But perhaps that is not true. They have found their answer in the iron of blades and arrowheads. Their absence must speak for them, and it speaks clearly enough.' He lifted his head. 'You must speak for them too,' he said. 'Though I do not want you to.'

'Why not?' said Kai.

'I think that you carry my death with you, in the words that you will speak,' Mor said, as simply and plainly as though he spoke of some idle matter. 'If only I could keep you silent, perhaps I could live forever.' He smiled thinly. 'But, in truth, who would wish to live forever? It does not seem to bring the gods much pleasure. So speak, then, and tell me of my death.'

And they did. Under the light of the moon and beside the calm water of the sea, they spoke of the Painted People, gathered in the forest. Of Corvus standing before them, made anew into the Maimed King. And of the cauldron of black iron that the Painted People worshipped as though it were the shrine of some fearsome god.

Mor said nothing for a time. The sea was still, so still that they could see the stars reflected in the black water – a second sky beneath them, as though it were a glimpse into another world. Mor stared at that water, a needful look upon his face, as though wondering whether he might step into that other world to save himself.

Finally, Laimei said: 'Which do you fear more? Corvus, or that cauldron he carries?'

'It brings me no joy to know that Corvus lives,' Mor said. 'He always was a warleader, one who knew well how to speak with a poisoned tongue, a teacher of how to hate. Now, he is something greater and more terrible than that.' He shook his head. 'But the Burning Cauldron is far more fearsome than any king or champion.'

'You shall tell us of it now?' said Kai.

'Yes,' Mor answered. 'And you must forgive me for my secrecy. With all my heart, I hoped it was not true. With all my faith, I prayed that it had been lost forever. For, to my great shame, I sought it once myself.'

They waited then, together in the silence. As the wind blew cold across the waters of the sea and the waves began to grow tall, washing and rattling across the shingle, they waited for Mor to find the courage to speak. Waiting for some portent written upon the water, sung by a howling wolf, or etched upon the stars that might let Mor remember what it was to be brave.

'You have long known,' Mor said at last, 'that we have no druids left amongst our people, no seers who may hear the whispers of the spirits. We have stumbled blindly in the dark, unguided by our gods, for more than a hundred years. Now, I shall tell you why. It is an evil story – ill luck has always followed the telling of it. For it is a story of the shaming of our gods, and they do not like it spoken.'

Mor reached out to the remnants of the fire and began tracing patterns in the ash. 'For as long as any man could remember,' he continued, 'the home of the gods was to be found far to the south and the west, on the island of Yns Mon. They called it the Dark Isle, for the groves of sacred trees grew so tall and thick that the sun was seldom seen. No one could say quite how ancient the oldest trees were – as old as the gods, some said. Older, perhaps.

'All the tribes of this island have made war against one another for as long as any could remember. We have lived by feud and cattle raid, passed down our hatreds the way a father might gift a fine spear to his son. Yet there was no war on Yns Mon. The druids of every tribe made their pilgrimages to the western sea and spoke with the gods there. That was where their magic came from – the magic with which they saw the future, and blessed the crops, and brought victory in war. It had been so for a thousand years.'

Mor's fingers ceased their tracing path through the ashes, and with a sweep of his hand he wiped away the markings he had made. 'Then the Romans came,' he said. 'They had no fear of chieftains like me. They could buy or bully or kill the leaders of all the great tribes. We have always hated each other more than the Romans, and understood too late the danger they brought. But the Romans knew the druids would never surrender to them.' Mor lifted his head. 'I do not know if the druids were mad or brave or stupid, but they would not submit to Rome. And so, more than a hundred years ago, the Romans drove them west, butchering and killing as they went. Until the last of the druids gathered upon Yns Mon, for one final battle.'

Mor hesitated then, turning his gaze to the south and the west. As though he might not just peer through the darkness, but through the veil of time itself. 'It is out there, somewhere, across the darkening sea,' Mor said. 'I have never been to Yns Mon, nor met any man who has. The trees were burned long before my father's time. Yet still, in the worst of my dreams, I always find myself there. All of our people dream that same dream, from time to time.' He looked to Kai then, his eyes wide and very pale under the light of the stars. 'And so I tell you now what I have seen a thousand times before, when I sleep at night. I see those druids dancing naked, screaming their curses, tending their ghost fences of skull and bone. I see the Legion marching forward, bearing iron, bearing fire. And all about them the great forests of ash and yew and oak, branches reaching up into the sky as though making offerings of themselves to the gods.

'In my dreams,' Mor said, 'I smell the ash, I taste the blood. I hear the druids screaming. And I hear the Romans laughing as they kill.' He licked dry lips. 'It is said that the fires were burning for a year and a day, so much blood spilled that it stained the earth like a rich red dye. And in the end, there was nothing left. The groves destroyed, the last of the druids killed. A thousand years of ritual and magic lost with them, for nothing was ever written by the druids, only spoken. Some say our gods died with them, there upon the battlefield. And if they yet live, they are silent now, and answer no prayers.'

And they were all silent too, for a time. Sitting together

upon the beach, listening to the waves, thinking of the dead gods.

'What of this cauldron?' Laimei said at last.

'After the groves were burned and the killing was done,' Mor answered, 'a druid's apprentice crawled from the ashes. He knew no lore, had no mastery of prayer and magic. But he took a sacred cauldron, forged from cold black iron, and in it he gathered all that he could – ashes from the trees, blackened bones from the druids who died there. What magic is left on this island, what power of the gods remains, it resides there, in the Burning Cauldron.'

Mor shook his head. 'Once,' he said, 'the druids had spells that might make the rain fall and the crops grow strong. They could pierce the veil between worlds, speak with the dead, and know the answer to all mysteries. But there is only one kind of magic left in that cauldron now – the magic of death and bloodshed, and of revenge. It is an evil thing, and no good may come of using it.'

'And the Painted People have it now,' Kai said.

'Yes,' Mor answered. 'I do not know how. Perhaps it was passed down in one of the tribes, or taken in raid. Who can say? They must have hidden it for years, and not dared to use it until they were truly desperate. But now they have, and this is an opponent that we cannot defeat – not with spears, at least.'

Laimei spat upon the ground. 'There is no man that cannot be killed, no warband that cannot be broken. You speak as though we fight a god of yours.'

'No,' said Mor. 'This is something worse than a god. For there is a madness that lurks in the hearts of my people. Perhaps every tribe has its own particular evil that it must always contend with. For the Romans, it is their longing for power that will destroy them eventually. You Sarmatians... I think it is the joy of killing that may drive you mad. But for my people, it is the whispering temptation of death. Ever since Yns Mon, I feel it there in my dreams – I think all my people do. And with that cauldron, it is no longer a whisper. It is a voice that screams and sings, and my people will not resist it.'

A shiver passed through Laimei then – so slight and subtle that only Kai could have seen it, knowing her as well as he did. 'How may we defeat them, then?' she said.

Mor smiled sadly. 'Lucius asked me that same question once, when Corvus first came south towards the Wall with the Painted People, five years ago. I told Lucius it would take magic to defeat the Painted People then, and it is the same answer now. But it was an iron magic we needed five years ago – strong spears, and bonds between warriors that are stronger than iron. I think it is a bloodier magic we shall need now, to defeat those who bear the cauldron. And, in truth, I do not know what that magic may be. But I know where we might find it.'

'Where?'

And Mor looked up at Kai then, his gaze closing upon the Sarmatian like the jaws of a trap. 'We must go south. To the Wall and beyond, if we must. We must find Lucius.'

'No,' Kai answered softly.

'The Romans betrayed you,' Laimei said. 'When they burned your lands, it was Lucius who held the torch. When they chased you into exile and death, it was he who hunted us.'

Mor nodded slowly. 'I do not know how we may defeat such an evil. But, if any can do it, it is Lucius who will guide us to the magic that we need. And if any are to stand in battle against the Painted People, it shall be Romans, and Sarmatians. This is an enemy that my kinsmen cannot face.'

'You speak as though it is the only way,' said Laimei. 'But there is another path.' She lifted a finger to point towards the North Star. 'We are so few now. The Painted People move south, and they leave only the dead behind them. Let us go north instead. To the empty, open country where we shall be free.'

Mor said nothing for a time. Then he said: 'Yes, you are right. That is another choice. But I never thought to hear you say such a thing. That the one they call the Cruel Spear would think to run from her enemies.'

Those words were as lightning on the plain, and Kai waited for the thunder to follow – for his sister to pull her sword and open the chieftain's throat, to scream down curses of all the gods and demons that she knew. He knew the laws of the world that he lived in: the sun rose in the east and set in the west, winter always followed summer, and Laimei would let no insult go unanswered.

But this time, the sun held still in the sky, and winter did not come. For Laimei made no reply, not with her words or with the iron of a blade. She held the chieftain's gaze, defiant and unspeaking, until he looked away from her.

'I pray that we shall go south,' he said slowly. 'There is a common soul that all the tribes share on this island, something precious and beautiful. I would not see it destroyed by the Painted People, even if I could live as king of those empty lands to the north. It would be a hollow throne to sit upon.'

Mor stood. The wind caught at his cloak and his hair like an unseen caress from another world, as though he had some lover from the spirit land, a fey creature that longed for what she could not have. 'I cannot go south without you,' he said. 'Whatever this magic might be, I shall need you to find it. If you wish to go north, we shall go north. Speak with one another now – when the sun rises, I must have your decision.' And he was gone, into the darkness of the camp, to join those sleepers and dreamers of the Votadini who so strongly resembled the dead.

Kai pulled his cloak close around himself and watched Laimei pace restlessly back and forth by the shore of the sea. A gentle sound reached him – the splash and whisper of stones skimming across the surface of the water, the game they had played when they were children, long before.

'There was a time,' said Kai, 'that you would have killed a man for speaking to you as Mor did.'

'Aye,' she answered. 'There was once such a time.'

'Why didn't you?'

She shook her head and said: 'It was the truth he spoke. It is ill luck to kill a man for speaking the truth. For I am afraid.'

'So am I,' Kai answered.

Laimei smiled sourly. 'Aren't you always?'

'Yes, I am. And so perhaps this fear is an enemy that I know how to fight better than you do.'

She stared back out towards the sea and thought on that for a time. 'Our people have always praised the hunters, have they not? The wolf, the eagle, the snake. We think them courageous warriors – I always have. But they rarely risk their lives. Perhaps it is braver to be hunted, to be afraid, and to face death every day. Perhaps it is braver to be a deer than it is to be a wolf.'

'It is dying that you fear?'

'No,' she said. 'I am afraid of not having enough time.'

'For what?'

'To become something other than a killer.'

Kai looked down at the empty fire, the scattered patterns of the ash. 'When we saw the Painted People dancing by the fire,' he said, 'I thought I saw something. A mark of your heart upon your face. I thought that you did not want to leave the forest.'

She gave an appreciative grunt. 'Perhaps you are not as foolish as you once were. Your eyes did not lie – I wanted to stay.'

'To fight and die against them?'

She shook her head. 'No, no, not that. Once, perhaps, but not now.' She hesitated. 'I wanted to join them.'

A familiar fear was upon Kai then. For he knew well the taste of iron in a dry mouth, the sudden touch of cold that danced across the skin, the twisting of the guts as though some living thing stirred within him. More than half his life he had spent afraid of his sister, during the long years of their feud. And for all that they had learned to love each other once again over the past few years, that fear came back in the single beat of his heart, strong as it had ever been. Because he could see the truth of it there in the moonlight – a lover's longing in her shining eyes and the turn of her lips.

She gave a wry smile. 'Why be so surprised? I saw my future there. For if one lives by the way of horse and spear as I have, then why not join the Painted People? Killing is all that matters to them – they have made it their god. Amongst them, I would truly belong. I would not be so aware of what I lack.'

'But you shall not go to them.'

'No,' Laimei said. 'I shall not. At the last I flinch. I do not have that purity of belief.'

'Or you have something else to fight for.'

And she laughed then – a bitter, mocking sound. '*That* is what you think? Perhaps I believed it too, once. But it is not so.' She looked down at her hands – worn and scarred, a groove of calloused skin marked in the centre of the palm from a lifetime of practice with the spear. And perhaps she saw blood there, all the blood she had spilt in raid and war and feud. For then she said: 'Blood is better than gold – is that not the saying of our people?'

'Yes,' said Kai. 'For all that is truly valuable is bought in blood and not gold.'

'Yet I now wonder what it has brought me – all the blood I have spilt – if I cannot love or be loved.'

'You do not think that you may change?'

'I told you before, I do not know how to.' She hesitated. 'I have told you my fear,' she said. 'Now you must tell me yours.'

Kai looked out upon the starlit sea, on that mirrored world beneath the waves – a world close enough to see, to touch, but never to reach. 'I am afraid to see Lucius, and Arite. I am afraid to see those that I left behind.'

'If we went north, perhaps at last you might forget them,' Laimei said quietly.

Kai shook his head. 'I could be one of those heroes of the old stories, gifted with a thousand years of life. And yet I do not think I could live long enough to forget them, any more than I could forget you.'

A bark of a laugh that echoed across the water. 'Fine words,' said Laimei, 'but I do not believe them.'

'If you went to the north, perhaps you might live long enough to become something more than a killer.'

'I do not believe that either,' she said. 'Perhaps Mor is right. Perhaps it is foolish to go to the north, if we gain nothing more than a few more years, spent in fear of what we have run from.'

'Though our lives be short...' Kai said, offering the words to her and expecting the customary answer, for her to complete the proverb.

But she made no answer for a long time. She was a champion, for whom thought and action had always seemed one and the same, who trusted in the guidance of the gods to make right any course that she chose. Yet she stood silent, hands upon her hips, staring out upon the waves.

At last she said: 'Perhaps it should be spoken the other way around. Great lives, and little fame. How many heroes have gone into the earth unsung? Perhaps we may still make our lives mean something, brief as they are – a campfire upon the steppe, struck once and never to be seen again in that place. But still, for a moment, there is fire, and there is light.'

As though summoned by her words, Kai saw the first touch of light in the sky – a sign of the coming dawn, the gods impatient for their answer.

'What shall we do, then?' said Kai.

'If you were not here, I would go north,' she said quietly.

'If you were not here, *I* would go north,' Kai answered.

And she smiled once more – not her usual wolfish grin before battle, or the sour smile she gave in answer to something that displeased her. But something wild and merry, a child's smile from a time long since lost.

'Let us both go south, then,' she said. 'Perhaps together, one last time, we might remember what it is to be brave.'

10

On her third day upon the Wall, that Arite saw the messenger come from the northlands. And when that rider appeared on the horizon, a shadow of a man upon a shadow of a horse, she did not know whether he was a messenger from the living or from the dead.

For Cilurnum had teemed with ghosts ever since she had arrived. While her son spent all day on the ramparts of the Wall, staring out hungrily into the wild lands of the north, she seemed to see Bahadur and Kai in the doorway of every wine shop, their faces on the sentries that patrolled the walls and stood guard at the gates. At night, while Lucius sat hunched over the maps of the north and conferred with his captains, making ready for the journey beyond the Wall, she heard the whisperings of the lost and the dead in her dreams.

And so on that third day, when she sat beside her son on the ramparts and saw that messenger coming towards the Wall, at first he seemed nothing more than a spirit gone astray, a ghost for her eyes alone.

But then, beside her, Akkas was crying out and pointing, wild-eyed with wonder at the figure who approached. An alarm call sounded close by, the horns blowing the call to arms as the sentries upon the Wall notched arrows to their bows. If it was a ghost who rode towards the Wall, it was one they could all see.

For a moment, her hope and her fear seemed to have come true – a moment where it seemed that a Sarmatian rider approached the Wall, that Kai had answered the call of the dream. Until the messenger drew closer and she saw that it was a warrior of the northern tribes who approached, riding one of the shaggy-haired ponies their people favoured. Even so, he had the look of a man who had ridden out of a dream – or a nightmare. His pale eyes were a shocking white against skin blackened with grime and ash, his cloak and his spear alike dressed in truce leaves. It was as though he were a creature of forest and moor, a warrior born from tree and earth. A monster, not a man.

He rode within bowshot of the Wall, the truce spear held high for all to see. Soon the Sarmatians were calling down challenges in the many tongues of the northlands. Then they uttered threats, commanding the stranger to speak or die. Finally they jeered at him, offering every insult they knew.

That rider from the north made no answer. He sat, still and silent upon his horse, and waited.

The sentries upon the Wall fell silent, and even the wind was still. Then there were footsteps coming up behind Arite – the steady, even pace with which Lucius always walked.

'Keep your eyes on the hillsides,' Lucius said to his sentries upon the Wall. 'There may be others with him.'

'I have been watching the hills,' Arite said. 'He is alone.'

'What does he ask of us?'

'He says nothing at all, so far.'

But it seemed that the moment the messenger had been waiting for had come at last. For he spoke then, in the Sarmatian tongue, with the halting, clumsy tone of one speaking from memory in a language that was not his own.

'If our lives be short...'

Arite shivered then, as though it truly had been a ghost that rode to the gates. 'Let our fame be great,' she answered, just as she heard other voices echo around her – the other Sarmatians on the Wall, who repeated the proverb as solemnly as a man might a speak a prayer.

The messenger from the north was looking at Lucius then. 'I know you, Lucius. Do you know me?'

And as the wind blew the cowl of the cloak from his head, Arite saw golden hair shining in the sun. The man had been hunched low in the saddle, but now sat upright – a tall man, he would have towered over her had they stood face to face, and he was thin, too thin, as though driven by some relentless hunger that he could never satisfy.

Lucius went still at the sight of him – so still that he might have been one of the spellstruck heroes of the old stories, turned to stone by the word of a witch or the whim of a fickle god. 'Yes, Corvus,' he said. 'I know you.'

A rattle of spears and the creak of bowstrings across the Wall – the Sarmatians remembered him too. A few remembered what it was to face that man in battle, and far more of their people were nothing but bones now, buried less than a mile from where they now stood. It was the war chief of the Painted People, the man who had brought a horde of death to the Wall five years before, who stood before them now.

'Remember the truce spear,' Lucius said to the men upon the

Wall, the words slow and reluctant. 'Do not shame yourselves by spilling blood upon it.' Then, to Corvus, he said: 'What brings the king of the Painted People back to the shadow of the Wall?'

'A king no longer,' said Corvus. 'And the Painted People are scattered back to their tribes, and shall never ride south again. You need have no fear of them. There is something else that you must fear now.'

'And what is that?'

'A thing best spoken softly,' Corvus answered, 'not shouted out for any man to hear. Will you come down and speak with me here, in the shadow of your Wall?'

A muttering up and down the ramparts, and all around her Arite saw the Sarmatians staring down with hard eyes upon that ghost from their past. But it seemed that Lucius paid the doubts of his men no mind. 'It will be done,' the Roman said.

Arite reached forward, laying her hand on Lucius's arm. 'Do not go, Lucius,' she whispered.

'I do not fear a man come alone with a truce spear in his hand,' Lucius said.

'It is not his spear that I am afraid of,' she said. 'Nothing good will come of speaking with him.'

Perhaps if Corvus had called up to mock him then Lucius would not have gone, for Arite had always thought that he was a man who could not be goaded. But Corvus simply waited, hunched up in the saddle and cloak pulled tight against the cold, patient as the carrion crow that gave him his name.

'I must go,' Lucius said at last. 'I must know what he will say.'

'Then at least let me come with you.'

'Why?'

Arite stared down at Corvus once more. A lone rider upon the plain was always thought an ill omen amongst the Sarmatians, who did nothing without company – only the exiled, the dishonoured, or the doomed rode alone. 'He seems to be able to poison the minds of men,' she said. 'Let us see if he can do that to me.'

The gate swung open before them. As Lucius and Arite rode out, the Wall towered above them and kept them in its embracing shadow, yet from the first step the horses took through the northern gate, Arite felt a shiver pass over her. She tapped the hilt of her knife, a wish for luck to the nameless Sarmatian god of war, and followed Lucius forward.

For all his proud talk upon the ramparts, Lucius rode forward carefully, hands light upon the reins and his spear held close. He checked his horse a good distance away from Corvus – some superstition, perhaps, to keep within that shadow of the Wall, as though it might offer fortune and protection.

'I thought you dead,' said Lucius.

'You hoped for it, you mean.'

'Yes,' Lucius said quietly. 'I hoped for it. You brought much evil with you. Many of my men died because of you.'

'I brought honourable battle to the Sarmatians,' Corvus answered. 'They love nothing more, do they not? Those that you buried, they would thank me for their brave death in battle – what Sarmatian would ask for more?'

Lucius remained silent. No doubt he knew the truth of what Corvus said.

Corvus shook his head. 'But we would never have come

south to make war on you, were it not for one of your people. The Roman, Caerellius.' At this Corvus's eyes glittered. 'I would very much like to see him again, some day.'

'Oh,' Lucius said, 'it would please me greatly if I could let the two of you tear one another's throats out.'

'You hate him too? So you see, we may agree on something.' Corvus shifted in the saddle, laid his fingers upon the leaves that bound the truce spear. 'Perhaps we may find accord on something else too.'

'Speak what you must, and speak truth,' said Lucius, casting his eyes back to the Wall. 'My men would like nothing more than to spill your blood upon this land.'

'Ill luck,' said Corvus, 'to kill a man bearing a truce spear.'

A ghost of a smile upon Lucius's face. 'Do I look like a man with any luck left to lose?'

'Ah, but all know you for a man of honour. It means everything to you. That is why your men love you. It is why Kai once loved you.' Corvus shrugged. 'But he is a weak and fickle man, is he not?' And Corvus looked at Arite then, and said: 'I think that you might know that better than most. You are Arite, aren't you?' His eyes traced up to the Wall, to where Akkas peered past the merlons, straining to see and hear. 'And that must be your son, up there behind you.'

'How do you know of me?' Arite said.

'I saw you, at the battle beneath the Wall. You led the Votadini then, with Laimei.' A thin, bitter smile. 'I once had spies in the fort, who would tell me every secret of that place. They told me of you and Kai. But he has betrayed you too. He has betrayed you all.'

'How?' she said.

'All the tribes speak of it, north of the Wall – the burning forts, the maimed dead. The Votadini return to their old lands. Laimei longs for war and glory, and Kai goes where his sister goes. With Laimei to lead them, they attract many to their banner, and they kill those who will not join them.'

'And so what must be done?' said Lucius.

'You know what must be done,' Corvus answered softly. 'And I know that you have the courage to do it.'

'And you do not?'

Corvus shifted on his cloak, like a crow fidgeting upon its perch. 'My courage matters not,' he said. 'I am no war chief of the Painted People – not any more. Nothing but a man without a tribe, waiting to die alone. And so I offer this revenge to you.'

'I do not want revenge,' Lucius replied, but his voice was unsteady as he spoke. He had never been a good liar.

'Then you shall fight because you must – perhaps it is better that way.' Corvus looked over his shoulder, towards the north. 'The Votadini are close,' he said. 'They return to their old sacred places, the ones that you burned long before. They must have the blessings of their ancestors before they go to war. That is the way of their people.' He turned back to Lucius. 'An open plain beside the river, where a great tree once stood. I think you know this place, Lucius. That is where they shall be, soon enough.'

Arite shivered then, at both the words and the memories they brought with them. She knew that place, for she herself had travelled there once before. It had been at night, and she had followed the great river northwards, its water shining silver under the light of the moon, until it had been time to strike out towards the distant mountains that were nothing but towering shadows in the darkness. She had found the Votadini gathered in their sacred place, searching for an omen – in the end, she had been their omen, leading them southwards, to war and to death. And she could feel that place beckoning to her once more, for she knew that the gods loved nothing more than to close a circle, to see a warrior journey and return.

'You shall find them there in but a few days,' said Corvus. 'They shall linger there briefly, to commune with the old dead gods, before they vanish back to the north. They shall be few, for only the Votadini gather there and not their allies. You must destroy them in that place, or they shall come back in countless numbers, and bring fire and death to the Wall.'

'Worse than the Painted People?' said Lucius.

'Very much worse. For the Painted People did not hate the Sarmatians – you were simply in our way. But the Votadini have spent five years learning how to hate you.'

'What proof have you of what you say?' Arite said. 'Why should we believe you?'

And Corvus made no answer, not with words at least. He simply pulled his cloak open. And Lucius and Arite saw that he was naked beneath that cloak – they saw too the terrible, familiar wound that he bore.

'You have seen something like this before, I think?' Corvus said. 'Upon one of your people?'

'I have,' Lucius whispered.

Corvus pulled the cloak close about him. 'It is what they do to their prisoners. To those who will not join them.'

'Why do you come here?' said Lucius. 'Why tell me this?'

And Corvus looked once more upon the land – the heather beginning to purple, the bracken rich and green, the sound of the river like a loving whisper in the air. 'I thought this place a prison,' said Corvus, 'when you Romans brought me here. An empty land of wind and rain, whose gods are dead and whose people are beaten. Yet I see now, too late, that it is beautiful. I would not see it destroyed.' And without another word he stirred his horse, and rode away to the north.

The rain began to fall heavy about them, rain as thick as mist. Soon, they could not see Corvus, the distant hills, the plain. Even the Wall was made nothing but a shadow. Lucius and Arite were alone in the rain.

'Do you think that he speaks true?' Lucius said.

'I think there is truth in what he says,' Arite answered.

'That is not quite the same thing.'

'No,' Arite said. 'It is not.'

Arite had seen Lucius face death many times before. When he was a prisoner of her people, when he had fought a great king of the Sarmatians, when he had led his warriors against the Painted People. Perhaps for the first time that she could remember, she saw him afraid.

'It does not matter,' said Arite. And a sadness was upon her then, knowing the truth of the words that she spoke. 'You will go to the north. You have no choice.'

'Why?'

'If there is a chance that Kai will be there, you shall take it. You shall always regret it if you do not.' She shivered, then clutched her cloak close against her skin as the rain fell harder. 'May I ride with you? I can steady a spear as well as any man in the warband.'

'Better than most,' said Lucius. 'But no. If it is to be war, I shall not make you watch Kai die.' He swallowed heavily. 'And if he must die, let his son live. You must stay, and guard him.'

'But you shall try to speak with him first?' Arite said. 'Go to him with a truce spear, before you go to fight. Will you promise me that?'

'Yes,' Lucius answered. 'I shall.'

Afterwards, when it was much too late, she would curse herself. For the signs were there – the way that his gaze slid away from hers, his too-tight grip upon the spear, and above all the way his horse tossed its head and muttered to itself, as if ashamed.

For it was always said amongst her people that horses loved the truth, and could not stand to hear their masters lie.

THE SACRIFICE
AD 180

11

It was a great company that Lucius led north of the Wall – five hundred heavy cavalry, the scales of their armour glistening in the sun, the hollow dragon banners they carried drinking in the wind and flying high above them. Horses twice as tall as the ponies of the northlands, men made giants by their tall helms and the great lances they carried, they were a company of heroes who should have nothing to fear beyond the Wall. And yet Lucius could not shake the feeling, as they followed the river north, that they had already been beaten. That they had lost the battle long before, and rode now through the lands of the dead.

Once, this had been the home of the Votadini, their hunting runs and grave barrows, their grazing grounds and sacred places. Until five years before, when Lucius had led his Sarmatians north of the Wall to burn and drive the Votadini away.

He had seen that land blanketed in fire, crops burned and herds butchered. Of the Votadini, he had killed mercifully few, for most had fled before the Sarmatians came north. But Lucius could still remember those unlucky ones who had been left behind. A Votadini shepherd who returned from a distant grazing ground with a wave and a smile, not knowing that he greeted his murderers. An old man in a shieling, his mind fallen to pieces, who was too sick of mind and body to flee, who had wept as the Sarmatians came, mistaking them for some invaders of half a hundred years before. The sick and the lost, the old and the mad – they had been Lucius's bloody prize in that war beyond the Wall.

Little trace now remained of what they had done – a forest of trees they had cut down had become a sea of bracken, a cluster of burned shielings was now overgrown with grass, and the ruined croplands were snarled up by thistles and wildflowers. The land had forgotten them, but he was certain that its people had not. Ghosts seemed to watch them from every forest and bank of heather, unseen eyes clustering thick about the cairns on the hillsides, peering up from the swift-running river. It was as though an army of vengeful spirits closed about them, and what use were spears against the dead?

They followed the river north into the wild country, until at last they came to an open plain whose shape Lucius half remembered, like a vision from a near-forgotten dream. And though it had been many years since he had stood in that place, he dismounted and walked to a single unmarked patch of ground. He knelt there, pressing his hand through the tall grass until he found what he was looking for – a hard shape pressing into his palm, rough against the skin. The remnant of a root, the ghost of a tree.

The sound of a horse whickering close by, and when Lucius turned, he found it was Tasius who approached. Now a captain of the Sarmatian *ala*, he bore a twisting scar where the Novantae arrow had cut through his cheek, giving him a gruesome, permanent smile.

'Can you settle a wager, sir?' Tasius said.

'Perhaps,' Lucius answered. 'What is it?'

Tasius nodded back towards the company. 'The men wonder what it is you search for. One of them thinks it is a stone to mark buried treasure. Another thinks it is a door to the underworld, and you mean to summon the dead to fight alongside us.'

'A door to the underworld?'

Tasius hissed through his teeth. 'The youngest amongst us, Iodas. He listens to too many campfire stories. He has a fanciful mind, but he means well. If there was such a door, he would follow you through it into the underworld if you asked.'

Once more, Lucius let his hand rest upon the ground. 'There was a tree here once,' he said. 'A sacred oak, from which the Votadini hung their trophies of war, their gifts to the gods. As great a treasure to them as the golden eagles are to a Legion.' Lucius hesitated. 'We cut it down, and burned the roots. And yet they still grow.'

'Stubborn, and strong. I like this tree.' Tasius turned away, and looked towards the river. 'The Votadini will come here?'

'They will,' said Lucius. 'They meet their friends upon the plain. Their enemies, they meet beside a river. And we are no friends of the Votadini. Still, I think they shall speak with us.'

'Why?'

'I earned that much love, from Mor and from Kai,' said Lucius. 'Even if we are to fight, they will come here first with truce leaves on their spears.'

'When shall we see them?'

'Tonight, I hope,' Lucius said.

'I do not think it wise that we stay out here after dark, sir.'

'We will have little choice. But I think that they shall come to parley with us.'

The captain scratched at his jaw, and nodded towards the forest. 'I shall send riders out to the woods.'

'Why?'

'We shall need truce leaves for the spears, if we mean to parley with the Votadini.'

'We shall not need them,' said Lucius. 'There will be no truce.'

'Sir?'

A long breath in, and then out, yet still Lucius's voice trembled when he spoke once more: 'I must ask you to do something for me tonight.'

'Anything, Great Captain,' Tasius said. 'Iodas is not the only man who would follow you to the underworld.'

'I ask something worse than that. Something shameful.'

'Evil things are done in war. When they *must* be done.' Tasius hesitated. 'Must this be done?'

'Yes,' whispered Lucius, 'it must. And so this is what I need from you.'

Nightfall came slowly, the sun seeming to hang still before it fell fully from the sky – perhaps some god of light and honour wished to give Lucius every chance to change his mind. But when at last the darkness fell, Lucius was glad of it. Evil deeds were better done by night.

Once the sun was gone, there were long hours spent waiting. That endless, maddening waiting that often comes with darkness, each minute seeming an hour. The Sarmatians gathered close about him, the horses restless, the men impatient. Longing for an enemy that they could see, and touch, and kill.

Yet for all the misery of that waiting, still Lucius found himself praying to the gods that the Votadini would not come. That the whole night might pass, one agonising moment at a time, and they would see no sign of their enemies.

But even as he whispered that prayer, he saw movement across the water.

Shadows gathered upon the bank of the river, faceless and insubstantial at first. Then the clouds broke open, and the light of the half-moon was upon the Votadini. The spear blades dulled with truce leaves, silver torcs glimmering about the necks of their captains, their cloaks dyed brightly in blue and yellow and red. For always the Votadini had treasured beautiful things, even in war.

They would go to their graves beautiful, at least.

Lucius could not help but look north then, to the woodlands that fringed the river. His shameful secret waited there – that was where he had sent Tasius and two hundred of his warriors, to ford the river under cover of the trees and the darkness.

A shiver ran through Lucius, to think of what would come when the signal was given. Tasius and his riders coming out of the woods, the Votadini pinned against the river with no hope of escape. The blood running thick in the water, a tribe killed by a coward's trick.

He had promised Arite that he would speak under truce with the Votadini. But he knew, in his heart, that he could not keep that promise. There would be no peace in the north until the Votadini were destroyed. There would be no peace for him until Kai was dead. And so Lucius stirred his horse forward, gave a wave of the hand to bring his men with him. He did not trust himself to wait any longer.

Step by step, his horse made its way towards the bank of the river. And a calm was settling upon Lucius, for in a single turn of the hourglass, it would all be done. One hour of terrible killing, and then back beyond the Wall. If they could return before the dawn, perhaps that killing might seem like nothing more than a dream, fearsome but fleeting. A single hour, and then a lifetime spent trying to forget that hour.

The Votadini struck torches, beacons welcoming the Sarmatians to the parley, and when those flames flared high Lucius was afraid once more. He could see the war host clearly now – the bright spears decorated with feathers and shields daubed in lime – but it was not they who made him afraid.

For beside the warriors there were children, scurrying from place to place, and women who bore no weapons of war. And Lucius remembered the Novantae, when they had come to fight and die beneath the Wall – not a war party come to claim the favour of their gods, but a wandering tribe, exiled and dwindling, that had come south to die. And there was doubt creeping in, with each slow step his horse took forward.

Closer they rode, close enough to see the twisting tattoos upon the skin of the Votadini, the breath of their ponies frosting in the air. Beside him, Lucius heard the music of bronze scales shifting, the scrape of horn across iron, as the signalman who rode at his side readied himself. For the Votadini were drawing close to the water, stepping into the jaws of the trap. It was almost time.

But he could hear horses calling then. Sarmatian horses, breaking the silence as they whickered and snorted from the far side of the water. And from the ranks of the Votadini two riders came forward – Kai and Laimei.

They still rode their Sarmatian warhorses, old and war-weary now, princes and giants amongst the little ponies that the Votadini favoured. Those horses must have given up all hope of seeing their kin again, and perhaps they had even thought themselves the last of their kind. And now those horses saw their brothers and sisters across the water, and they called out in joy in the knowledge that they were not alone.

And Lucius could see Kai was smiling then, as light and carefree as though this were some chance meeting upon the steppe. He rode to the edge of the river, and he was waving and beckoning to Lucius as though five years had not passed. As though they had never abandoned one another. Two friends meeting by a river after a long absence – what could be more beautiful than that?

For a moment, a mad desire to call out to Kai, to warn him away, to warn him of Lucius's own treachery. But instead, Lucius licked dry lips, and made ready to speak the words that would kill his friend. And, to his shame, he knew then that what drove him was not revenge, but fear. Lucius was afraid to hear Kai speak, of how those words might unman him. He would have to act now, or he would never have the courage again. He raised his hand as if in greeting, drew his breath in to give the order.

But a different horn was blowing then – high-pitched and wavering, as though in mockery of the sound it replaced. And with it came drums, beating like rolling thunder, and war songs sounding out from behind them, sounds that Lucius had not heard for many years, that he had hoped to never hear again.

The war music of the Painted People.

12

At first, Kai thought it to be a waking nightmare, one of those dreams where spirits are made flesh and come from the darkness as though made from the night itself. The shadows of men were taking form as they rushed down from the hillside, gripping knives and spears and moving like they were carried by the wind, and when the light of the moon fell fully upon them, he saw them all too clearly – the Painted People, numberless and terrible, sweeping down from the hills towards the Sarmatians. Towards Lucius.

As though it truly were a nightmare, Kai found he could not move or speak. If he had been able to say anything in those first few terrible moments, it would not have been to cry a warning, to order an advance or a retreat. It would have been to offer a wish to the gods – to change places with Lucius. To have the Roman live, and for Kai to die in his place.

'The ford,' he said. 'To the south. We must—'

'It is too late,' Laimei answered. And her voice was calm, and weary. A champion of a hundred battles, she had seen men die in a thousand different ways – there was nothing here to surprise her or move her. Only the certain knowledge of what would come next.

Kai heard the Sarmatian horns sound the alarm, the music of those notes achingly familiar, saw the Sarmatians wheel as one to face the Painted People. They showed no sign of panic to find themselves so outnumbered – they still had the horseman's faith, a belief as strong as a holy man's love of the gods, that the Painted People would not be able to stand against them. Five years before, that was how the Painted People had been defeated, broken over and over again by but a few Sarmatian cavalry in the shadow of the Wall.

But when the charge came, this time the Painted People did not part before the wave of horse and spear. Once again, they threw themselves willingly onto the long spears to drag them and break them. Once more they made a fortress of their dying flesh and glittering spear-points, and the Sarmatian charge shattered against it.

A moment of stillness, almost of intimacy. The horses and men could have been the stitching of a tapestry, the close press of the battle fixed to a single unmoving moment. Then, almost as one, the Painted People stepped forward, and with their grasping, bloodied hands, they reached up and began to pull the Sarmatians from the saddles.

Kai was at the riverbank then, screaming in the language of their people, calling for them to run, to ride to the river and turn south towards the ford. But they could not hear him over the sound of the killing.

All was shadow and motion in the darkness. Spears rising and falling, the glint of the stars and moon upon the murderous little knives that the Painted People favoured. The horses biting and kicking, and for a moment it seemed that there was something that the Painted People were afraid of – no fear of death at the hands of men, but some horror of the animal that their mad faith could not still completely.

But once more, that mocking, high-pitched horn sounded from the darkness, and step by step the Painted People began to drive the Sarmatians to the river. They would soon be trapped in the place where heroes always fought to prove their valour, the soft ground beside a water that was the undoing of heavy cavalry. Already Kai could see horses stumbling and slipping and falling, panic spreading through men and horses both. For there were no heroes there beside the water now, only desperate men who were soon to die.

It seemed as though that was to be Kai's fate – to watch, helpless, as his kin were cut to pieces in front of him. Until, from close by, he heard the ringing sound of hooves, and warhorns singing out once more.

For upon Kai's side of the river, riders were approaching from the darkness. There was a moment of terror when he thought them to be more warriors of the Painted People, until he saw the tall spears of Sarmatian warriors, the rippling scales of their armour like the hide of a dragon. He saw too their war gear cinched close and marked with soot, no dragon banners flying above to drink the wind and scream war cries of their own. The marks of those who rode in silence for only one purpose.

But their captain held his spear horizontal before him – the old sign of the peace offering on the steppe, the gift of a weapon to a war leader. It was a man that Kai knew from long before, a man called Tasius, who rode straight to him and said: 'Tell me how to save him. How to save Lucius.'

'There is a ford to the south,' Kai said. 'Deep, but perhaps they may make it through.'

Each moment counted, and with each beat of the heart, another Sarmatian died across the water. But the captain spoke once more before he gave the signal, the words halting and pained: 'We came to kill you, when you thought it to be a truce,' Tasius said. 'A shameful thing. Forgive me, before we fight and die together?'

'I forgive you,' Kai said, his voice hollow, the words as ashes in his mouth. And then the Sarmatians' horns were ringing out and sounding the rally, his horse's hooves beating against the grass as he made for the ford. And on the other side of the river he heard a horn call an answer, just once, before it was cut off forever.

He found the place of the ford the Votadini had marked many years before, a part of the river which seemed like any other but where a steady horseman might cross. No time to test the water – a touch of his heels to his horse and he plunged into the river, his horse tilting her head up and gasping for air at the shock of the cold.

Behind him he could hear the others – Laimei, cursing to see her brother ahead of her, and the Sarmatians, their armour chiming like music as the men whispered prayers to the gods of war and the hunt. Above it all the horns calling, over and over again, for their companions to rally to them.

Before him, Kai could see Lucius and his warriors fighting their way towards the river. They were so few now, their spears broken and armour hacked apart, painted in blood and their horses staggering with exhaustion. Lucius was there amongst them – unhelmed, his golden hair streaked with red blood, the sword still bright in his hand. His face was grey, and marked with that terrible, eerie calm of those who know they are soon to die. A life measured in moments, and so he would spend those moments precisely. Each stroke of the sword, each command given, every word of love a captain may offer to those who are to die with him: all of them would be perfectly measured.

Some god must have whispered in Lucius's ear to make him turn at just that moment. And he would have looked on what must have seemed impossible to him – Kai on his side of the uncrossable river, as though carried there by the whim of a water spirit. And Lucius stood tall in the saddle with his sword held high, a banner of iron for his men to follow, as he called the retreat and led them to the river. Close behind, the shadows of the Painted People pursued them like vengeful spirits.

'Let us buy them time,' Kai said to the Sarmatians who had followed him through the ford, and they answered him as though he were their captain – the echoing rattle as the lances came forward, the horses dancing to the charge, the sweet songs of death sounding out around him.

The Painted People were before them in a moment, arms open and offering themselves to the lances as though they sought to embrace their own deaths. But Kai called for the Sarmatians to break and turn, and they parted at his words – a few reaching out with the lances, striking at the Painted People as a fisherman might thrust at the water, and he heard a cry of victory from Laimei as her lance found its home in flesh. Only a few of the Painted People were slain, but he had checked the horde for a moment, and above the war songs and the splintering of spears, Kai could hear the crash of horses entering the river.

'Ride for your lives!' Kai called, as he led those warriors back to the river, and together they plunged into the water, like swimmers to the sea.

All about Kai then horses were tripping and falling, men thrown into the water and disappearing in a moment, pulled down by the weight of their armour, clutching up helplessly towards the surface. For the Sarmatians knew each river to be a warrior that hungry for battle. That was why their waters surged forth in the flood season to claim their bloodprice, carrying away careless children as trophies of war. This river was no different – it too longed to hunt and to kill.

And so they fought against it as much as they fought the Painted People. Kai felt hands reach out and grasp his, saw as horses leaned against one another to remain upright, and it was as though all of them, men and horses, sought to lash a raft together of their flesh, and make themselves one against the fury of the water. And beside Kai, he saw that it was Lucius that he held upright in the river, Lucius who in turn held him safe.

At last they were across the river. The horses lurching and staggering, up to their knees in black mud, the warriors bearing broken weapons, ashen-faced with defeat. Together they turned back, exhausted and shivering, to guard the ford against their pursuers.

But the Painted People did not follow them. It was as though they were monsters from the old stories, the blood-drinkers who could not cross running water. They simply stood there, still and silent, dead Sarmatians and butchered horses scattered at their feet.

'Why do they not follow us?' Lucius said, his voice hoarse.

'Fifty of us could hold this ford against ten times their number,' Kai answered.

'They do not care if they live or die.'

'They do not,' said Laimei, her spear black with blood. And she pointed to the other side of the river, to a shadow in the darkness. 'But he has use for them yet.'

For there before them was the shadow of a man, a tall shape that was hauntingly familiar, who danced from one Sarmatian corpse to another like the carrion bird that gave him his name. It was Corvus they saw, the Maimed King, who clasped the faces of the corpses in his hands and wiped away the blood and the dirt, as though he sought some boon companion, some beloved friend, there amongst the dead.

'Corvus,' said Lucius. 'He searches for me.'

'Yes,' Laimei answered. 'He still thinks that you matter.'

To that, Lucius gave no proud warrior's answer, no curse upon her name. Kai had never seen him look so defeated, as he huddled in the rain and stared at the men that were left to him. Of the five hundred men he had led to that place, a few dozen remained. Many of them, hacked and bloodied and slumped in their saddles, would not outlive the night.

Kai knew well that there was no greater shame for a captain than to have led his people into an ambush. But he found he could offer no words of comfort – not to Lucius, not at that moment. For he remembered the men who had ridden from the forest, their armour darkened and their banners held low. The murderers at Lucius's command, who had come there to kill him and his people.

13

They fled from the river like travellers from the underworld, those fools or heroes from the old stories who so desperately try to crawl out of a land of death. Wet leaves pressed against them like grasping fingers, the blood slowly drying upon their skin like the ritual paint of a festival, the only sound the ragged breathing of horses pushed beyond exhaustion.

For Lucius, it was a journey between waking and dreaming too. For though it should have been impossible to sleep, time and time again he would drift away between one breath and the next – in one moment riding exhausted through that shadowy country, and then he would be drowning in a river of blood, or having his skin peeled from his body by laughing, twisting shadows of men, or watching Kai and his men burned alive by a fire that Lucius himself had set. Then the dreaming world would begin to tilt and tip, and Lucius would wake to find himself about to slide from his saddle.

It was exhaustion in part that cast him into sleep, that weariness after battle that is like nothing else. But perhaps, more than that, his mind was in its own retreat from what had happened, and it craved the forgiveness of sleep. Even the nightmares he had were kinder than the shame he felt now.

A shifting in the column of riders, a man moving beside him, and Lucius did not have to look to know who it was.

'May I swallow your evil days, Lucius,' Kai said tonelessly.

Lucius closed his eyes – hoping, just for a moment, to slide once more into sleep. But his body betrayed him and would not grant him that escape. And so he opened his eyes once more, and said: 'You want to know why I came to kill you?'

A whisper answered him: 'I do.'

'Corvus,' said Lucius, the name like a piece of rotten meat in his mouth. 'He told us that you had burned the northern forts and killed our people. That you meant to bring a war to the Wall.'

'And you believed him?'

A bitter laugh broke from Lucius's lips. 'Why not? You were already a deserter. And why should the Votadini not come seeking revenge, after what I did to them?'

A moment of silence. Lucius kept his gaze low, upon the neck of his horse. But he could well imagine the look of disappointment on Kai's face.

'You gave the Votadini great cause to hate you,' Kai said at last. 'But I did not think I had done such a thing, to earn such hatred from you.'

'Why should I not?' Lucius said, meeting Kai's gaze at last. 'You fled north of the Wall. Leaving me when I needed you most. Leaving Arite behind.' A hesitation then, but he could not resist using the weapon he had. 'And you abandoned your son too.'

The words struck home, for Kai was silent, his eyes wide and solemn, the face of one condemned to die. And there was a longing from Lucius to call back the words he had spoken, to undo what had been done. A foolish hope, he knew, for not even the gods had such a power as that. They too had to live in the shadow of the things they had done.

And so Lucius turned from Kai then, and rode on unspeaking. He wondered if it was true that a man might die of shame.

At last, it seemed they had ridden far enough through the fells to be thought safe from their pursuers, and beneath the light of the moon and in the shadow of the mountains they came to a halt. Lucius went to tell his Sarmatians to rest, but there was no need, for without waiting for his command they slid from the saddle and unlaced their armour, curling up together in blankets and sharing the comfort of touch. *By the law of the Roman army, I could have them flogged,* he thought, and felt a bitter smile steal across his lips. How little that law meant now, in this place.

He desired the mercy of sleep himself, but he knew it would not be granted. For he saw those familiar shadows gathering in a circle around him – Kai, and Laimei, and Mor. How many times he had seen such a vision in his dreams. How much he had longed for it before, and feared it now.

They could not risk a fire, so they sat together in the dark. A shadow offered him a skin of something to drink – once Lucius's eyes had adjusted he saw that it was Mor, a sad smile upon the chieftain's face. When Lucius drank, it was the taste of heather beer that greeted him, sharp and harshly sweet upon his lips. He offered the skin in turn to Laimei and to Kai, but neither of them would take it from him.

They sat in silence together for a time, each waiting for the other to speak.

'We came south to find you, Lucius,' Mor said at last. 'And I am glad that we have.'

'And he came north to kill us.' It was Laimei who spoke, with a kind of quiet, almost disinterested hatred.

'No need to speak of that now,' Mor said. 'We have all done shameful things, have we not? But none of that matters now. Only the Painted People matter.'

'You came to find me?' said Lucius. 'Why?'

'*He* thinks that you may help us,' Laimei said.

Mor nodded. 'Yes,' he said, 'we came to find you. The people north of the Wall will not fight the Painted People. Many of them have joined Corvus already, and those that have not are dead or in hiding.' He gestured around him, to the men and the women and children scattered about the darkened camp, the remnants of a dying people. 'We, the Votadini – we might be the last who have not fallen under his spell. And we cannot stand alone. Will you fight with us?'

It took Lucius a long time to answer. 'I have seen the best Legions fight against the most desperate, blood-mad tribes upon the Rhenus,' he said eventually. 'I have fought with Sarmatians too, whose courage I thought unmatched. But I have never seen men fight like that.'

'Yes,' Mor said. 'They are different now – worse than what you faced five years ago. For they have an evil magic with them. The Burning Cauldron.'

A chill touch across his skin, the kind all warriors knew as the sign of an omen – a glimpse of death from the spirits beyond. 'Tell me what that is,' said Lucius.

And Mor spoke then – of burning groves and dying druids, butchery upon holy islands and evil magic gathered into a cauldron of iron. Even as the tale was told, it seemed a story that Lucius somehow knew already, that he had waited his whole life to hear again. A story that offered a road to follow, a path before him that led to his death, and all he wanted to do was turn from it.

When at last Mor had fallen silent, Lucius said: 'And you think they mean to break through the Wall?'

'Much more than that,' the chieftain answered. 'They mean to bring the whole island under their sway. To fill all these lands with that terrible kind of worship, and make a throne for their Maimed King to sit upon.'

'There are still near four thousand Sarmatians across the Wall,' Lucius said. 'The Sixth Legion stationed near Eboracum. They shall not break through the Wall, or take the island. There are not enough of them.'

A look of grief then upon Mor's face. 'You speak of walls and numbers,' he said. 'They shall do no good, not against men who carry the Burning Cauldron. The whole island will bend the knee to them. What we need to defeat them, it is—'

'Magic,' Lucius answered flatly. 'You have said so before. You think this magic may be found by me?'

'I do.'

'What magic did you see upon the banks of the river, when I led my men to be cut to pieces?'

'Any captain may make such a mistake,' Mor said softly. 'And the magic was never with you alone. It was with all of us, together, and the love that we shared for one another. And here we are once more.'

The light of the moon went dark for Lucius as Kai stood up before him. 'If it is from love that you hope to find such a magic,' Kai said, his voice trembling, 'then there is none left to be found here.' And with that, he stalked away into the darkness.

Laimei made to rise and follow her brother, but was stilled by a gesture from her chieftain. 'Let him go,' Mor said. 'He is not himself.'

'He is right,' Lucius said. 'There are only broken bonds between us. What use are we together now?'

The chieftain of the Votadini said nothing for a time. 'I heard what you said to him,' he said at last, 'when we came here. That he abandoned you, and Arite, and the son he has never seen.'

'I spoke truly.'

A shrug. 'True words may be cruelly spoken.' Mor cocked his head to the side. 'Did you think to ask him why he went to the north, and left you behind?'

Lucius made to answer, but found that he could not.

'Not even I know that,' Mor continued, 'and often it has been said of me that I may see into the hearts of men.' The chieftain hesitated. 'Ask him,' he said softly, 'before you decide. Before it is too late.'

Slowly, Lucius shook his head. 'It shall do no good,' he said. 'It is already too late.'

He could see a quiet kind of sadness marked upon Mor's face, a fatherly disappointment. 'Then what shall you do instead?' said Mor.

'In the morning we shall go south to the Wall.' Lucius looked at his remaining men, who lay huddled upon the ground like a pack of dogs sharing warmth. 'I shall see them safely home. Then send a rider to Eboracum, and call for the Governor to send the Sixth Legion north.'

'You think that Caerellius may help you? He was an ally to Corvus, once.'

'I must hope that he will see the greater danger here.'

'Hope.' Mor shook his head slowly. 'That shall not save you, or us. Not even a Legion may stand against the Painted People. The only thing that can—'

'Do not say it,' Lucius said quietly. 'I have heard enough.'

And then another voice spoke from the darkness: 'Fools,' said Laimei.

Lucius had almost forgotten she was there. For she had sat in silence as they spoke, picking at her teeth with a thumb, her eyes moving about as though she stared into a dancing fire rather than the empty air. Lucius had thought her lost in some memory of the past, some former glory that she had brought out like a treasure from her mind, turning it over and trying, impossibly, to recapture that feeling once again.

'You are both fools,' she said, 'and both wrong. It is always the way of men. To see what you wish, and not what is truly there.' She stood, and hooked her thumbs into her sword belt. 'It is the champions such as I who are cursed to see the truth.'

'Tell us, then,' said Mor.

'How many of the Painted People do you think there are?'

Mor thought for a moment. 'Ten thousand, at least,' he said. 'From all the tribes they have gathered in the northlands.'

Her grey eyes were upon Lucius then, empty and unreadable as they always were. 'How many of the Painted People did you fight beside the river?' she said.

'Perhaps two thousand,' Lucius answered, a cold touch of fear dancing across his skin.

For he knew he had been wrong – Laimei had not been lost

in her memories. Her champion's mind had been working like a Greek mathematician's, thinking to solve the mysteries of the universe with numbers alone. The weight of a spear, the courage of a man, the exact moment that a shield wall might hold or break: all could be known and counted if one had the art, and she had seen it all.

'So, then,' said Laimei, 'where are the rest of the Painted People?'

And, as if brother answered sister, he heard a wordless cry ring out. For Kai was staring to the south where, impossibly, it was as though the sun rose in a different place.

A great fire upon the horizon – a new dawn rising from the Wall.

14

The sound of horns calling, soft and distant, like the sound of a distant festival, and a scent of smoke in the air that brought memories of campfires and festivals, nights spent free upon the steppe – these were the sensations that woke Arite from her sleep.

There was a smile upon her lips then, as she reached out into the shadows, her half-awake mind thinking that she might feel a lover's skin against hers, might find Kai waiting for her there in the darkness.

But her smile was gone a moment later, cold fear clutching at her heart. For they were horns of war that rang in the air, the Sarmatian calls of alarm and the victory knells of the Painted People. The smoke was not the comforting scent of campfire, but the acrid smell of a burning building. In a moment she was at the door of the *principia*, the commander's quarters where Lucius had insisted that she stay, and she knew at once that it was already too late to run. When she looked out upon the fort of Cilurnum, she looked out upon the prelude to her death.

The Painted People must have struck suddenly that night.

Lucius had taken the best of the fort's men beyond the Wall, with only the fort guard left behind. Those men must not have seen the Painted People creeping to the Wall until it was too late, until the arrows were sweeping the men from the ramparts, the gates were staved in by the blow of a ram, the fires lit and tearing through the fort.

Already parts of the fort were aflame, that acrid smoke in the air scented with oil and wine and grain from storehouses and barracks. Upon the Wall she could see the Painted People swarming, raising their victory banners unopposed. And the last flicker of hope died as she saw the southern gates closed and burning, tattooed warriors standing before them. The trap had closed about her.

She saw Sarmatians wandering the streets, laughing to see their deaths upon them, stumbling on their bowed horsemen's legs and calling challenges to any who would face them – in search of a warrior's ending, all hope of victory gone. And she too felt the madman's laughter rising in her throat, the careless joy with which her people had been taught to meet their deaths when the time came, that longing to go out into those streets and try to find a good way to die.

She felt her hand close about the handle of her sword, took half a step forward, and it was as though she watched another acting through her body, as though she saw some half-remembered dream. And then, behind her, she heard a scraping of feet across the tiles. She looked back to see Akkas walking towards her with tottering steps, his hands outstretched.

For all the tales of bravery that he loved to hear, Akkas was still so young. In that moment he was a child knowing, perhaps for the first time, what it might mean to die. He looked to her with a child's beautiful ignorance, the belief that she could somehow keep him safe.

She could hear the war songs echoing loudly in the streets outside, the sound of the killing drawing closer. She knew then what she must do.

She fell to her knees, rapping the hilt of the sword against the floor tiles until she heard them ring hollow, and then she was stabbing out the mortar and clawing under the edges. Her nails were splitting to the quick and her fingers were soon slick with blood, but the tile was lifting, and beneath it, she could see a hollow place. The hypocaust, Lucius had called it, where wood was burned to heat the tiles from below. Still unswept and thick with ashes, looking for all the world like a funeral pyre that had already been lit, a place for the dead and not the living.

Akkas recoiled from the sight, for he must have known then what she intended. 'Please,' he said, clutching at her arm. 'Do not make me go down there.'

'You must,' she said. And the lie came easy then, the loving lie, as she knew what she must say: 'It is how you will save my life. Lie down there, and make not a sound. No matter what you hear. That is how you may save me.'

She saw his courage return – it was a hero's task she had given him, to lie and cower in silence, and at once he was crawling into the floor, then looking back up at her with a face already greyed with ash.

She placed the tile back down, as though sealing her child within a tomb, and she stood once more. She waited for the Painted People to come.

She knew then that it was not courage that sent the Sarmatians outside hurrying towards their death, but a

particular kind of cowardice. For it was an easy thing to give
up all hope, and charge gratefully to a quick death. The more
frightful thing by far was to stand there and wait for death
to come, and it took all of the will that she had to hold her
ground, a bare sword held in a shaking hand.

All that time, she was speaking an endless, tumbling rush
of words – words of love to her child, tales of his father that
she had been too stubborn to speak before, dreams of the
life that Akkas might lead, and confessions of her own that
she had never told anyone. A lifetime of words to speak, a
hundred beatings of the heart to speak them.

The sound of footsteps close by and the howling laughter of
the victorious, of those seeking trophies of gold and flesh. Her
shaking hand went still around the hilt of sword, and Arite
knew that she was ready. Her death at their hands would be
slow, a thing of nightmares. But if she sold her life well, and
if, bloodied and exhausted, the Painted People did not think
to search that place too closely, then her son might yet live.

They came to her then – a band of six, their flesh blackened
with soot and daubed in blood, their eyes dull and already
weary from the killing. They were panting for breath, for they
must have run there, outpacing their companions, eager for
the shining prizes they hoped to take from the commander's
quarters. They found her instead, and they grinned at first,
their teeth shining wolfish white against their filthy skin.
Until they saw the sword in her hand rise, saw her slide one
foot back, graceful as a dancer, into a practised swordsman's
stance.

'Do you have a champion,' she said, 'brave enough to face
me alone?'

There was only silence to answer her. For there was no

warrior's code here, it seemed, or even the base cruelty of the conqueror – either of those she might have understood. They looked at her as they might have looked upon a sickly animal they had to butcher. It was an act to be done from bloody duty, and nothing more.

They spread out in a ragged line, tested the weight of their weapons. She looked between them, trying to guess at which one would move first. She hoped she might fight well enough that they would have to kill her quickly.

One last moment of perfect stillness. She felt each drop of sweat that beaded upon her skin, the coolness of the tiles beneath her bare feet, the binding of the hilt pressed tight into her palm. She saw a shifting of weight from one of the Painted People, an echoing ripple of motion that passed through them all.

And she heard a voice behind them speak a single word: 'Stop.' Then, like something from an impossible and terrible nightmare, she heard her name spoken: 'Arite.'

A figure came forward, tall and thin and golden-haired, his eyes shining wildly, so alive and so in contrast to those men that he led, as though he were the only living man left in an army of the dead. There was no surprise for her, but only a feeling of fate, to see that it was Corvus who stood there before her.

'Do you have the courage to face me?' she said. 'Or did they cut away your courage too?'

He smiled at her. 'You cannot make me angry, Arite. For I know why you chase death so eagerly.' The smile faded, and he said: 'When last I saw you, you had a child who watched us both from the ramparts of the Wall. Tell me, where is he now?'

Arite made no answer, but she saw his eyes fall upon her fingers, taking in the blood and the mortar dust and her broken nails. And then he was circling around her, careful and patient, his eyes hunting across the ground until at last they fell upon the broken tile. He bent down and rapped his knuckles upon the tile, listening to the hollow echo that answered it.

'In the hypocaust,' he said. 'Very clever.'

A coldness then, bitter and deep. The kind of cold she had felt before when she had been badly wounded, when her life had threatened to bleed away from her. Now it was hope that was bleeding then, leaving only something hard and hollow behind it – the empty longing for a revenge that she could not have.

Corvus must have seen it. Perhaps her eyes were now as dull as those of the men he led, and perhaps it was a look he knew all too well. For he said: 'There is a way that you may save him. Put down the sword, and I shall tell you how.'

A longing to believe him – a foolish, impossible longing that she tried to push aside. 'How may I believe anything you say?'

'There is an oath that my men will hold me to,' he said softly. And there was a flickering of life in the dead eyes of the Painted People, as they turned their murderous gaze upon their leader. 'Upon the Burning Cauldron, I swear there is a way for your child to live.'

She made no answer at first. A glorious death was something that her people treasured above all else – what better chance would there be than this? The king of the Painted People was tantalisingly, maddeningly close. Perhaps she might cut her way to him, before they killed her. A chance in a thousand, one that any hero would choose.

Then, above the sound of the fire and the butchery outside, the victory cries of the Painted People and the death songs of the Sarmatians, something else could be heard. A soft, echoing weeping that came up from the floor beneath them, as Akkas could hold his silence no longer. The sound of a child, begging for his life.

A ringing clatter echoed through the chamber as Arite cast her sword to the ground. 'Tell me, then,' she said. 'Tell me how I may save my son.'

15

Upon the horizon, the flames burned brightly – the night sky above a bloom of red and gold, the stars hidden by smoke. All about Kai, the others gathered, Sarmatian and Votadini alike, to bear witness to that fire.

There were some amongst the Votadini who gave soft calls of victory to see the Wall broken, the fulfilment of a dream long wished for – revenge against the Empire that had burned them from their own lands. The Sarmatians were silent. That fire spoke of death to them, a great pyre for the friends and companions they had left behind. A little grief in that silence, but, more than that, the hope that those men had met their deaths bravely. For them, there was no shame or sadness in a death well met.

But even so, from amongst them, a single voice cried out in the night.

It was Lucius, his hands raised, trembling and shaking, towards that fire upon the Wall. The Roman tried to speak but it seemed the words would not come. He turned away, pressed his face against the mane of his horse and wept.

'What grieves you so?' asked Kai. 'What matters that fort to you after the lives you have already thrown away today?'

And Lucius lifted his face, and his horse's mane shone with the tears he had left there. 'Arite is there,' he whispered. 'Your son is there. Can you forgive me?'

It was as though Lucius spoke some lost language, some secret tongue of an ancient people that held no meaning any more – Kai's mind, in some strange act of mercy, sought to keep the truth from him for just a little longer.

But then the words echoed once more: *Arite. Your son.* And at last he understood.

He had seen men and women driven mad with grief, tearing at their faces and screaming at the sky, but such a madness did not come. Nor did hate, or a promise of revenge; nothing, save for a pitiless kind of clarity. The knowledge that he had abandoned Arite and his child, and so doomed them to the worst of deaths.

He felt a heavy hand upon his shoulder – Mor, offering what comfort he could. 'A cruel jest the gods play,' he said.

Kai kept his eyes upon the fire – a victory trophy to the Painted People, a funeral pyre for Arite and the son that he would never see. 'What can we do now? How can this end?'

'The only thing that might stop them,' the chieftain answered. 'We must take the Burning Cauldron from them.'

A hiss from Laimei. 'You say it is as though it is some childish trick to take their greatest treasure,' she said. 'You might as well ask us to pluck the noonday sun from the sky.'

'It is no simple thing,' Mor said. 'Perhaps it cannot be done at all, and not without great sacrifice. But when did a champion fear such a thing? How it may be done, I cannot say, whether it shall be by bravery or magic or the cunning of a trick. But it shall be done.' Mor turned to the Sarmatians and the Votadini who were gathered about them, watchful and silent, waiting for an omen from god or man. 'All I know,' he said to them all, 'is that if there are any who can do it, it shall be us. Together, our peoples defeated them once before, and I know that we may do so again.'

Kai saw those words take hold of the men and women gathered there, settling amongst them like snow. There in the darkness, for a moment the Sarmatians and the Votadini did not seem to be two different tribes born half a world away from one another – just for a moment, it seemed as though Mor might truly forge them into some force that could stand against the Painted People.

But the moment was gone as soon as it had come, and Kai saw them as they were once more: a pair of beaten, broken tribes, driven from their homes. No magic there to perform a miracle, just the weary, doomed fury of a wolf too tired to run any more as it turns upon its hunters. They would fight and they would die, but they did not believe that they could win.

Mor must have seen it too. 'But that is for tomorrow,' the chieftain said. 'For now, I ask that you try to sleep, and listen to your dreaming. It is there that the dead cry out for vengeance. It is there that they shall tell us what we must do.'

All about him then men and women began to drift away, hunters in search of sleep. The Sarmatians and the Votadini, reaching some wordless kinship, exiles gathering together in the darkness to share a silent companionship. The passing of a wineflask, the shy exchange of some small gift of a brooch or a glass-bead necklace. Here and there, they even managed the sharing of a song – a few fragments of verse sounded out with half a heart, before lapsing into silence once more.

Laimei vanished with them, as quickly as a figure from a dream. In but a moment, only Lucius and Kai remained in that clearing.

Kai stared at the Roman under the light of the half-moon, to see how much had changed since last they met. Lucius's hair was silvered now, like a blade charmed against spirits, and there was a certain stoop in the way that he held himself – an older man stood there, older than those five years apart might suggest. And Kai could not have said quite what it was he felt, to be there with the Roman. Some half-forgotten feeling was there, like an echo of love, a hollow cut out of the heart. An absence or a memory, and that was all.

'What is his name?' Kai said at last.

Lucius hesitated for a moment. 'It is Akkas,' he said.

'Akkas,' Kai repeated softly, testing the name upon his tongue. 'And why did you take Akkas and Arite to the Wall, when you knew there was such danger in the northlands?'

'I thought that I would keep them safe,' Lucius said. 'Caerellius...'

'Stop. I do not care about him, or his foolish Roman scheming.'

Lucius bowed his head. 'They may yet live,' he whispered.

'It is worse if they do,' said Kai. 'I have seen what the Painted People do to their prisoners.'

Lucius made no answer. Kai turned instead to those strange, familiar, beautiful shapes that moved in the darkness – the Sarmatians and their horses.

For the first time in five years his people were all about him, and memories returned unbidden – the countless nights he had spent upon the steppe in the easy companionship of those who had sworn to fight and die together. In the air was the sharp and sweet scent of the horses, and he could see their shadows stalking around the campground, as proud and powerful as demigods. How much he had missed the company of his people. How much he had lost in those years spent north of the Wall.

'Tell me of my son,' Kai said.

'He is a wild little thing,' the Roman answered, after a moment's silence. 'Always playing with a stick for a sword, challenging any Sarmatian in the street to a duel. Strong of spirit, and a dreamer too, ever hungry for the stories of heroes.' He hesitated. 'The men loved him, and thought him lucky. They missed their own children, I suppose, those that they left behind.'

Kai thought then of another child lost to him. For he had a daughter, Tomyris, that he had left behind on the steppe with nothing but a promise of return. A promise he had given believing that it would be true, but that he would never be able to keep – Lucius and the Romans had broken it for him. She would be almost a woman now, ready to take her place in the warband. Waiting for a father who would never come back.

He heard Lucius speak once more. 'Mor said that I should ask you,' he said. 'Ask you why it was that you left.'

Kai lifted a hand to his cheeks, felt the old scars there where he had cut away the marks of his clan long before. 'An oath,' he said. 'An oath sworn to a dying man. Bahadur asked me to leave Arite behind, and so I did. I have broken many oaths in my life. I wish that I could have broken that one.'

A moment of silence from Lucius. Then: 'I did not know.'

'How could you?' said Kai. 'I had hoped that you would know at least that I had good reason to go to the north.' Then, softly: 'I had hoped that Arite would know it too.'

'You could have told us why,' Lucius said. 'You should have sent word. Or you could have stayed, and never spoken to her again.'

'I was afraid to,' Kai said. 'I was afraid I would not have the courage. And would you have truly let me go? A deserter, gone north of the Wall with your blessing?'

'Perhaps you are right,' Lucius said. He had turned his face to the north, towards the sharp mountains that pierced the sky like spears. Seeking an omen, perhaps, or simply some of that clarity that sometimes came to one who stood upon the high clear places and looked out upon the world, the mountains that promised a man that he might make his life anew.

A deep breath in, and Lucius spoke once more. 'I asked you,' he said, 'before you left, if there might be peace between us. I ask it again now. I do not think it is the gods who have brought us here, or destiny. But it seems a shame to come so far and nurse our wrongs, our hate.'

And so, there it was – an offer of peace, made in Lucius's own particular way, quiet and open and brave. It must have cost much for him to make it, yet he had done so. And Kai felt a longing then, to forget what had passed between them. They had founded their brotherhood after meeting upon the battlefield, their spears set against each other. It had survived betrayals before, and so why could they not build it anew?

But Kai looked once more towards the fire upon the horizon, and saw there an omen of his own – not of clarity and peace, but of death and courage. An omen born of fire and not the mountain, the beautiful, terrible kind of omen most beloved by his people. And he knew then what he had to say.

'I do not need the friendship of a man who came to kill me,' said Kai. 'I do not need the brotherhood of a man who has killed my son.'

If those words wounded Lucius, he gave little sign of it. A shiver passing across his skin, a slight shift in his weight to find comfort in a swordsman's stance, the way that men often sought a warrior's comfort to their pain. And Lucius gave the slightest dip of the head, the soldier's farewell, before he walked away – his steps a little lighter, or so Kai thought, a man unburdened. For the Roman had tried his best, and spoken bravely. It was to be Kai's shame that he had turned down such generous words, and they both knew it.

Once more, Kai let his eyes rest upon the burning Wall. As though it were a beacon lit for him alone, a challenge issued that he would have to answer with his life.

At least now he knew that, when the time came to do what he must, Lucius would not try to follow him.

16

The great Wall was broken open, and the Painted People swept through it.

With each step that they took beyond, the world itself was made anew, the old rules no longer holding governance. For half a hundred years the distant Empire had decided upon that border, cut a careless line through the grazing grounds and hunting runs and burial sites of a dozen different tribes. That barrier was now broken and, at first, it seemed as though it might be a return to an old order and the lost way of things – that they might return to a time when the tribes had wandered freely across the northlands, writing their own borders in the blood spilt in feuds, in the passage of herds, in the dreaming of seers and the songs of poets.

But this was not a return to the old ways. Arite saw it all as she stumbled, exhausted and defeated, in the army of the conquerors, her last child clutched close against her. No bindings were upon her wrists, no watchful men kept close guard upon her, for there was nowhere for her to run. Her thin leather riding boots were worn almost to pieces by the end of the first day as the Painted People moved southwards unopposed – a nightmare dragged from the world of dreams and made flesh beneath the light of the sun.

For what they did was not the feuding and raiding of rival tribes that balanced itself like the seasons, feuds that sought prizes of victory and not the utter destruction of their adversaries. The Painted People were birthing something new into that world, something terrible that had never been seen before.

They were not wild or bestial – all their frenzy had been spent in breaking through the Wall. It was a patient kind of butchery, done without passion, committed almost with boredom. No hate guided the hands that they bloodied, and nor was there a pattern in what they did – sometimes they burned full fields of crops and marched hungry the next day; sometimes they killed half a family and left the rest alive for no reason Arite could discern. Messengers carrying the sacred truce leaves upon their spears were pulled down and gutted; farmers offering tributes in cattle and grain and silver and iron had their treasures cast upon the ground and their children taken instead. No rhyme or reason to whom the Painted People butchered or allowed to live, just the blind faith in their dead, murderous gods that guided them.

And at the end of the first day south of the Wall, that faith was answered with a blessing, as they came across the greatest prize in flesh that they could have hoped for.

Marching beside one of the great Roman roads, they saw a gilded carriage, seeming abandoned. And within it, sleeping soundly, was Caerellius, the Governor of Britain.

His guards must have seen the fire on the horizon or heard the fell march of the Painted People approach. Perhaps they had judged that they could not escape with the carriage, and none of them were willing to offer their master a horse, to trade their life for his. For all Caerellius's ambition, for all that he had sought to bribe and charm his way to the highest seat of power, that was what it came down to in the end – a Roman centurion looking down upon his sleeping master and deciding that he was not worth saving.

The Painted People gathered about his carriage, in absolute silence, and waited for him to wake. A strange courtesy, respecting the dreaming of a doomed man.

When at last he did rise from his sleep, Caerellius had a smile upon his face – it must have been some sweet dream of ambition or revenge that he woke from. He did not seem afraid at first when he saw the Painted People waiting for him. Perhaps he thought at first to be in one of those dreams within dreams, when he woke to see the nightmare before him.

Their hands were upon him then, strangely gentle as they led him to the side of the road. He wept and gibbered and made promises of silver and gold, entreaties to their mercy and threats of vengeance, until he saw what awaited him – Corvus, the Maimed King, standing quite still, his tall, thin frame like a stone idol erected to a vengeful god.

'Where are my guards?' Caerellius whispered.

Arite saw, for just a moment, a smile dance across Corvus's lips. 'Do you ask because you care whether they live or die, or because you wish to know why they abandoned you?'

Caerellius hung his head low and did not answer. She wondered what he was thinking then – a life of scheme and ambition and it had come to this. Not to see once more the sun falling upon the hills of Rome, to stand upon the Capitoline and hear the crowd chanting his name as though he were a god upon the earth. But to die upon his knees as the rain fell about him, here at the furthest edge of the Empire. For a moment, Arite almost pitied him.

'They left you sleeping,' Corvus said eventually, 'and they ran. To the south, I suppose.'

Caerellius lifted his head once more. 'What have you done, Corvus?' he whispered.

'I have united the tribes of the north and broken open the Wall. Once that was your desire, was it not? When I was a dog upon your leash.'

'It could be my desire again,' said Caerellius. 'Tell me what you want, and it shall be yours.'

'I want nothing from you. I need nothing. I am beyond such things.' And a strange kind of sadness seemed to settle upon Corvus then – a hollowing of the face, a stoop of the shoulder. Perhaps it was that he understood the truth of his own words. That this revenge was a hollow thing, an empty settling of a debt, nothing more.

And Caerellius saw it too – that there was to be no bargain made here. For he looked at Arite then, and it seemed that he had debts of his own to settle. 'I came looking for you,' he said, 'if you shall believe it. That is what sent me hurrying to the Wall.'

'Why?' she said.

'I was furious that Lucius had taken you from my grasp. That he had defied me like that.' Caerellius risked a look towards the north, towards the Wall. 'Does he live, do you know?' he said.

A flicker of anger across Corvus's face. And in spite of the danger it might bring her, Arite found herself smiling. 'I think that he does,' she said.

'Perhaps I may have my revenge through him,' Caerellius said. But the words were empty, and it seemed that they brought him no comfort. 'I am not sorry for what I have done,' he said to Corvus, blinking against the light of the sun in his eyes.

Corvus nodded to himself absently. 'Tell me,' he said, the words spoken as if by rote. 'When were you loved most?'

'Why do you ask me such a thing?' Caerellius whispered.

'Consider it a gift,' Corvus answered. 'A good memory, before the end.'

Caerellius did not answer for a long time. He merely stared at the ground as though hoping to see his memories etched there in the heather and the stone, the way a seer might read their omens. And Arite thought at first perhaps he sought merely to prolong his life, to hold on for a few useless moments more in the hope that something might change. The way Arite had once seen a brutally wounded man, his guts unspooled and bones shattered, a man who had screamed himself to a hoarse silence, still hold up a pleading hand as she came forward, a merciful knife in her hand, and beg her to wait a little longer.

But Caerellius lifted his head at last, and said: 'I do not know. My mother, perhaps, before I grew old enough to disappoint her. Perhaps never.'

And though he shook and trembled then, the stink of fear sweat rising from him, at the very end there was something in his eyes, a certain sense of steel that made Arite think of the man he might once have been. There, facing the worst of deaths, Caerellius remembered at the last what it was to be brave.

The grasping hands were upon him, the knives rising

high. And as they took him apart a piece at a time, while he screamed and wept and prayed to the skies, as though the rain that fell might hold some blessing from the gods that might somehow save him, Arite felt the useless scream clawing at her throat, fighting to make its way out and be heard.

When the bloody work was done at last, Corvus stood tall and spoke once more to his people. 'This shall be the first of many,' he said. 'This is the fate of all Romans in this land. But not of the Brigantes, the Parisi, or the Carvetii. Not all of them, at least.' He nodded towards the captives. 'Soon, we shall hold our ritual. It is nearly time to gift others with our blessing, to make brothers and sisters of those who were once our enemies.'

No chants of victory or songs of heroes greeted his words. Here and there amongst the Painted People, a gently nodding head, a dull eye growing bright for a moment. No joy at the thought, only a grim kind of satisfaction, a weary acceptance of what was to come. And for Arite, a fear once more, sudden and strong, like the touch of a hand to a broken bone when the pain has been dulled for a moment, as she thought of what that ritual would mean for her and her son.

And, as though answering her fears, Corvus turned and spoke to her then: 'Yes,' he said softly, almost with kindness. 'Soon, you shall have the chance to save your son.'

17

The stars stretched out above Kai, clear and sharp and beautiful. They were often hidden by the clouds in this cold, hard country, but on that night, the last that Kai expected to see, the sky was shining like silver, open and endless. And as he waited for the others to fall asleep, he remembered nights upon the steppe as a child, lying beside his sister as she taught him the meaning of the stars. He lifted his finger to trace the patterns of those lights in the sky, to remember the stories of old heroes that his people told with the constellations. All their stories were of courage, in the end, and that was what he sought there now.

Soon, he told himself. For he knew that he would not have to wait much longer.

As the Painted People wandered south, Kai and the Votadini had followed them. They pursued a trail marked in ashes and blood, the earth torn and raked by the passage of countless feet as though by the talons of some crawling monster. Each day, they studied the dead in the fields like priests judging an augury, reading a story in flesh and rot, running their fingers through the ashes and trying to judge how old the fires were.

As they had travelled, night after night, Kai had sat around the campfire and listened to the plans that the others made – of stealing into the camp of the Painted People by night, of challenging Corvus to a duel, of waiting for some omen of lightning or rain that they might use to their advantage. A thousand ways that they might steal the Burning Cauldron, each plan as useless as the next, and none of them mattered to Kai. For he knew that he would not live long enough to see any of them put into action.

At last, they had come to a place where the dead in the fields could almost have been sleeping, and where the ashes of the fires still bore some trace of heat, deep within the embers. The Painted People could only be a day or so ahead of them now.

And so that night, when the campground had fallen into near silence, when more of the Votadini and the Sarmatians lay in the dreamlands than in the waking world, he rose from his blankets and made his way towards the horses, his spear in his hand.

It would be a simple thing, to make his way past the sentries of the Votadini. For they were not like the Romans or oathsworn Sarmatians, who regarded desertion as the worst dishonour. To wander in the night, chasing ghosts and omens, was the practice of their Votadini. To seek death too, if that was what the word of a god or the whisper from their hearts might command them to do. A man riding out to seek his end would not be stopped or slowed by his companions, merely offered some last gift of wine or heather beer before they vanished into the mist and the heather. But Kai knew that Lucius and Laimei would try to stop him if they saw him. Perhaps Mor would too. And there would be no answer to give them, except for the truth.

So he moved softly through the darkness, light-footed as a thief, until he reached the corral. There, his own horse was once more in the company of its kin – no longer towering alone above the ponies of the Votadini, but delighting in the scent and touch and feel of its own kind, once more part of the whole and not alone. And yet as soon as Kai approached, she looked at him solemnly, the way that horses always seemed to know when a journey lay ahead, a journey towards death. A little nod, as though of assent, a single step forward all the blessing that the horse could give him, but it was enough.

But the deep black eyes of the horse were looking beyond Kai then, and she gave a low mutter that might have been a curse or a warning. And when he looked back, he saw that a shadow trailed him in the darkness. Then, as it drew closer, it was no longer a shadow but a reflection – a face much like his, a Sarmatian warrior carrying a spear that was the mirror of his own. It was as though Kai faced himself there in the night, like the old stories of heroes hunted by their twins. But the eyes were unlike his – they were the eyes of a killer. The eyes of his sister, Laimei.

'You make a habit of this,' his sister said as she approached him. 'Fleeing in the night.'

'You knew that I would try to leave?'

She gave him a slightly pitying look. 'Of course,' she said.

'I could never conceal anything from you,' Kai answered.

'And I could always hide everything from you. And so we are as we are – distant as the stars from the earth. I wish it were not so.' She nodded to his spear. 'You intend to make war upon the Painted People alone, I suppose?'

'I do not go to fight.'

'No,' she said. 'You go to die.' She hesitated, as though afraid to speak again. Then she said: 'What will you do?'

'I shall go and offer myself to Corvus,' Kai said, the words coming slowly. 'I shall ask him to free Arite, and my son, in exchange for my life.'

'They may already be dead.'

'It is a chance that I must take.'

And Laimei laughed then – not with the bitter mirth of the champion in mockery of death, but with the gentle laughter he had last heard when they were children together, long ago. 'You go to trade your life away,' she said. 'The same trade I have tried so many times before. And I am trying to stop you, the way that you have always sought to stop me. It is as though I argue against myself.'

'I have tried that many times,' said Kai. 'I can tell you that it does not work.'

'Perhaps so,' she answered, and the laughter was gone from her then. A kind of hollowing came over her – a lifetime of sadness from which the champion's code had shielded her, and that now was upon her all at once.

'Laimei—'

'If it is true what you say,' she said, her voice quiet and flat, 'if you are as determined as I am, then there is nothing that we may say to each other. There is nothing that we *need* to say to each other. I will not try to stop you.' And her eyes were shining again as she lifted her head towards him. 'I only ask if you will do one thing for me?' she asked.

'What is that?'

'Will you stay but a little longer?' She looked away then, as though ashamed of what she asked. Then, softly, she said:

'Will you hold me one more time? The way you did when we were children?'

Kai reached forward and took her hand in his. 'Yes, my sister,' he said. 'I will.'

She started at his touch as though struck or burned. Her eyes blazed fire, as the killing rage was upon her once more – he had seen it so many times in the past, when the nameless god of war touched her upon the shoulder and whispered to her, told her to kill. And though every instinct Kai had spoke to him of death and commanded him to release her hand, he held fast, just a little longer.

She went still, the fire fading from her eyes. And then she was weeping against him, in a way that he had never known, not even when they were children together – wretched, aching sobs that shook her like a fever, her hands gripping into his shoulders like talons, her weight so fully upon him that she would have fallen to the ground if he had stepped away. And so he held her close, held her upright, as she cried a lifetime of tears away for the life that they would never share.

They stayed close to the horses, for they had always liked to be near to the herd when they slept as children. Each of them laid their spears on the ground – hers dressed in the tuft of red felt, his marked with the mementos of those he had known and loved – and then they lay down together beside those weapons, as though keeping them company.

He was the taller now, but they lay down as they had back then, forming a shape like the curve of a bow, her at the outside and wrapped about him. Her forehead against the back of his neck, her arms looped around his waist, her hands clutching his. How much more time he wished they could have had. How much time they had wasted in hate.

Kai only meant to lie there for a little while, but there in her arms, sleep came over him like a spell – sudden and irresistible, a sensation like falling, then swimming, then flying. Perhaps, just for a moment, he and his sister might share one last dreaming, going together to a place where all things were possible.

One last time, he let himself sleep in his sister's arms. Before he would go to the south, to trade his life for a son that he had never seen.

18

For the Painted People, no sign or omen marked the time of the ritual.

It was not noon or dawn or dusk, those times when the sacred things were done. They had reached no sacred place of standing stones or shrine to a long-forgotten god, just an empty plain ringed by the distant hills. There was not even a flash of thunder or a sudden gust of wind that many would take as an omen – Corvus merely turned his face to the black night sky, let the rain fall upon his face, and said: 'Now. It shall be now.'

And so, as she stood beside him, Arite knew that the time had come for her to die.

She had walked all day in fear of that moment, searching for the slightest chance of escape – a fast-flowing river that she might throw herself in, a horse that she might try to steal, a thunderstorm that might give her some chance to flee. But her mind, numb with fear, could not seem to think fast enough. All she could think of was putting one step in front of another as her exhausted son stumbled beside her, hunched over as though he were sickened by her fear. Together they moved the way she had seen cattle go blindly forward towards their deaths, even as the herdsman's knife was dark with the blood of those he had already slain.

And so at first there was a shiver of relief when Corvus spoke, the way that a soldier before a hopeless battle will weep with joy when he hears the horn that calls him to the fatal charge and signals an end to his fear at last. But then she saw the Painted People dragging the other prisoners forward, and a new fear came to her – that her son would be made to watch the others die first. That he would understand, in his last hour upon the earth, just how cruel the world could be.

And she turned to Corvus then, and said: 'If it is to be done, let us be first.' She spoke again, more softly, so that only Corvus might hear: 'Let my son be first.'

'I told you that he may be saved,' Corvus replied. 'You may even save yourself.' And he spoke so lightly, as if of some trifling thing. 'I ask only that you join us, and swear an oath that I know will bind you.'

She made no answer.

'Why not?' Corvus said. 'I know you are a warrior. You could fight with us, against those who brought you in chains to this place. Against the Romans.'

She kept her silence as she weighed the choice before her. Perhaps, as a Sarmatian, such an oath should have been easy enough to swear – her people worshipped war and death above all else, after all, and to die against the Romans was as good a cause as any.

But she had no longing for the dance of horse and spear, no reckless love for the joy of battle. What she wanted now was a simple song sung about the fire, the smell of her son's hair as she held him close. Even the rain falling around her sounded as music in her ears, the scent of the sodden earth and the bracken rising like a rich perfume. That life she was soon to lose, that was what she worshipped now. It had never seemed so beautiful to her, until she knew she was to leave it.

'It is not just against the Romans that you fight,' she said slowly. 'But against all who will not join you. It is against life itself you fight, I think, and I shall not pledge myself to you.'

A singing in her heart then, to know the truth of the words that she spoke. The sense of a challenge being met, a question answered.

'I thought as much,' Corvus said. 'You do not have the courage.'

'To fight?' she answered.

'To do what you must to survive. As I have.'

'Is that the story you tell yourself?' she said.

This time, it seemed, it was Corvus who had no answer.

And so she spoke again: 'You might have passed your life as a mystic in a cave, a farmer tending a field, a hunter of the woods. It is not survival that brings you here. It is because you cannot bear to be defeated.'

Those words seemed to find a home in the Maimed King – the slightest tilt of the head or a shimmer in his eye, as he glimpsed, just for a moment, the life he might have chosen.

And then it was gone. 'I see that I have no more use for you,' he said.

Arite turned her face from him and looked towards where Akkas sat – blank-eyed, gone to some distant place in the very heart of fear, perhaps even some place beyond pain. 'Do not make him watch, when you kill me,' she said quietly.

'And what shall I do with him?' Corvus said, a terrible

smile spreading across his face. 'Shall he join you in death, or join me in the killing?'

'He is a child,' she whispered.

'It is the children we need most of all. It is for them that we fight – we build this new world for them to inherit.'

'You want him to join your people?' Arite said.

'I do,' Corvus answered. 'But I have no place for the faithless. You must give him this faith. Or he will be made an offering to the gods of the Burning Cauldron.'

Arite did not speak for a long time. She wanted so desperately for her child, her last child, to live.

She thought of what Akkas would become if he were raised in that warband amongst the Painted People. A killer amongst many, dragging children away from their mothers, carving men open as bloody tributes to long-dead gods. Meeting his own death upon some forgotten battlefield, hacked down by the Legions of Rome or spitted on a Sarmatian spear. The bright-eyed child she had raised on stories of heroes, patiently shaped to become a killer of men.

And if she refused, he would be tied to the ground by the Painted People and given a death from the worst of her nightmares.

But there was a third choice there – delivered suddenly to her mind, a gift from the gods. Arite knew then, in a heartbeat, what she would have to do.

'I can give him the faith that you need,' she said to Corvus. 'If you let me speak with him alone.'

For a moment she thought that wish would be granted. But something must have given away her purpose – some murderous, testing twitch of her hands as she thought of what she must do, the shining light of a liar in her eye or a hesitance to her speech. For Corvus said: 'Speak to him here, in front of us. I wish to hear what you say.'

She nodded slowly – suddenly calm, at peace with what she must do. She turned to look for the last time upon her son.

Five children had she buried already, lost to fever and sickness and war, and this was the last cruel joke from the gods. Akkas, her miracle child born against all odds, would have to die by her own hand.

For that was what she knew she must do. She would not let him become one of those blank-eyed murderers, and she would not let them carve him to pieces as an offering to their dead gods.

She knew that she could do it – she knew that she had the cruel and loving courage. And she did not feel grief or fear or horror, only a kind of terrible pride, kin to evil and cousin to madness. She found herself unafraid of killing, unafraid of death, laughing at the gods who thought to test her so, and that laughter was a prize and a victory in itself.

When she looked upon her son, she saw the softness of his brown eyes, the little scar upon his thumb that only she knew of, the wild dark curling hair that he took from Kai. And even there, in that place, a shy smile breaking out upon his face when he saw her walk towards him.

She would have to do it quickly. It would be only a moment before they were upon her, and it would be worse to leave the killing half done than not to do it all. There would be no time to tell her son why, no sign that she might give. She could only trust that he would understand at the very last moment – that when she pressed her hands so hard to his throat that she felt the crack of bone beneath her fingers, or if she took up a stone from the ground and beat his little head to pieces, it would be done as one last gift of love.

She took a step towards him, smiling all the time, and slowly raised her hands.

But then, all around her, the beating of a drum – the warning cry of the Painted People.

She thought that alarm was for her at first, that some warrior of the Painted People had seen a sign of her intent and struck the drum in his hand to warn the others. But no eyes were upon her now, as all about her the Painted People were pointing to a shadow upon the horizon, clearly outlined by the light of the moon and bearing fire in its hand.

It was a lone rider upon a horse, carrying the tall spear of a Sarmatian warrior in one hand and a burning torch in the other. He was dressed in the shining scaled cuirass of their people, with a great helm upon his head that turned him into a faceless man of iron. No truce leaves upon the spear, for it seemed this man came to fight the army alone. It was something from the myths and old stories, where a single hero might stand against ten thousand and be victorious.

The rider showed no fear or hesitation to see that terrible host gathered before him. He rode forward with a kind of weary relief, slow and steady, relaxed in the saddle with the spear carried low and the torch held up as a signal of peace, the way a traveller upon the steppe will ride when they see the winter campground before them and know themselves safe at the end of a long journey.

Closer now, and she saw the Painted People take up their spears and nock arrows to their bows, ready to give the fool the death he had come for. And she was frightened for the rider then, though she did not know why – it was not her place to come between a stranger and the death that he had chosen.

Then her eyes settled once more upon the Sarmatian spear, richly lit by the fire of the torch, and she knew why she was afraid.

It was marked with charms and gifts, the way her people always liked to decorate their spears. But she saw a familiar strand of wolf fur twisted about the haft – a gift from a child, a daughter left back upon the steppe. A little band of gold wire that her husband, Bahadur, had given to the bearer of that spear. And bound there too, a single strip of leather, a token that Arite herself had offered up many years before when she had nothing else to give. It was Kai's spear.

One final cruel curse from the gods, that she would have to see her child and the father of that child die on the same day. And Arite was screaming then, screaming at Kai to run, even as all about her the Painted People roared with laughter, their hands clutching at her and holding her still, forcing her to watch.

And then Corvus spoke.

'I know that spear,' he said. 'I know this man. Let him come to us.'

A moment of doubt, there amongst the Painted People. Arite saw it in a hand that whitened around the haft of a spear, in lips that pursed to speak but remained silent. She had seen enough in those few days amongst them to understand that there was no bargaining or parley for the Painted People, no man thought more or less important than another – in this at least, there was a cruel sense of fairness. Their dark, miserable faith was all the Painted People had left to them now, and they did not like to see one of its few rules broken.

The rider came amongst them, into a ragged circle of the Painted People, a chain of flesh that soon closed around him. And that warrior seemed almost glad to be surrounded – for the Sarmatians, all true and sacred things were done inside a circle. Born in a circle of women, loving in the round tents of the steppe, dying in an executioner's circle if they lived to be too old to steady a spear.

The rider checked his horse, thrust his spear in the ground and cast away his torch. Slowly, he slipped the helm from his head.

A face much like Kai's lay beneath that helm – the coppery skin, high cheekbones, the black hair that she had always loved to run her hands through. But those cold grey eyes were not his. And beneath the nicks and scars of half a hundred battles, it was a woman's face that stared back at her. The face of Laimei.

'You are not the man I hoped to see,' Corvus said flatly. 'Not a man at all.'

Laimei ignored Corvus at first. 'Kai would have come,' she said to Arite in the Sarmatian tongue, 'if I had let him. Do not think ill of him that he is not here.' Then, to Corvus, she said: 'We met in battle, once before. But I was not certain you would know me.' She shook her head, and spoke the next words almost to herself, seemingly heedless of the horde that surrounded her. 'In my own land, it is my name that all men know. And yet here, it is my brother whose spear might win me passage. What a strange sense of humour the gods have.'

Corvus rocked back upon his heels, a slow smile spreading across his lips. 'You are Laimei. The one they call the Cruel Spear. I think you have come to find a cruel death of your own in this place. And we shall give it to you.'

She shrugged, seemingly unconcerned. 'If that is what you mean to give me,' she said, 'then I shall take it. But I offer you something else instead.'

'And what is that?'

'I will fight for you,' she said. 'Your people need warriors, and I am a champion like no other. Your people bring death, and that is my great love.'

A murmuring then, amongst the Painted People. For though they had laughed at Laimei before, and although their dark faith had no use for champions, perhaps stirring deep within them were the old stories of their own tribes, the people they had once been – the Damnonii, the Venicones, the Taexali. The memory of a time, almost forgotten to them, when they had still loved courage, still believed in heroes.

'I am to believe that you will fight against your kin?' said Corvus. 'Your brother?'

She laughed then, bright and merry as a summer's day. 'Why not?' she said. 'I have fought against my kin before. My brother too, for most of my life.' She shifted in the saddle and a sword was in her hand, bright and brilliant beneath the light of the moon. 'You know the value of a sword oath amongst my people?' she said.

'I have heard that it cannot be broken.'

'Just so. Like an oath your people swear upon that black cauldron of yours.' She laid her fingers to the point of the blade. 'I shall swear it here, and my word shall be my bond. But you must offer an oath in return, and meet the price that I shall ask.'

A thin smile spreading across Corvus's face – perhaps he too could not help but admire such courage. 'You think to bargain?'

'I know my worth.'

'And what do you ask of me?' he said.

Laimei levelled her sword at Arite and Akkas, the way a chieftain of the steppe would pass judgement on one of their people. 'You shall let them go from this place unharmed,' she said. 'None of your warriors shall touch them.'

There was silence for a time. Only the scattering sound of the rain falling upon spear and shield, the wind rolling across the bracken on the hillsides.

Then Corvus shook his head and said: 'It is an impossible thing that you ask.'

'I have done many things that men have thought impossible,' Laimei said. 'This shall be another. I shall do more impossible things in your service, beneath your banner.' She hesitated. 'Let me bring death,' she said. 'It is all that I was ever good at.' She nodded once more towards Arite and Akkas. 'But let them go free. They are not strong enough to see the truth, as you and I do.'

Arite could see the temptation on Corvus's face. She knew that she could not allow it.

'Kill him, Laimei.' It was in the Sarmatian tongue that Arite spoke, desperate and urgent. 'You are close enough. Take your spear and kill him.'

A crooked smile answered her. 'You would die if I did,' Laimei said. 'I have done enough killing. I thought I might try to save a life instead.' The smile faded then. 'And I came in my brother's place, and I must do what he—'

'Enough of that,' Corvus said. 'How can I let her go, not knowing of what you speak?'

'She wanted me to kill you,' Laimei said, matter-of-factly.

'I shall swear to fight for you, and kill for you. But you shall swear upon the cauldron in return. That is my offer.'

Corvus kept his eyes on her for a long time, and she stared back unblinking. Perhaps, for them both, it was like staring into a mirror of the soul – each seeing a killer before them, a worshipper of death. Each seeing how much they were alike, and how different.

And at last Corvus spoke again. 'It shall be so,' he said. 'The Burning Cauldron is not here for me to swear upon. But I will give an oath that cannot be broken.'

'Where is it, then?' Laimei said, grinning. 'Did you lose it upon the way? Careless of you, to cast aside the grave of a god.'

From the Painted People, a mutter of anger at the blasphemy. And something more than that too – once more, Arite saw some sign of feeling in those dull-eyed killers. They came alive once more, in the doubtful, resentful looks that they cast at Corvus.

And then Corvus raised his voice and spoke to his people with the quality of a ritual, a prayer: 'What was lost has been found again,' he said. 'And what was burned…'

A thousand voices answered him: 'Shall grow once more.'

He turned back to Laimei. 'You see the faith they have. You see how much it matters to them. I shall swear upon the absent cauldron and my people shall hold me to that oath.'

For some time, Laimei looked upon the Painted People, perhaps judging them with her champion's eyes, eyes that had spent a lifetime bargaining in life and death. And it seemed that she saw some truth there that satisfied her, for she nodded to herself. 'Very well,' she said, 'we shall swear our oaths.' She turned then to Arite. 'Go now. Ride north and follow the star of Arkash, and you shall find your way home.' She hesitated, and then she said: 'You shall find Kai.'

'What should I tell him of you?'

Laimei shrugged. 'Nothing at all, for he knows it all already. I speak my love in deeds and not words. Now take your son and go.'

Corvus spoke again: 'No. Only Arite may go free. Her son stays here.' And his hand was upon Akkas then – a gentle, almost fatherly touch. 'A life for a life. That is a fair trade, no?'

A clawing terror was upon Arite at those words – no fear so strong as to think her child safe only to lose him again. And as though from some great distance, she saw Laimei lift her chin proudly. 'I would think my life worth more than one,' Laimei said. 'But if that is to be the trade, let Akkas go free.'

'No,' Corvus said, his hands working through the hair of the child as though he soothed a skittish horse. 'I have need of the children most of all. We shall need warriors to raise.'

The child stared up at Arite, glassy-eyed and trembling. But she could see the comfort of touch already working upon him, how easily he might be moulded to be one of the Painted People. And the courage came back to her then – a reckless smile upon her lips, as she made ready to speak the words that would doom her.

But another voice spoke first: 'Do not waste this,' Laimei said. For a moment, all the champion's careless arrogance was gone from her, something desperate and needful in the way that she spoke, before those grey eyes were hard and empty once more. 'Tell Kai and the others what you have seen here, and heard here.'

And so that was Arite's choice – to run and live a coward, or to stay and have her son watch her die. As though seeking his counsel, she looked towards Corvus, and she saw the longing in his eyes, for her to stay and offer herself up to useless death. And, in that moment, she found the comfort that her people had always found in defiance, the promise of vengeance. She let it kill the love in her heart.

'I will return,' she said to Akkas. 'Have no doubt of that.'

'What must I do?' he whispered.

'Whatever you must do to live,' she said. 'Live for me, and I shall come back for you.'

At every moment, as Arite mounted the horse and rode away from the Painted People, she expected to feel the sudden touch of iron – an arrow passing into her ribs, the stroke of a sword flensing her thigh, a spearhead twisting through her belly. But there was no trick or betrayal. The Painted People did not even look at her as she rode, as though she were already dead.

She was almost out, almost through. And then, like those heroes fleeing the underworld who, with the light of the world before them, still cannot help but glance back and doom themselves, she looked back one last time.

She saw Laimei, her hand upon her sword, swearing her life away to the worshippers of dead gods. She saw Corvus give an answering oath, his hands cupping an invisible cauldron in the air as tenderly as he might have held a babe in his arms. She saw her son, lost and weeping, a child amongst murderers. And then she saw the worst sight of all. When, like a trap closing around Akkas, Corvus took her son into a loving, fatherly embrace.

19

K ai slept, and his dreams were beautiful.

They were shapeless and shifting, and even amidst them he could not have said whether they were dreams of places he had once been or visions of strange and unknown lands. All he knew was that they were dreams of motion, for amongst the Sarmatians, the most joyful dream was to feel a horse galloping beneath them or to take to the sky in the form of an eagle and wheel through the clouds. It was in their nightmares that they were held frozen in place, as monsters from the dark stalked towards them. The living were ever in motion. Stillness was for the dead.

But a coldness came upon him, there in his beautiful dream – the coldness of the traveller in winter whose fire slowly dwindles, or the wounded man who knows that chill to be the prelude of death. And as he woke, somehow he knew that coldness spoke to him of an absence, a thing of beauty that he had lost and would never recover.

The light of the sun was upon his face, and he felt the blind terror of a child that has fallen asleep watching the herd – he had meant to rest for but a moment, but the whole night had been stolen from him by his sleep. And, a moment later, his terror doubled to feel the cold hollow beside him where Laimei had been.

He looked to the place where he had placed his spear the night before. He had borne many such weapons throughout his life – when one broke in battle a new one took its place, and each of them he had marked with the same charms. For the Sarmatians did not write their stories in words the way he knew the Greeks and Romans did, no scratchings of ink onto parchment or marks chiselled into stone. They told the stories of their gods and heroes in the stars, the songs about the fire, and the markings of their spears.

He had seen men etch them with dragons and wolves, with the creatures that they wished to be. He had dressed his own spear with trophies of friendship, and of love. And now, looking down, he did not see the trinkets of those he had loved and lost, the gifts of Bahadur, Arite, Lucius, and his daughter Tomyris. He saw only the tufts of red felt that Laimei always favoured, symbols of all the blood she had spilt with that weapon. For she did not write her story in love, sought no favour from the gods. Only victory and death had ever mattered to her. She had taken his spear, and left hers behind. And he knew then where she had gone, and what she intended to do.

Through the morning mist, he saw a figure approaching – a man half formed or half glimpsed, like something from a dream or a creature from another world. There was a fool's hope at first that it might be Laimei, turning back from her chosen path of death. But the shadow from the mist resolved itself into greying red hair and coiling tattoos, eyes that were at once kindly and ever grieving.

'Laimei has gone?' Mor said, as he laid his hands upon Kai's shoulders.

Kai nodded dumbly, unable to speak. But his eyes must have asked a question, for Mor shook his head in answer.

'No, I did not see her go,' the chieftain said. 'I did not know it for certain, until you spoke. But I dreamed last night of a wolf that hunted the moon itself, that fought the stars as though they were a legion that stood against it, and died laughing in battle. I knew that something beautiful and terrible had happened. I know now what it means.' Mor sat heavily beside him. 'You meant to go yourself?' he said.

'I did,' Kai whispered. And there was light shining in his eyes then – from above the mountains, the light of the dawn breaking upon them – and Kai knew the sun would make golden rivers of his tears. 'She was always braver than me.'

'No. She saw the chance for great courage, greater than any she had known before. To offer up her life without a hope of victory. Who are you to deny her such a chance to prove herself? She must have envied you greatly, if she was so willing to take your place.'

Kai said nothing for a long time. He had never thought that his sister might envy him anything. 'What is to be done now?' he said.

'We wait,' Mor answered, 'to see what comes of her sacrifice.' And he laid a finger to his arm, to one of the twisting, looping tattoos that marked his skin – not animals in the way that the Sarmatians favoured, but knots and chains that twisted back upon each other.

'What do they mean?' Kai said. 'Those tattoos of yours?'

'That we are stronger together than we are alone. That

all things join to one another, given enough time.' And Mor turned his gaze north towards the Wall, broken and burned upon the horizon. 'That is what will happen to us and the Romans. Together, we shall become something new.'

'Like the Painted People?'

'No,' Mor said. 'Like so many people on this island, they long for the old times, the dead gods, the lost world that will never come again. That is why we shall defeat them, or they shall defeat themselves.'

'You truly believe that?'

'Now, or a hundred years from now, or a thousand,' Mor said.

'A long time to wait, if so.'

Mor nodded. 'For men. But not for gods.'

'I wish that I had your faith,' Kai answered.

Together, in silence, they turned their eyes to the south. And in time, others gathered around them.

The Votadini had risen ready to give chase to the Painted People, but sat down silently beside their chieftain without a word of protest. For they were followers of the dream, the whim that might lead them to chase a beam of sunlight across a barren moor, or follow the distant whisper of the waves just to look upon the sea. The Votadini saw their chieftain waiting, and they joined him without hesitation. Watching the south. Waiting for an omen.

It came at last, as the sun rose high above the mountains – some unseen signal passed through the air or the earth. It was no sound, not at first, but something more like the touch of wind in a place of stillness, the sense of a lover waking beside you. Then there was sound, the gentle fall of hooves upon sodden earth, the rattle and jingle of tack. Through the morning mists, pierced by golden sunlight, Kai saw a single rider come towards them then. A woman.

Nothing but a shadow in the mist at first, but Kai knew that it was not his sister. For Laimei there would be no changing of her mind, no sudden grip of cowardice sending her fleeing from death. Only if she had done the impossible would she have returned, trailing a river of blood behind her as a signal of her victory.

This woman rode towards them with no spear in her hand, no proud armour shining upon her body – nothing but filthy clothing marked with soot and ash and blood. Her head hung low, and Kai could see the sun falling upon the twisting braids of gold and silver hair that had partly unravelled to spill upon her shoulders, the way that Sarmatians wore their hair in mourning.

It was Arite, and there was a shiver of joy to see her that lasted but a moment. For he knew then what it must mean, for her to be riding alone. For his son, their son, to be dead at the hands of the Painted People.

At last, she brought her exhausted horse to a stop before them. Arite's eyes were upon him then, and he knew that kind of gaze all too well. It was the way his sister had looked upon him long ago, in the depths of their feud. The way that Arite's husband, Bahadur, had stared at him as though upon a dead man. It was how Lucius was learning to look at him too – the steady, patient gaze of hate.

Time and again, he had held such a meeting with her in the wordless land of dreams. But he did not know how to begin. Any single word alone would be the wrong one, no matter what followed it. He had only a longing for some impossible word that could say it all in a moment – that could ask for forgiveness, offer love and a vow of vengeance, all in the passage of a single breath.

And so, instead, he said nothing.

At last, she shook her head – some moment passing, some test failed. 'It should have been you,' Arite said. 'It should have been your life traded, and not your sister's. But that has always been your gift, has it not? To live while better men and women die.'

The wind came calling then, blowing hard across the hills. The leaves shivered and sang in the trees, as though the gods raised that echoing music and wished to hear no more words of men.

'It is true, what you have spoken,' said Kai. 'Laimei and Bahadur, they were braver than I ever could be.' And he took in a long and trembling breath, and said: 'But I sought to die before both of them – you know this to be true. The gods keep me here for a reason. Let us find out what it may be.'

Arite gave a little shake of her head. 'You may tell yourself such stories if you wish,' she said. 'It means nothing to me. Not any more.'

20

Upon a hillside close by stood a circle of stones. Old and abandoned, some fallen to the earth and breaking the sacred circle, scattering what power remained to the wind and the sky. All of those stones webbed with lichen and moss, the altar at the centre broken and long since bare of gifts.

The broken Wall loomed behind them and the trail of the Painted People, that great column of churned earth and trampled heather, lay ahead of them. And there, in that ruined world, they sat together upon the bare ground, in the Sarmatian style – Mor, Kai, Lucius, and Arite.

It was a place that Lucius had led them to – five years before, in another life, he had sought to bargain there with Caerellius, to save the Sarmatians at any cost. Now, it seemed, it was where the fate of the whole island might be decided. When Mor asked him how he knew of that place, Lucius had smiled thinly.

'I have been there before,' he had said, 'when all hope seemed lost. It seems a good place for us now.'

And so there, within the broken circle, Lucius and the others gathered, to decide what must be done.

What few supplies they had left, they brought there. Arite would take no food, though her skin was grey and her cheeks were hollow with hunger, but when Mor offered her a skin of strong heather beer she drank it down as if it were water. What further numbness it could offer her, he did not know, for her eyes were empty. As though she were a corpse, conjured by some dark magic to speak once more before she collapsed to dust.

'What shall I speak of first?' she said. 'I shall only have the strength to tell the story once. So listen carefully.'

'Tell me of the Wall,' Lucius said. 'Tell me how they got through.'

She nodded slowly, and in time she began to tell of what she had seen – of awakening to smoke and fire, and the screams of the dying.

A shiver of grief when she spoke of the breaking of the Wall and the burning of Cilurnum, a flood of memories passing through Lucius like icy water, memories of the Sarmatians he had left behind. A boy with shining eyes who looked upon Lucius as though he were a hero, a man alone upon the parapets singing to the moon as if it were his lover, a warrior with silver in his hair tending the horses in the fields. A hand striking a drum around a fire, the sound of laughter echoing out of the barracks, a cup of wine offered, an embrace in the darkness – all of them gone, now, and nothing but the memories left.

'I should never have left them,' said Lucius.

'It would not have mattered,' Arite answered. 'You would have died there with them, that is all.'

'What came after?' Mor asked.

She told them of the burning and butchering, the relentless

march of the Painted People to the south. Of the death of Caerellius, cut open and made a sacrifice to the old dead gods.

After that there was silence for a time.

'I had every reason to wish him dead,' Kai said at last. 'Yet it brings me no joy to hear of this.' He shook his head. 'For all the evil he did, he was a petty little man.'

'It is often so,' Mor said. 'The great heroes die swiftly – a few brilliant battles, and the gods snatch them away. It is those petty men who linger, and do greater evil.'

'You think Corvus is such a man?' said Lucius.

'Yes. For all that he has done, there is something paltry to his dreaming.'

After a time, Arite spoke once more – of the coming of the lone Sarmatian rider bearing Kai's spear. 'It was the bravest thing I have ever seen,' she said. 'And now Laimei is lost. And we are lost with her. What hope can there be, when the best of us fights with the Painted People?'

Nothing spoken for a time. Around the stone circle, Lucius could see that those words had struck home. The Sarmatians hung their heads low as they murmured their songs of death, and the Votadini were smiling bleakly, the way their warriors had been taught to greet a doomed cause. Laimei had been a god-touched champion, a hero from the old stories – perhaps the last one that any man there would see in their lives. And each of them knew, from their stories and their myths, that when the last of the heroes died, the rest of the tribe soon followed.

From somewhere close by, Lucius heard birdsong. Not the kind of sound that spoke of gods and omens, no cawing of a crow or cry of an eagle, but merely the gentle singing of a sparrow. He saw the bird then, dancing and sparring with its mate in the air around the stone circle, as though they practised some hidden ritual of their own in that place, to gods that were deaf to men but were still worshipped by the songs of the birds.

Perhaps that was to be the fate of this land – abandoned by the gods, stripped bare of men and women by the Painted People. A land where the beasts ruled and worshipped gods of their own, and knew nothing of the sorrows of men.

It was Arite who broke the silence. 'What is the Burning Cauldron?' she said, and her voice sent those sparrows dancing away through the sky, their ritual broken.

'What do you know of this?' said Mor.

'Laimei knew what it was,' Arite answered. 'And to the Painted People it seemed sacred. Corvus swore an oath by it, and I think they would have killed him if they thought he would break it.'

'They would,' Mor said. 'For it is a thing of evil magic that is holy to our people. A tomb of the dead gods of this land. You saw the cauldron?'

'No,' she answered. 'Corvus did not have it.'

A stillness then, as even the wind fell silent. As though the world itself seemed to hold its breath and listen to what was spoken.

'What do you mean?' Lucius said at last.

'Laimei asked him to swear an oath upon the cauldron,' Arite said slowly, 'and he could not. He swore upon its memory – it seemed that was enough.'

Mor, Lucius, and Kai all looked to one another – a flicker of hope kindling in their eyes.

'Tell us everything that Corvus said,' Mor whispered. 'Everything that you remember.'

Arite did not answer at first. A shiver passed through her, a whitening upon her skin, for it was with great cost that she went back to that place in her mind again.

'They were angry,' she said. 'In the days I spent with the Painted People, I never saw them show such feeling for anything. They were never afraid, and they were almost bored as they butchered and killed, but they were furious with Corvus for leaving the cauldron behind.'

'And how did he quiet that anger?'

'He spoke words, and they answered him. As though it were a prayer or a ritual. "What was lost has been found, what was burned shall grow again."'

Silence followed those words. And Mor was smiling wildly, a berserker's grin upon his face as he rocked back and forth like a delighted child. 'He would not take it south of the Wall,' the chieftain said. 'He could not take the chance of losing it. It is somewhere here, in the northlands.'

'Then we truly are lost,' Lucius said. 'There was a chance in a thousand that we might find some way to take the cauldron from him as he marched to the south. We shall never find it now.'

Mor could sit no longer, it seemed, for he sprang to his feet and began to pace about the stone circle, as though enacting some spell or ritual of his own. 'I know where he has hidden it,' he said.

'Oh yes?' answered Lucius, and knew that his voice was weary. 'You saw it in a dream, no doubt. A falling star pointing to a cave in the mountain, a raven flying over a wood by the sea. We shall be old men, grey and weary, chasing across the hills and the heather all our lives.'

'No.' And Mor's hand reached out to the standing stone

beside him, tearing away a handful of the moss. 'Our gods do not live in iron or stone,' he said, 'but in the earth and the trees. In the sacred groves of Yns Mon that were burned to ash. He means to plant the cauldron like a seed, and let a new grove grow on top of it. He means to make the dead gods live once more.'

Lucius shivered. 'Where?' he said.

'Of this land, and apart from it. In this world, and reaching out to touch the world beyond. Just as it was on Yns Mon.'

Kai spoke then: 'An island,' he said, his voice cold and empty.

'Just so.' And there was a longing in Mor's voice as he spoke. 'He thinks to grow the sacred groves once more. To make the dead gods live. The people of this land, of half a hundred different tribes – they would follow him forever, if he could do such a thing.'

'It tempts you, doesn't it?' Lucius said.

Mor smiled sadly. 'To hear the whisper of the gods as my ancestors did, and to feel the touch of their hand upon mine? Yes, it tempts me. It is a terrible thing to live in a cemetery of the gods. We have been alone without them for so long.' The smile faded then. 'But they would be evil gods, reborn by such bloodshed. Let them remain dead. We must learn to live without them. We must go to the island and destroy the cauldron.'

'There are dozens of islands off the coast,' Lucius said. 'There could be hundreds, for all I know, for we have never mapped them.'

'But there is only one that it could be,' Mor answered. 'It shall be close to the shore, just as it was with Yns Mon.' Mor looked at Kai then. 'I think you know where it is.'

And Kai sat up then, his face relaxing – almost a smile upon his lips. 'The Island of Spears,' he said.

'Just so. You remember when we sat upon the shore and looked to that island but a few days ago, and saw firelight there? We did not know what it meant, then. But I do now. It is a signal for us.'

'Then we go,' Kai said. And Lucius saw that he had the kind of lightness that blessed a warrior before a battle, that came with the acceptance of death. That parting gift of the gods, to make the last journey bravely.

Then, with all the fervency of an oath, Arite whispered: 'Not all of us.'

'No,' Mor said softly. He looked around the circle then – at Lucius and Kai, at the Votadini and the Sarmatians, those remnants of tribes nearly lost. Embers from a fire that had once burned brightly, and perhaps might again, one last time. 'Some of us shall follow your son to the south,' he said. 'That is my path, and yours. The Painted People grow stronger and greater with every step they take and every tribe that they conquer. Those that are left in the south must gather against them.'

Lucius shook his head. 'You think you may defeat them in battle, where the Legions and the Sarmatians could not?'

'No.' And there was a rueful smile on Mor's face as he spoke again: 'We were always better dreamers than warriors in this land. That is why, to make those people strong enough to defeat the Romans, Corvus had to turn them into a nightmare.' And Mor reached out and laid his hand upon one of the standing stones once more, his fingers gently working against the lichen and the moss. 'But perhaps we may hold them for a little time, while you do what you must. Perhaps we can help them remember the dream that they once were, even if only for a moment.'

'That is not much to hope for,' Lucius said.

'No.' And Mor turned to the south then, as though impatient to be going, to hurry towards his death. 'But it may be enough. Not to fight, or to win. But to die in a way that matters.' To Arite, he said: 'Will you still come with me, knowing that?'

Arite nodded, solemn as a priest at the sacrifice. 'I take not one more step further away from my son. I have brought you your message. I shall ride with you to the south. When I die in battle, it will be against Corvus. Not on some island far from here, chasing some useless piece of iron.'

A silence then, and a shadow passing across Mor's face. 'We go south, then, with my people,' he said. 'Lucius, the Sarmatians shall go with you, to the island. Perhaps a dozen, no more than that. You must travel fast, and in secrecy.'

Silence once more. The question hung unspoken in the air and Lucius waited for a time, waited for someone else to speak. But he saw that Mor would make him ask it.

'What of Kai?' Lucius said at last.

A nod from Mor, one that spoke of gratitude, a recognition of courage. 'You will need a guide, will you not?' he said. 'Kai knows these lands as well as any of us.'

Lucius turned his gaze to the circle around them, the ring of stone and the people gathered beyond. Not to the Votadini, those strange dreamers who held no love for him, but to the Sarmatians – those who were left. He saw how Mordos had reached out and taken the hand of Ossious, with the easy intimacy of men who fought together, loved together. He saw the way that Gosakos paced back and forth, impatient as a wolf before the hunt, a little smile dancing across the Sarmatian's lips at the thought of the journey ahead. And he saw the weary, loving patience with which Tasius looked upon him, the way that seconds had always looked upon their captains – an old warrior, broken and wounded and weary, ready for one final battle. He looked upon all those men who had followed him from distant lands, who had kept their oaths without hope of reward, who would follow him to death without hope of victory. And then he looked at Kai.

'No,' Lucius said at last. 'I shall go in search of your Burning Cauldron, for what else is there for me to do? But if I go to die in the darkness at the edge of the world, it will be beside those that I love, and that I trust. I have no place for him.'

THE DREAM

AD 180

21

At the heart of the stone circle, the Sarmatians and the Votadini struck a fire – two peoples who had fought alongside and against each other, feasting together for one last time.

As she sat beside that fire, leaning back against a broken stone, Arite saw men pass around skins of wine and heather beer, simple treasures that they had saved for just such a moment. A rich scent soon filled the air: the venison roasting and spitting. As she watched the flames lick higher and the shadows dance across the once sacred stones, she wondered if it was a blasphemy to feast in such a place. She supposed that no man of the Votadini could say for certain – the druids had never written down their teachings and so that knowledge had been lost more than a hundred years before, burned away with the sacred groves of Yns Mon. But there on that morning, to share food and wine within that circle of stone, it felt like something sacred.

There was no question of sacrilege for her people – amongst the Sarmatians, fire was holy. The gods were said to live in the dancing flames, in the beacons and campfires that the nomads of the steppe followed from one place to the next all their lives, until the funeral fires that marked their graves. And so, together, with wine and meat and fire, they prepared to say goodbye.

All about her, Arite heard the voices of people making peace, pledging love, swearing oaths, and taking vows of bravery. She could see others seeking omens from the gods – one man casting a bag of stones upon the ground and reading their pattern, a woman rubbing the tooth of a wolf and whispering silent prayers, a Sarmatian warrior staring into the fire and hoping to hear those sacred flames speak. And she too stared into the fire, but she did not expect to hear any whisperings from the gods. She wished only to be left alone.

But in time, she became aware of a presence close by. A man sitting beside her, waiting.

A weariness settled upon her then. How many times had she seen men come to her, supplicants before a queen, asking for some blessing she could not provide – love, or wisdom, or forgiveness? How much they had taken from her, and how little they had offered in return.

She tilted her head to the side, and as her vision swirled with the smoke and the fire, for a moment she thought she saw Bahadur sitting beside her – the husband she had betrayed long before, whom she had seen die upon the battlefield many years ago. But when she blinked twice and her vision cleared she saw reddish-gold hair, the kind and weary eyes of Lucius staring back at her.

'What is it you wish to say?' she asked him. 'Is it a question, or an apology?'

'Perhaps a little of both,' said Lucius. 'You are wise...'

'You can spare me the praise,' she said, impatient. 'I am no vain chieftain you must flatter to get your way. Say what you wish to.'

Lucius stared into the fire for a time. 'I should never have taken you to Wall,' he said at last. 'Akkas would still be free. What a fool I was, to fear Caerellius more than the Painted People.'

'I chose to go,' she said softly, her eyes upon the broken Wall to the north of them. 'Do not pity yourself, it does not suit you. And it is of no use to me.'

'You are right.' Lucius looked down at his hands. 'I came to ask if you would forgive Kai. But I cannot. So why should you?'

'You thought to make me forgive him, when you could not? That was to be my burden to bear.'

He nodded. 'As I say, I am sorry for it.'

She turned away from him then, and looked beyond the stone circle at the open country about them – a scattering of clouds across a beautiful sky, the achingly beautiful light of summer shining across the hills and the heather. All those little gifts offered by the gods to those who are soon to die, for the world always seemed at its most beautiful before a battle. 'He has been given love enough in his life,' she said. 'What should it matter to us now, if he chose to throw it away?' She hesitated. 'I only ask of you this – that you be brave, and take Kai with you in search of the cauldron.'

He did not answer for a time. 'It is much that you ask,' he said eventually, his voice soft and thick.

'No. It is the simplest of things. It is your pride alone that you must put aside. Does that matter so much?'

'You do not seem so quick to forgive him yourself,' Lucius said.

'You do not have to forgive him,' she answered. 'He has done much to hurt us both. The gods do not let him be happy, but they give him their favour, in a strange sort of way. You have a better chance with him than without him – nothing else matters.' She hesitated, and then she said: 'You have always made each other brave.'

She watched Lucius test the thought she offered him as he might have tested a new sword – feeling the weight of it, turning it this way and that, searching for a flaw. A little smile then, as if in mockery of himself, and he said: 'Very well. It shall be so.'

It seemed to Arite that he did not speak those words in defeat, but with a kind of acceptance, a burden being lifted. And in spite of herself, she felt some glimmer of pleasure to see it. Once more, she had helped a wound to heal. 'Thank you, Lucius,' she said.

'I will be brave, as you ask,' he said. 'And you should be brave, and ask him why he left.'

She said nothing for a time. Then: 'I am afraid to.'

'I know. But you shall regret it if you do not ask. You must be brave too.'

Lucius stood then, and he needed to speak no command or give no signal to gather his men – all at once the Sarmatians were casting down their food half eaten, pouring the last of their wine into the fire as an offering to the gods, calling to their horses and making ready to depart.

'Tell Mor to gather the tribes west of Eboracum,' Lucius said to her. 'Hold the Painted People there, if you can – fight them, lead them on a merry chase through the hills, whatever you can do. I shall meet you there, if we succeed.'

'You think that you shall find the cauldron?' she said, as she rose to stand beside him.

'No.' And he tried to smile then. 'But Mor is a dreamer. Kai is too, in his own way. Let us try to believe in their dream.'

'Very well,' she said. 'Let us be brave, and dare to dream one more time.'

His arm was about her shoulders then, as he gave a chaste, brotherly kiss to her forehead. A wonder that, in spite of all the years they had spent in Eboracum together, both of them lonely and mourning those they had lost, she and Lucius had not become lovers. She would have thought nothing of it herself, for the people of the steppe were accustomed to loving freely, sometimes carelessly. But perhaps Lucius's love was for the Sarmatians he led in battle: a love that had something of the father to it, something of the brother, and something of the priest. A proud kind of love, joyful and unyielding. But lonely too.

She watched Lucius go amongst his people, preparing them for the journey ahead. A man going to his death, saying farewell to those going to a death of their own. A ragged man, armour hacked, leading but a scattering of the men he had led north of the Wall. He should have been the very picture of defeat, a doomed man seeking to salvage a little honour before his death. Yet, to her, he had never looked more the hero, more the king, than he did in that moment.

She paced across the stone circle, one steady foot in front of the other across the earth, until at last Kai was before her. He had one knee to the ground, his hand pressed against the grass, his head bowed low – the look of a man making a vow, some silent prayer witnessed by the spirits of the earth alone.

'Lucius shall take you with him to the west,' she said. 'I have made certain of that.'

Kai lifted his head, his eyes shining in the light of the sun. 'Thank you,' he said.

'I did it for him, not for you.'

Kai nodded slowly. 'I know,' he said. 'And he asked you to speak with me, I suppose? It is not what you want.'

'It is not,' she said. 'But that is courage, is it not? To do what we do not wish to do. Or have you forgotten what it is to be brave?'

'I have not forgotten,' he answered quietly.

She tossed her head as though struck. 'I knew it,' she whispered. 'As soon as Akkas was born, I knew it would end this way. Lucius liked to call him a little miracle. But I knew him as a mockery from the gods, a black jest made flesh. For I have lived longer than all of my children – why should this one be any different? It is my curse to bury them all.'

'You do not know him dead.'

'Ah, yes,' she said. 'Of course, you would not be brave enough to face the truth. Why should you be? You were not brave enough to stay.'

'Do you wish to know why?' he said.

'I do,' she said.

She saw him lay his hand upon the standing stone beside him – seeking some comfort in the coldness against his fingers, perhaps, or some secret courage that the gods might have hidden in that stone long ago, waiting for just such a moment.

'It was a promise to a dying man,' he said at last. 'A promise to Bahadur. He asked me to leave you behind, and so I did.'

And, as though his ghost was conjured by the speaking of his name, once more she could almost see Bahadur then – the husband who had died five years before, and been lost to her long before that. They had loved one another for so long, raised and buried children together, shared everything in word and in deed. But, even so, perhaps she had not truly known him until that moment. She looked away and wiped irritably at her eyes. 'He was a broken man, by the end,' she said. 'His promise should not have bound you.'

'He was a broken man,' Kai said. 'But I loved him as much as you did. I thought to honour him then.'

'And now?'

'I wish that I had stayed,' he said quietly.

'Your wishes are no use to me.'

'I know.' And Kai stood then, as grave and solemn as a priest before the sacrifice. 'But I shall make another, even so,' he said. 'I wish to come back from the Island of Spears. I hope that I shall see my son before I die.'

And he waited then, perhaps hoping to hear some answering sign from the gods that might acknowledge the words, to hear the omen marked by a peal of thunder or the calling of an eagle.

There was nothing, save for the low whisper of the wind.

She watched him mount his horse and take his place once more at Lucius's side. Thirteen warriors setting out to the west: a hopeless journey, as Lucius had said. A chance in a thousand that they might find the Burning Cauldron, a chance in ten thousand that they might succeed in bringing it back.

Yet still, in spite of all, she found herself making a wish of her own. She did not even dare whisper it, for fear that the gods might hear her and mock her desires, as they always seemed to.

She wished, against all hope, that she might see Kai again, just one more time.

22

O ver the hills and across the broken Wall they travelled, heading north and then west. They were hunters in pursuit of the setting sun, the way the champions of the old stories, their minds broken by the gods and longing for death, sought an impossible battle with a mountain or an ocean or the stars above.

By day, Kai led his companions through the old hunting runs of the Novantae and past the burial grounds of the Selgovae, charting the path as safely as he could. Occasionally there was the sensation of being watched from afar – a glimpse of shadow upon a hillside, a rustle from a tree. But there was no telling whether it was truly a sentry or merely some phantom of their own minds that watched them. For the northern tribes had been swallowed up in the passage of the Painted People, and any who remained had taken to the deepest forests, the caves in the mountainsides, all the hidden redoubts known to the tribes beyond the Wall. They were ghost lands that the Sarmatians passed through.

In the nights, they sat in a circle once more. Sometimes around a little fire when they had hunted some meat to cook, more often together as shadows in the darkness, staring up at the stars and reading the old myths and stories that were written there. It was no close brotherhood that the Sarmatians offered Kai now, deserter and exile that he was. Some of them would not look at him at all, as though he were a ghost that they refused to acknowledge. Others offered him the barest courtesy. Only one went further than that – the scarred warrior called Tasius, who shyly and reluctantly offered Kai a wineskin when he thought that no others would see.

On those nights they sat in silence for the most part, except to exchange whispered stories of those they had lost – the Sarmatian way of honouring the dead. Every once in a while, one of them would sound out some fragment of a song, a few wistful, winding verses before it faded back to silence.

It was only on the third night, when the first hints of the sea mist had been sighted on the horizon, that the pattern was broken.

It was the youngest of the Sarmatians who spoke first that night: Gosakos, more of a boy than a man. Thick dark hair fell about his face and golden, wolfish eyes looked out through those locks towards Lucius, his Great Captain.

'Do you think we shall succeed?' Gosakos said.

A reproachful hiss from another man about the fire, and a few of the others shook their heads. It was bad fortune to speak of such things, in their warrior's tradition.

But Lucius came alive at the words – they had risked a little fire that night, and in the light of the embers his eyes shone as though he were a father speaking to his son. 'None can say but the gods,' he said. Then, gently: 'Are you afraid?'

'Only a little,' Gosakos answered, and Kai thought it was truth that he spoke – perhaps he was too young to consider the life that was being taken from him, only thinking of the glory that might lie at the end of the journey. Perhaps, in the way of young men, he had more fear of failure than of death.

'All I know for certain,' said Lucius, 'is that I am glad to be in this place, now, with all of you. All I know is that it is a brave thing we do, with the eyes of our ancestors upon us.'

'To try is enough?' Gosakos said. His voice was hesitant, doubtful – perhaps, in all of the dreams of death and glory, he had never let himself think of defeat. Of dying alone upon an island in a lost cause.

'It is so,' Lucius answered.

And the others were murmuring around the circle then, echoing the words. 'It is so.' A prayer, a war chant, an act of faith that it seemed they all believed in.

All except for Kai. The old words, the familiar lies – how many times before must Lucius have spoken to men like this, young and drunk upon tales of glory? How many times, making them ready to die? For Kai had seen a shadow that passed across Lucius's face, and perhaps he alone knew how hollow their Great Captain's words were. And Lucius's gaze met his then – a challenge was there, a warning to keep silent.

And so Kai tipped his head up, looked towards the stars, and tried to remember when he had believed such stories himself. Of honour, and courage, and duty. He would need that courage soon, for what was to come.

He would need it the next day, when they rode to the end of the world and looked upon the sea.

They heard it before they saw it – the crash of the waves that sounded like the footfalls of a marching army, the calling of the gulls ringing in the air as though they were the heralds of that warband, singing of war and victory and death.

And when they crested the hill at last and looked out upon the ocean, they could see nothing but the water before them. The sea mist lay thick, and there was nothing but white fog and the churning grey-blue of the sea, stretching endlessly before them. The edge of the world, the ending of the world, and it was as though they could somehow see that vast gulf between the land of the living and the land of the dead.

They stayed there for a time, watching the waves rising and sweeping towards them like a line of white-painted cavalry, listening to the rattle and clatter of those waves breaking upon the shingle with a sound like splintering shields. And then, as if in answer to that image, the Sarmatians stirred their weary horses to one last charge.

Their banners drank in the screaming sky, their long spears tilted down towards the waves, and the old war songs sounded out across the stones and the sea. For their long road was ended, here at the edge of the world; those great warriors were travelling to a place where neither horse nor spear could help them. Their one final charge was made in defiance of death – a celebration, and a farewell.

Then the waves were washing over the hooves of their horses as the salt spray kissed their skin, and they frolicked in the surf like children, careless and free. Until all at once the old songs fell silent, as they gathered together and stared out across the water. All lightness gone from them then, for the sea mist was parting, carried away by the wind, blown away by the breath of a god. Before them, at last, they could see the Island of Spears.

It was a shadow, squatting upon the water. Easy to see how

it had earned its name, for the sharp hills upon its spine rose up like a thicket of blades, just as the curve of its coast resembled the shape of a shield. A shiver of fear to see it, for Kai's people were born of the steppe and not the sea. It seemed impossibly far away from them, guarded by the press of the waves and the depths of the water. They might as well have sought to fly to the moon, or pluck the stars from the sky. And it seemed the Sarmatians all felt it together – a coward's longing to turn their horses back to the hills. To flee the coast, and the death that waited upon the water.

On the beach before them, Lucius swung himself down from his horse, let his fingers run gently through its mane. 'Our horse-brothers can carry us no further,' he said. 'We travel now upon the waves of the sea.'

'Should we tether them here?' Kai asked.

'And let them starve, if we do not return?' Lucius said. He gave a long, patient caress to the face of his horse. 'No, let them go free.'

Slowly, reluctantly, the Sarmatians dismounted, as each man chose to say his farewell in a different way. Kai saw one man lay his forehead against his horse's face, whispering words that no one else would hear. Another led his mount down to the water and walked with it upon the beach, the water lapping about their ankles as they stared together out upon the rolling waves. As for Kai, he put his arms around his horse's neck, his nose filled with the sharp, sweet smell of horse sweat perhaps for the very last time. A moment later, he felt that long neck curl about him in an answering embrace.

Then all of the Sarmatians together were stripping away the barding from their horses and casting it to the ground, slipping the saddles loose and freeing them of rein and bit, working upon the horses as though they were cutting away the bonds of prisoners that they had rescued. And when it was done, the horses did not understand at first. They simply stood there, naked before their masters, and waited. They had been bred for war, trained to obey and to kill. They had never known the freedom of choice.

There was nothing but stillness for a time: just the horses staring at the men, a silent question in their eyes. The Sarmatians stared back, an unspoken answer in theirs, as the waves, falling softer now, made their gentle music upon the shingle.

And then, at last, it seemed that the horses understood.

There was no shaking of the earth beneath the sudden thunder of hooves. There was no rush, no hurry to do anything at all. As one, moving as a wild, free herd, the horses began to wander away from the beach, moving gently towards the slope of a hill that shone a promising, verdant green in the light of the sun. Soon enough, they were shadows on that hillside, taking their place in nature with a natural, careless ease.

Kai knew that this land had never seen horses like that wander freely. They would tower above the ponies of the northland – they would be giants, princes, and kings, and their children would roam freely across hill and heather and know nothing of war.

On the beach, the Sarmatians were scattered and solitary, each man mourning his horse alone. Only Lucius did not watch the herd upon the hillside, for he was staring out towards the Island of Spears. Kai hesitated, but then thought once more of the horses, remembering how they had always taught him to be brave. He walked to stand beside his Great Captain, the man who had once been his friend.

Together, they listened to the waves.

At last Kai spoke. 'What I said before…'

'I suppose,' said Lucius, 'that you shall tell me now that you did not mean the words.'

'I thought to trade my life for Arite's. For my son's. I thought to drive you away, for I could not have you following me.'

'You could never hurt me with a lie,' Lucius said. 'Only with the truth. And I think it was the truth you spoke, even if you did not know it yourself.'

'Lucius…'

'What was between us was lost long ago,' said Lucius, as his eyes followed the motion of the waves. 'You asked me once, long ago, whether I fought for hate or for love. Before the duel with that king of the Sarmatians. Do you remember?'

'I do,' Kai said. For it had been a beautiful day, aching bright, as Lucius had fought to save his people. A battle fit for the old stories, a hero standing alone against a cruel king. Never had Kai and Lucius been closer than at that moment.

'I answered that I fought for love, then,' Lucius said. 'Perhaps it shall be for hate now. Perhaps that is all that is left to me.'

'We shall find out, upon the Island of Spears.'

'Yes, we shall.'

'If we return,' said Kai at last, 'do you think the horses will come back for us?'

'We shall not find out,' said Lucius as he looked towards the island. 'We go there to die.'

'Then why go at all?'

A moment of stillness, as Lucius thought it over. 'I do not

think we can take the Burning Cauldron from them,' he said. 'But to see it... I would like to see it, at least. Perhaps that will be enough for me.'

'You did not say this to the others.'

'Better for them to have hope. I can lie when I have to.' And there was a bitterness to his speech, then, as he said: 'My greatest gift, inspiring men to die for lost causes.'

Kai turned to Lucius, then – a hand half reaching towards his Great Captain's shoulder, before he remembered himself and drew it away once more. 'Do you truly believe that?' he said.

Lucius said nothing for a time. Then: 'I am glad you are here – for this at least, that I may confess the lie to you. But I need you for nothing more than that. I do not care whether you have hope or not. And I need nothing more from you.'

And with that he was gone – walking across the beach, laughing and joking with each of his men as though he had not a care in the world. Gathering them together to wait for darkness and the hope of another omen, another miracle.

23

'No.' The chieftain of the Coritani shook his head, the torcs about his neck clinking together like chimes, his lime-stiffened hair tall as a lion's mane above his impassive face. 'What you ask, it cannot be done.'

For Arite, it was no surprise to hear those words. She stood now in the hunting runs of the Coritani, with the great white limestone cliffs towering above them like pale monuments to forgotten kings. But she could have been in the hillside fortress of the Deceangli or the sacred beach of the Parisi, where, it was said, the gods had once spoken through the music of the waves. In each of those places, they had spoken to a great chieftain of the southland tribes. Each time, Mor had asked them to face the Painted People with him. And one by one, over and over again, each chieftain said: 'No.'

Beside her, Mor shook his head. 'You say it cannot be done,' he said. 'What you mean is, you shall not do it.'

Pertacus, chieftain of the Coritani, said: 'Call it what you will. What does it matter?' And he cast a disdainful eye over the people Mor had brought with him, who were gathered together in the meadow below the cliff.

They must have seemed a ragged band to him – Sarmatian horsemen, usually so impressive upon their tall, beautiful horses, now with their armour hacked and broken and the shame of defeat hanging heavy upon them. The Votadini had a bandit look about them, like wolves at the end of winter, with their hollow cheeks, their skin grey and near translucent, their eyes that seemed too large in their heads. They must have seemed to be the kind of men who would say anything for a scrap of bread and a cup of wine, the kind of men who had nothing to offer a chieftain except for ill fortune.

'You do not believe what I say?' Mor said. 'What I swear upon my honour and my ancestors?'

'No,' Pertacus answered. 'Because you speak in stories fit for children, and nothing more. These tales of a horde of tribes descending from the north, what do they matter to me? These Painted People shall take the lands of the Brigantes and the Carvetii, perhaps. But no tribe may conquer the whole island.'

'The Romans did,' Arite said, loud enough for the words to echo up the cliff to where the Coritani watched them. And a ripple passed through the warriors of the tribe as those words struck home.

Pertacus ignored her, and said: 'You ask me to join with the other tribes – our people have been enemies for centuries. Why should we cast aside a five-hundred-year bloodfeud to face men who have never wronged us?'

'Because the Painted People do not mean to play the game of cattle raids and honourable feuds,' Mor said. 'They come to take your lands and your people, and destroy you, once and for all.'

'We shall treat with them,' Pertacus answered, 'and they shall leave us alone. All chieftains may be bargained with.'

'This is no chieftain,' Arite called up. 'This is the Maimed King. And with him there shall be no bargaining.'

'You are not of our lands,' Pertacus answered flatly. 'You know nothing of our ways. Why do you question me so?'

At this, Arite felt the last of her patience go. 'I only wonder why you refuse to see sense,' she said, gripping her spear a little tighter. 'Is it because you are a coward, or a fool?'

The chieftain went white with rage. 'Brave words,' he said, 'for one who insults me with truce leaves upon your spear. That is a true coward's trick.'

With a single stroke of her hand, she plucked those leaves away and cast them to the wind. She held the spear out, point towards the chieftain – the traditional Sarmatian challenge. 'Try me,' she said, 'if you have the courage.'

The chieftain hesitated for a moment – enough for her to see a glint of fear in his eyes. Then Pertacus spat from the top of the cliff, the spray of it falling down upon them like rain. 'It would dishonour me, to fight a woman such as you. A wandering mongrel with no clan to call her own. Now, begone from our lands before the sun sets. Or you shall find my warriors shall take up your challenge, and you shall not like the result.'

'Very well,' she said. 'I have the answer to my question, whether you are a coward or a fool. I need nothing more from you.' And with a twitch of the reins and her spear held high, a banner to her people, she turned her back on the chieftain and led them from that place.

Behind her she heard the jingle of tack, the rustle of stumbling steps, as the ragged band of the Sarmatians and the Votadini followed her. And rising above it all, the jeering mockery of the Coritani, echoing from the cliffs like the howling of wolves, chasing them from those lands. The songs of doomed men who did not know themselves to be doomed.

On the journey away from the Coritani, Arite waited for Mor to speak – to curse her, or plead with her, or to tell her some story of dreams and omens that he thought might offer her hope. But the chieftain of the Votadini said nothing. He rode beside her in silence, wrapped up in some dark thought of his own, the sadness sitting heavy upon him as a bearskin cloak.

It was only after they crossed the river that marked the end of the Coritani lands, the water shimmering golden and beautiful in the light of the falling sun, that Mor broke the silence. 'You remind me of her sometimes,' he said. 'Laimei, I mean.'

'I do not know if you intend to praise me or curse me, when you speak so.'

'Perhaps a little of both.' He leaned down and dipped his fingers in the river, watching the brief trails they left behind before the water closed up and became whole once more. 'Pertacus might have listened, if I had been given more time. If you had not spoken the way that you did. What chieftain may bend before such insults?'

Arite shook her head. 'You are a fool if you think he would change his mind. When the Painted People come to burn his fields and butcher his people and tie him down to be flayed alive, he shall still believe he was right to refuse you. He shall tell himself that, all the way to the end.'

'You are right, aren't you?' Mor chuckled to himself, rueful and self-mocking. 'Perhaps I am the fool. Perhaps you are here to teach me so.'

'I am not one of your omens,' she said. 'I am not here to teach you anything.'

'But you are,' Mor answered. 'Don't you see? It is you that I fight against. You have no faith in me – neither do the chieftains. You do not believe that we may win, and neither do they. If I may persuade you, I may convince them. But you are an opponent I do not know how to defeat.'

'The Painted People have plenty of faith. See what it has brought them.'

'Yes,' Mor said quietly. 'It has brought them victory.'

They sat together for a time. Arite cast her eyes across that gathered company – the remnants of two broken peoples, both exiled and defeated. And her eyes fell upon the children that travelled with them, the last generation of the Votadini. A people soon to be lost to the world, with all their songs falling silent.

'What is it you see in your dreams?' she said.

Mor blinked, then, and lifted his head. 'What?'

'You show no fear in the waking world. You are brave for your people, a true chieftain. But every night...' And Arite fell silent then, not knowing how much she should say. For all of the Votadini knew how Mor trembled in his blankets at night, his lips moving ceaselessly in some desperate, silent prayer, his teeth bared towards the stars and sky. How he woke each day, slow and hesitant, as though he were a man rising from his own grave.

'It seems my mind betrays me,' he said. 'Yes, I have tried to be brave. Brave like you, or Laimei. You inspire us all, you know – that is how my people pray. "Make me brave as a

Sarmatian woman," they say. And in the day, I think that I show some courage.'

'You do,' she said softly.

He nodded. 'But at night, when I dream, I see something that does frighten me.'

'Your death?'

'No. I know that my death will come soon.' A hollow laugh. 'And it does not please me, but I do not fear it.'

'Then what?'

He looked all about them then – to the north and the south and the east and the west, where the countless tribes of that island made their homes. 'By day, I have a vision of all of these tribes gathering together, and facing the Painted People. A hopeless stand, perhaps, but it would be beautiful. It might mean that we are more than bandit kings marking our borders, lost in our feuds – that we are not the foolish, petty people that the Romans think we are.'

'But you see something else in your dreams.'

'I do.' He said nothing more for a time, and she tried to imagine the horrors that he must see when he slept – those he loved put to the slow death of torture, a terrible reign of the Painted People that would span across countless centuries, the dead gods rising from the Burning Cauldron once more, reborn in blood, living only to be worshipped in death and destruction.

But in the end, when he spoke of the evil of his dream, he simply said: 'An empty field – that is what I see when I close my eyes.'

'That is all?'

Mor nodded slowly. 'It should not frighten me so,' he said, 'but it does. For I know what that empty field means – that none of the tribes will join us. Divided and fearful, too stubborn to put aside their feuds, they shall submit to the Painted People. And we shall lose something that will never return. We will become an island of killers, like monsters from the old legend.' He hesitated. 'We shall become what the Romans have always believed us to be.'

He looked up towards the sky, where the sun fell to the horizon and painted the land in crimson light. 'And soon it will be time for me to return to that dream, and face that empty plain once more. But perhaps I do not need to sleep to see it,' he said, as he gestured to the open lands all around them. 'It is here in the waking world for anyone to see.'

And Mor laughed then – a sweet, crisp sound that had no trace of sadness or mockery to it, and that gave Arite no warning of the words he would speak next. 'But why do I speak of this to you?' he said. 'You do not care. You only wish to die – one of us, at least, shall get what they long for soon enough. Forgive me.' And with that, he stood up, whistling a merry, mad little tune as he went to wander through the camp.

Arite watched him as he made his way through the Sarmatians and the Votadini – always pausing to share a joke, a story, a fragment of a song, to speak some words that seemed to leave those beaten men and women a little lighter in his wake. Even there, at the ending of all hope, he fought to laugh and to smile as if to spite the coming darkness.

She wanted to believe the truth of what he spoke – that she did not care what became of them all. But as they made their miserable campsite and passed around what berries and little game they had managed to gather, as they drank the silty river water and tried to imagine it to be wine or heather beer, she began to feel something beyond the quiet, hollow, persistent longing for death. She found herself hoping that Mor's empty dream would not come true.

That night, once again, she watched him sleeping – a warrior going alone to a hopeless battle in that world of gods and dreams and omens. She listened to the songs and stories told around the campfires, the wind twisting and warping the words as they came to her, making the tales of the Votadini and the Sarmatians all blend into one another, telling one great story of relentless hope in spite of the darkness.

And there, beneath the light of the waxing moon that shone above her, once more she heard the whispering of a god, the speaking of an omen. Not in mockery, as she had expected, the cruel words of a god tormenting her once more with all that she had lost, but one last message from the spirits beyond, as true a gift as she had ever known.

Her hands were upon Mor then, shaking him awake. And he clutched at her in terror as he woke from the dream, weeping against her like a child, all his courage and hope spent at last.

'You need face that empty field no longer,' she said. 'For I know now what we must do.'

24

On the edge of the world, as the full moon rose above them and the waves lapped at their feet, the Sarmatians waited. They stared towards the Island of Spears and waited for the turning of the tide, for the darkness to grow thick about them. They waited for an omen to guide their way.

They had found the boats earlier in the day – a pair of battered coracles, the kind the local fishermen used. Boats made to float close to the shore, not fit for any kind of crossing, but even so there had been an appreciative murmur from the Sarmatians when they found them. In the presence of those boats, they saw the blessing of the gods.

Yet, to Lucius, it seemed that blessing was not enough. At night, beneath the light of the moon and stars, the water looked like a sea of silver – a place for gods and monsters, not for men. Before those metallic waves, the Sarmatians stared at the ground with bowed heads, afraid. They were people of the land and not the sea, and they saw only death upon the water.

Lucius knew that the fear of his men was not the kind that could be dismissed with a well-timed jest, an appeal to honour, or a pledge of brotherhood. He could not drive them forward in the Roman way, with threats of the whip, of decimation, of crucifixion. It was the kind of fear that could only be broken by an omen.

Amongst the Sarmatians only Kai seemed unconcerned, turning a smooth stone over and over in his sword hand with a confident, patient air as he waited for the turn of the tide. There was a moment of gratitude to have Kai with him, before Lucius angrily pushed it aside – that traitorous feeling was a weakness he could not afford.

A glimmer in the darkness, a point of light far upon the sea before them – perhaps it was Kai's quiet courage that had earned the notice of the gods, or perhaps it was Lucius's anger that pleased them. For there before them was the omen that they sought, just as the tide began to turn. Distant, upon the Island of Spears, they saw fire.

First one fire, then many – not the scattered campfires of a little fishing settlement that one might expect on such an island, nor the single great bonfire of a warband or pirate crew celebrating a victory. For Lucius saw a particular geometry in those points of light, the way the people of the northlands laid their circles of standing stones just so. It was a pattern of ritual, a message in smoke and flame that was written for the gods above and below.

Those flames should have been a fearsome sight – they spoke of a terrible enemy across the water, great in number and strong in faith, working towards a fearsome purpose. But all around him, Lucius could see the Sarmatians nodding solemnly. Fire was sacred to the nomads. They followed it all their lives, tracing a path from one campfire to the next until they reached the funeral pyre that would burn above their graves.

To the Sarmatians, it must have seemed as though those people of the island were lighting beacons, calling them home. And so, without anyone uttering a word or a command needing to be given, they pushed their boats into the water and took to the silver sea.

It was a fearful, fumbling journey – hesitant whispers in the darkness, the two boats rowed and steered with crude oars cut from branches and driftwood, fighting with the currents and the waves. The Sarmatians knew so little of ships and the sea. Lucius knew but a little more, enough to understand that to be on the sea in darkness was only fit for madmen and for fools.

Yet their omen held true at first, as the boats drifted across the water. The sea still and calm beneath them, no wind save for a caressing breeze against their cheeks, the gentle tug of the tide drawing them towards the Island of Spears. A rising hope that no man dared to whisper, that they might make it to that island unscathed.

There was a change then – soft, almost imperceptible. A sudden stilling of the wind, a darkening of the stars above, a distant roll of thunder, deep as the snarl of a wolf. A moment of eerie silence, when it seemed as though the sea itself were holding its breath. And then the air was screaming as the tempest swept over them.

The waves arched up into mountain ranges, black and terrible, as the water fell in torrents from above – the rain so heavy that it was as though a second sea had settled in the sky above them, that they might drown in the open air.

The sea beat against their coracles like spears against shields, as though some unseen spirits fought against them from deep within the water. And perhaps it was so – perhaps the fell gods of the Painted People, seeing their enemies approaching, had found their breath once more to drive them from the island, reaching with unseen hands to rend them apart.

Those dead gods grew strong, it seemed, almost ready to be born back into the world. For the coracle was groaning beneath Lucius then, a sudden wetness seeping up like blood pouring from a wound.

There was a moment where Lucius's stomach lurched with fear and not the motion of the waves. Then a sound like flesh tearing, as the coracle fell to pieces beneath them and the sea took him into its hungry embrace.

All about Kai, the black water of the sea.

There had been no time to think or to act as the coracle broke to pieces about him. A shattering beneath him, a sudden rush of water, and then the sea had been full of terrified, drowning men, each clutching at the other with a murderous instinct that they could not control, each fighting to force the other beneath the water and stay upon the surface themselves, each seeking to turn their sworn brothers into a raft of dying flesh.

A moment when Kai was free, head upturned to the sky and fighting for air, watching the lightning break across the sky. Then something took him – it might have been a drowning man clutching at his legs, a murderous wave that he did not see in time, or one of the fell spirits that was said to hunt in dark waters. One moment, he was fighting towards the island, taking half-breaths between the relentless waves. The next, he was plummeting down through the black water, rolling and tumbling as fell.

At last he reached a place of utter stillness, deep beneath the raging sea. All about him, light from the moon and the stars and the lightning shone refracted through the water. He might have been suspended in the night sky itself, caught up in one of those beautiful dreams of flight that he loved so much. No way of telling which way was up and which was down, for there was both light and shadow every way that he looked. In every way but one lay deeper water, and death. Only a single path led to life, and to freedom.

A moment where it seemed easier to stay where he was, suspended in that night sky, thinking himself deep within a dream. A moment where it seemed easier to drown in peace where he was, rather than risk journeying further into the deep. He kicked lazily in the water, and some unseen force plucked at his clothes – almost a caress from the current, a gentle touch that seemed an invitation from the gods, though whether it was to live or to die he did not know. And he trusted it enough to follow.

At once, he was out of that place of stillness – the water fought against him and Kai fought back, kicking and striking and raking and gouging at the sea, his lungs aching and his vision trimmed by a different kind of darkness. Until at last, separated by the veil of the water, once more he saw the moon and stars above him.

Gasping for air, born once more into the world of the

living, even as the waves tumbled over him over and over again, trying to drag him back down. Flashes of lightning broke through the sky, and he saw the island looming larger and larger before him – the tide held true and carried him towards it. At last, after what seemed like hours battling through the waves, he felt that impossible, beautiful sensation of sand beneath his feet.

Kai had given so much to make it that far, yet those last few feet, staggering and crawling up the sands of the beach, seemed to cost him more than all the rest of his journey across the sea. And so when he collapsed to the ground the waves were still lapping and pulling at his feet, but he was too exhausted to go any further.

There was a longing then, to sleep. It would be death to do so, for either the waves would drag him back out or some sentry of the Painted People would find him and slit his throat before too long, a fresh sacrifice for the dead gods of the cauldron. Yet even knowing all of that, Kai was certain that he could not stand again.

There was no hope of them succeeding; Lucius had said so himself. He alone lay upon that beach, and what could he hope to do without his companions? Perhaps it was enough for him to have made the journey that far – a man of the horse and spear had bravely faced the black sea at night. No more could be asked of him than that.

And then, in the darkness, Kai felt someone reach out and take his hand.

For he saw now that there were others there, lying exhausted upon the sand beside him. Seven shadows in the darkness, the rest made sacrifices to the hungry sea. And he saw the man beside him, the one who held his hand, was the scarred captain of the Sarmatians, the man called Tasius.

Kai turned his head away, feeling the wet sand clutch and scrape against his skin. And in the light of the full moon, a little distance away, he could see Lucius.

The Roman returned his gaze, too weary to mask his heart any longer. Even after all that had passed between them, they could hide nothing from one another – a blessing when they had been as brothers, and a curse now. For it was not with old affection, or even with that familiar, empty coldness that Lucius looked upon Kai then. It was with hate.

Kai stood from the sand – gasping with the effort, his sodden clothes as iron upon him as he rose upon trembling legs. He would not be defeated, would not become the weak and broken man that Lucius thought him to be. And but a moment later, he saw Lucius rise as well. Perhaps the Roman had felt that same longing to lie down and die. Perhaps the same thing had driven him to his feet – that pride, such a close cousin to hate.

If still they had loved one another, perhaps that would not have been enough to raise them from the sand. They might have died there together, content and defeated in each other's company. It was their hate that drove them from the beach and into the cover of the heather – a darker gift from the gods, but a gift all the same.

Somewhere distant before them, deep within the island, the sounding of a drum, the echo of a chant. Behind them, like dead men rising from the grave, the last Sarmatians rose from the sand and together they slipped silently into the hills, moving towards those sounds of dark ritual, towards the place where the dead gods might be born once more.

25

Beneath the light of the stars and full moon above, Arite waited.

It was at the centre of the island that they had chosen to make their stand, somewhere west of Eboracum and south of the Wall, where the omens seemed to sing from the trees and the stones and the sky above. For they had found a place seemingly shaped by the gods themselves – a great crag of limestone that curved in a horseshoe around them, a natural amphitheatre that might have been fit for giants, marked by a deep hollow at the very centre. She was there now to see if they might find something to fill that hollow at the heart of the island.

The last remnants of the Votadini and the Sarmatians huddled behind her in the darkness – no reborn gods or army of heroes, but merely a gathering of exiles desperate to share a dream, one last time. They had a great pyre built in that place, wood stacked high enough for a Beltane festival, flint and tinder ready to be struck. Beside it she could see Mor pacing back and forth, and Arite thought him restless at first, wracked by fears and nightmares. But when he turned to her, the moon shone upon eyes that were alive with childish joy.

'You really believe they will come?' she said.

'I do not know,' he answered. 'But there is a chance – a chance that we have made from nothing. And that is enough to smile at, is it not?'

Arite turned away to gaze towards the distant hills. She could not stand the way that Mor looked at her, for he was a man who saw the workings of fate in all things. She had no wish to play a part as one of his omens.

Yet even so, in those last weeks she had done her best to become one, as they scattered and went amongst the people of the island. She had spoken to lone shepherds upon the hillsides, as their flocks looked on in mute witness. She had watched as Mor played with children in a river, gambolling and pulling faces and playing the fool to make them laugh, before offering a few whispered words to the parents who watched close by. Around the cooking fires of farmers and the campfires of the hunters, they had spoken of the Painted People. She had not sought to frighten those she spoke to, nor to bully or command. She had merely asked them to gather at the stone heart of the island, beneath the light of the next full moon. She had offered them a dream of a world that might be, and given them a chance to be brave.

For that was what she had understood at last, after the chieftain of the Coritani had laughed at them and chased them from his lands. This was an enemy that the Romans could not defeat – they would huddle in their forts, waiting for orders that would not come, until the Painted People came to destroy them. And as for the chieftains of the tribes, they would never risk what they had so jealously hoarded, would not let themselves believe in the ending of the world as they knew it. It would be the people of this island who might stand and fight, and if they did it would not be under the war banners of their tribes and led by the commands of great men. They would come for the dream, or not at all.

The night drew on and the wind blew cold against her, whistling through a nearby copse of trees with a piercing, mocking whine. Arite tilted her head back and watched the full moon rising overhead.

'Is it time?' she asked.

'Not yet,' Mor answered. 'We must give them a little longer.'

Whether any allies would choose to join them there, only the gods could say. Arite knew only one thing for certain – that from the north, the Painted People marched towards them.

Day by day, she had seen the columns of black smoke drawing closer and closer – steadings and farms being put to the torch, corpsefires burning and casting the dead as ashes into the sky. They carved no straight line to the south, but wandered back and forth like a hunting dog coursing through the heather, eager to turn up any prize in flesh that they might have missed. There was no need for them to hurry, for their destruction of the island was a slow and patient thing.

But they were close now. A few days, a week at most, there was no doubt about that. The only question was, who would be there to stand against them?

Above them the last sliver of the moon shaded white – a perfect circle shining above them.

'Let it be now,' Arite said.

'Let it be now,' Mor answered.

The tapping of the flint, a crackle as the kindling caught

the flame. And soon the fire was roaring beside them, a lonely beacon in the night, the wind whipping sparks and embers past Arite as she looked out to the hills around her, hoping to see answering fires in the darkness.

There was nothing. Nothing but the wind, and the empty night.

From close behind her, Arite heard a little sigh from Mor – not a sound of sadness or fear, but merely a kind of acceptance. And a moment later she felt his hand in hers, their fingers interlacing together.

'I am glad to be with you here,' he said. 'We shall dream here together, at the end. And you must know that the dream will still matter, though we are but a few. It may still be enough to change the world.'

Other hands were upon her then, Sarmatians and Votadini alike coming in to share an embrace. A scattering of tears here and there, but little sign of true grief amongst them. She saw women draw their lovers close in the light of the fire, men gather up their children and place them upon their shoulders, hands clasping hands in one great circle. Cold comfort on such a lonely night, with death marching towards them, pitiless and implacable, but it was all that they had left now.

And then, from all about them, suddenly there was fire.

Light upon the hills at a hundred different points, scattered like dancing fireflies. They were not the columns and squares of the Roman army, nor the great towering pyres that the Painted People favoured to signal their dead gods, but the little torches of individual wanderers, nomad families travelling together.

Those torches drew close, and Arite could hear voices

calling out to one another, strangers greeting each other like old friends. For Arite it was like being on the steppe once more, where the Sarmatians wandered as the herds desired, chasing good grazing, following the channel of a river, or simply seeking the beautiful places where the setting sun would turn the grasslands into gold – gathering together and splitting apart, as naturally as birds wheeling in the sky.

Soon they were gathered together around the fire, those people from half a hundred different tribes, and the air was a cacophony of different languages. From time to time she could hear them ruefully resort to Latin, knowing the tongue of their conquerors better than that of their neighbours. A gift from the Romans greater than any of their secrets of stonework or treasures from distant lands – a language that belonged to all tribes and none.

'What do they say to each other?' she asked Mor.

'That they all shared a dream,' he said. 'A dream of this place. And so they came here to see if it would come true.'

Impossible to count them all in the darkness, but some nomad's instinct spoke to her of their numbers – a few thousand, perhaps, but no more. 'There are not enough of them to fight,' she said.

'No.' And he smiled at her. 'We shall not win, of course. But perhaps we shall linger in the minds of the Painted People, like a story or a song, something they glimpse while sleeping. That is what brought these people here – not to win, but to become a dream themselves.'

They were brave words that Mor spoke – the words of a druid, a holy man, who thought in spans of centuries, a man of faith in a better world to come. But as Arite looked to the north, beyond the black smoke that marked the approach of the Painted People, once more she found herself with a dream of her own. And this time, she dared to speak it aloud.

'I hope for one more miracle,' she said. 'Kai and Lucius, with that cauldron in their hands. I do hope we live long enough to see that.'

Mor draped his arm across her shoulder and said: 'So do I. Let us sleep, and dream of it, and perhaps it will come true.'

26

The black cauldron lay before them. Close enough for Kai to see the marks of wear upon the sides, to see that the handle had been replaced not long ago, and where a little indentation showed that it had once been struck or dropped. It was close, yet still so far away. For as the sun fell from the sky on their second day on the island, beside him he heard Lucius whisper the words that the Sarmatians had all been thinking, but were not brave enough to say themselves.

'It cannot be done,' Lucius said, and the words were spoken with the heavy air of defeat.

Kai made no answer at first, but he knew the truth of those words all too well.

At first, fortune had favoured them. Rising up from the beach at night, they had moved as fast as they could until dawn, making their way towards the distant fires on the hillsides. When the sun rose they had begun to crawl through the sparse undergrowth – the work of slow, terrifying hours, for on this hard, bleak landscape there was little to conceal them. A scattering of boulders, a few stubby trees bent in half by the incessant wind, the folds in the land as the hills rose and fell. At any moment, Kai had expected to hear the hunting cries ring out and echo from the cliffs, for the Painted People to descend gleefully and cut them to pieces, new sacrifices for the old dead gods.

But every time they reached a patch of open ground, it seemed that a squall of rain burst from the clouds or the sea mist rolled in, and they could move on unseen. They even dared to whisper to each other, when the wind blew strong enough, that they had gods of their own watching over them, guiding them to the Burning Cauldron.

They made it all the way to the valley at the heart of the island, a place shielded by mountains on either side. They had crawled to the edge of a grove, where a cluster of boulders and a few tall trees shielded them from view. But here, within sight of the cauldron, their fortune had failed at last.

Kai saw it all so clearly – the little stubby saplings that sprang from the red earth, too young to offer any cover for their approach. The holy men who wandered through the valley tending to the trees, their hair tonsured in the fashion of the ancient druids, heavy knives upon their hips. The sentries who sat upon the hillsides, like shepherds watching their flock. The last hope had been the night, that some ritual or superstition might drive the Painted People to leave the grove untended, but it was a hollow hope. For once the sun fell, he saw torches bloom and fire pits light the grove, the flickering light and dancing shadows making it even more fearful by night than by day. And at the centre, shining dully, was the Burning Cauldron – taunting, beckoning, inviting the Sarmatians to hurry forward to their deaths.

For hours he had watched as Lucius's eyes traced the paths of the wandering sentries, searching for a weakness and finding none. He was a captain and a general such as Kai had never known, who had done in battle what seemed impossible before. Now, at last, he was faced with a problem that could not be solved.

'I thought to see it would be enough,' Lucius whispered. 'To see the cauldron. But...'

'I know,' said Kai. 'But you have always wanted to win. It is the Roman in you.'

A ghost of a smile on Lucius's lips, before he remembered himself. 'Can you see a way through?' he asked, his voice cold once more.

'No,' Kai answered.

Lucius nodded slowly, in defeat, and there was a clutch of sadness at Kai's heart – how far had they fallen away from each other, that Lucius could not hear the lie in Kai's voice? There had been a time, long before, when they could speak nothing but truth to each other. Now, it seemed, they could speak only falsehoods.

Hesitantly, Kai laid a hand upon the Roman's shoulder. 'Rest an hour,' said Kai. 'You cannot think on it any longer. Something may change. We will wake you if it does.'

Lucius turned to the other Sarmatians huddled close by, as though asking their silent permission. They gave it to him in little gestures – touches of a finger to the heart, a clasp of a hand around his ankle, the twitch of a brief smile. Lucius bowed his head in answer, and there was a kind of weary gratitude in the way he moved as he lay down beside the boulder and curled up like a child. Exhausted as he was, he was asleep within moments, seeking some answer in his dreams that he could not find in the waking world.

A moment of silence, as the seven Sarmatians looked at

one another. Each of them knowing the answer to the riddle of the grove. Each of them afraid of that answer, and waiting for the others to speak first.

Their captain, Tasius, crawled across and crouched down beside Kai. Together they watched the twisting motions of the Painted People who wandered the grove, the way the flames of the torches left traces of themselves behind for a moment in the darkness. They communed in the silent, honest way of the steppe people, a slow, patient attuning of one mind to another. Soon enough they would speak, and yet when they did, the most important matters would have been settled already in that silence. And there was an aching love in Kai's heart – for the Sarmatians from whom he had been exiled, for the wild open steppe that he would never see again. For it was of death that they communed, there in the silence.

At last, Tasius said: 'I learned to hate you these past five years.' He said it matter-of-factly, the words as plainly spoken as a greeting.

'Is that so?'

'It is so.' Tasius's eyes drifted down to where Lucius slept fitfully. 'We all love our Great Captain. We saw how much you hurt him, when you deserted north of the Wall.'

Kai made no answer. He merely waited, knowing that there were more words to come.

'I thought you a coward,' said Tasius. 'I still think that may be so. But perhaps it is because you give your bravery to others, and have none left for yourself. For I see the love you have for him now. And I see the courage that you give to him. Brave as he was, he has never been so fearless before. With you, he becomes what he is meant to be.'

A shiver passed through Kai then, to hear those words. 'Why do you speak of this?' he said.

'Because we both know how to pass through that cursed grove, even if Lucius does not.'

'There is no way past them,' said Kai. 'There are too many to fight.'

'And so some of them must be drawn away.'

'Just so.' Kai glanced down once more – even in dreaming, Lucius looked restless. His lips twitching, giving unspoken orders to those in his dreams, eyes dancing beneath closed eyelids as he surveyed some battlefield of the mind. The careworn lines faded away, the shadowy light hiding the grey in his hair. In sleep, he might have been a man half his age. 'I think he does know, in his heart. But he cannot bring himself to say it.'

Tasius nodded. 'It is why he shall never be a king, or an emperor, or any such thing. For all his bravery, he cannot stand to send men to die without him. He shall lead them himself, but he will not send them alone. Yet he must live.' Tasius hesitated, and then once more he said: 'He must live,' repeating the words like a prayer.

'Yes,' Kai answered. 'He must.'

'It is beautiful, is it not? Our world hangs in the balance and he cannot bring himself to cast aside the lives of seven men. Did you ever hear of such a captain?'

'No,' Kai said. 'He cannot do it, but we can.'

'Yes, we can.'

'There is only one question left.' And Kai looked at Tasius then, a challenge in his gaze. 'Which of us will go?'

'Yes,' Tasius said, 'That is the choice, is it not? One of us must stay with him. It will take two to carry the cauldron.'

'Just so.' A moment of hesitation, and then Kai said: 'And I do not wish for Lucius to be left alone.'

'We shall let the gods decide who goes and who remains.' Tasius lifted and opened his hand, palm towards the sky as though he made an offering to the gods of sun and stars, and Kai saw two stones sitting there. 'I took these from the beach,' Tasius said. 'For I knew it would come to this.'

Kai considered them for a moment – one was white and the other was black, each a sign amongst their people of good or bad fortune. 'Let the white stone go to his death, then,' Kai said. 'What could be luckier than that, to have the chance to show such bravery, and to die so well?'

Tasius nodded slowly. 'Let it be so.' He rubbed the stones together in his palm, and Kai heard the soft clink and rattle, a little echo of the sound of the sea.

A moment of waiting, of seeking some signal as to which hand held which stone. A moment too, for Kai to wonder which he truly wanted to draw. He felt some impulse guide him to Tasius's left hand, and so, trusting the omen, that was the one that he chose.

A weight settling into his palm, cool and round. Kai breathed in once, breathed out once more. He opened his hand, and looked down.

A whiteness, shining in his hand, the sight he had hoped to see. But it was a trick of the light, the full moon falling upon polished stone, for when Kai shifted his palm he saw it was the black pebble that he held.

Tasius held up the white rock between thumb and forefinger, like a conjurer showing a coin after a trick. 'I always heard that you were unlucky, Kai,' he said. He gave one more look to the sleeping captain, and Tasius's eyes were glistening as though he looked upon a lover. 'Take good care of him.'

Then the word was passing amongst the men – a whisper in the ear, a touch upon the shoulder. A sentence of death being passed from one man to the next, yet they were grinning, eyes bright as children playing in the fields, as they took up their knives and made ready to go into the darkness.

'Count to five hundred,' Tasius said. 'Then go.'

Kai nodded. 'Though our lives be short...'

'... let our fame be great,' Tasius said. 'Tell others of this, if you live beyond this night.' And with a single clasp of the hand, Tasius was gone into the darkness.

Kai laid a hand upon his chest, counted the beats of his heart, counted away the life of his companions. It would have been wise to alert Lucius then, to make him ready for what must come next. But he could not bring himself to wake his Great Captain. Let him sleep a little longer, dream a little longer. It would be a bleaker, colder world that he woke into.

Somewhere distant, a rattle of pebbles scattering down the hillside. As though in answer a hunting whistle sounded – torches and shadows moved across the slopes towards the sounds. But no alarm cries, not yet.

There were twenty beats of the heart left to count, when there was a stirring upon the ground – Lucius, blinking his eyes open as some unseen signal beckoned him from sleep. An instinct of danger, born of a captain's love for his men, and Kai saw his eyes hunt in the darkness, rolling whites under the light of the moon as they cast about, searching for his beloved Sarmatians.

Finally, they settled upon Kai, the last man Lucius would

have wanted to remain behind. The Roman made to speak but Kai put a hand upon his shoulder, a finger to his lips. For he had counted to five hundred, and there was no time left.

At that moment, a bubbling scream of agony broke through the air – the death cry of a man butchered in the night. And all at once the hunting horns were sounding, the Painted People taking up spear and sword and running into the darkness, the air filling with screams of rage, curses for the invaders and defilers.

The grove was alive with shadows – dozens, perhaps hundreds, of the Painted People, swarming in the darkness, a flood of men and women that swept through the valley.

And then, all at once, the grove was empty.

The campfires burned, the flickering light sending the shadows dancing and playing upon the saplings, making them seem alive with movement. But there was nothing living left there in the grove.

Together, without a word being said, Kai and Lucius stood as one and walked out towards the cauldron.

They did not run, or crawl, or try to scuttle from shadow to shadow. They walked steadily and openly, the light of the fires shining upon their faces. They went willingly, the way the sacrifices of old were said to go to the stone altars to offer their throats and their hearts to priests and gods.

It seemed impossible that they would not be seen. With every step, Kai thought to hear the whisper of arrows from the hillside, for war cries to sound from the shadows, for the trees themselves to reach out and bind them, blasphemers that they were.

There was nothing. Distant, the sound of men screaming, fighting, dying. But it was as though those sounds came from another world. Kai and Lucius could have been the only men left alive, the two of them walking upon an empty earth towards a tomb of the dead gods.

They drew close to where the cauldron lay, half buried in the earth at the heart of the grove, the firelight shining upon the black metal. Lucius strode forward then, as though seeking to be the victor in a slow and solemn race. Yet there was a hesitance before he touched the cauldron – perhaps even some sense of blasphemy. For warriors felt the will of the gods more than most, saw the senseless caprices by which good men died and evil ones lived.

At last, Lucius reached down and rested his fingers upon the black iron. And behind him, as though summoned by that touch, something rose from the darkness.

A creature of shadow it seemed at first, as though some unseen spirit clutched the night about its form to give it a body of darkness with which it might fight and kill. But a single heartbeat later, Kai saw clearly what it was – a man of the Painted People, rising from a shallow grave dug beside the cauldron. A last guardian planted there, ready to destroy the blasphemers. A half-buried man, guarding his half-dead gods.

In one hand a knife, and the other was grasping towards Lucius as though to tap him on the shoulder, to greet a friend found in an unexpected place. Kai went for him, but slowly, terribly slowly, as though he swam through a river towards the man who would kill his friend.

But the world held still, for just long enough – some god holding the sands of time suspended, a gift to the brave. Lucius was sent tumbling to the ground, away from the killing blade, the warrior of the Painted People screaming in rage. And then that guardian of the cauldron turned upon Kai, and bore him to the ground.

The warrior's stinking breath was hot against Kai's cheek, their hands slippery with sweat as they clutched at each other. Kai's grip was slipping, and somewhere the hand with the knife was free, working against Kai's body with a strange coolness, as though it were a blade of ice carving into his skin. But the blade could not find Lucius, and Kai felt no fear. It was as though his heart and lungs were carried in the body of the Roman, his blood beat in the body of another, and no blade could harm him unless it was turned upon his friend.

Then there was the coppery smell of blood in the air, a choking, whispering sigh from above Kai, a heavy weight settling upon him. Lucius pulled him free from beneath the corpse of the warrior, and there in the darkness, painted in blood, he and Kai stared at one another.

Kai felt Lucius's hands upon him once more, intimate as a lover's, searching for a killing wound – the fountaining blood that sprang from a thigh carved open, the spilling coils of a gut wound, a dagger in a pierced heart that quivered with every beat. But he found nothing but a cut across the ribs. For a second weight was upon Kai then, as Lucius caught him up in a desperate, needful embrace.

From over the hills, a howling, distorted war cry sounded out – some final cry of victory from the Painted People.

'We do not have much time,' Kai whispered.

Remembering himself at last, Lucius stood. They took up flaming brands from the fires nearby and cast them into the grove – the saplings smouldering, blazing, and then burning. And in the light of the rising fire, Kai's eyes fell once more upon the knife that had almost killed him. Blackened and filthy, marked with blood and earth so heavily that he could not see the blade. A chill touch across the skin, that feel of an omen that he had known so many times before.

But there was no more time to think of it. Together, they each put a hand upon the cauldron. Together, they began to run.

27

A rite heard them long before she saw them.

The Painted People marched without travellers' songs or war music, but still there was the drumming of their feet upon the ground, sounding out like the rolling of thunder. Then Arite saw the birds wheeling thick in the sky as they were driven from forest and copse and hedgerow, even though she could not yet see the force that chased them from their homes. At last, when the midday sun rose high above her, she watched the Painted People come from the north.

There were close to ten thousand of them now, their numbers swollen by all the tribes they had conquered, all brought together by the words of the Maimed King and the power of the Burning Cauldron. No doubt some had gone willingly, seeing in that killing horde a great and terrible purpose of which they wished to be a part. Others wept as they walked, fearful men made into murderers, their fresh tattoos seeping blood that mingled with the tears.

Perhaps the Painted People had sensed a confrontation was coming that day and knew some force gathered to oppose them. No doubt they thought they would face a

Legion of Rome or some great warband of the southland tribes. Perhaps they had hurried there as fast as they could, to that amphitheatre of stone at the heart of the island fit for gods and giants – a fitting place to seal their victory in blood, once and for all.

Yet when the Painted People came over the hill, they found no army to oppose them. No sea of red shields with Roman eagles dancing above them, no great warband of the Sarmatian cavalry mounted upon monstrous horses and bearing long lances. Nor did they find a war host of the tribes of Britain, skin daubed in woad and great chariots rolling across the open plain.

It was not an army they found there, but a festival instead.

For those who faced them, the People of the Dream, were not gathered for battle. They had hung up their shields for targets, blunted their spears for practice and the love of the game. No war paint marked upon skin now scented with rose and musk, their long hair cleaned and combed and braided, for they sought to be beautiful rather than fearsome. What might have at first been mistaken for blood upon their chins were the stains of wine and heather beer, and the music that rolled off the hills was the old courting songs of love and joy, not war music and battle cries.

They were feasting and singing, and when the Painted People came over the hill, they threw open their arms and called for the newcomers to join them. As though they were long-expected guests late to the feast, not a baleful host come to destroy all that those People of the Dream held dear. For even as they faced death, they would greet it smiling, and laughing, and singing.

That was how they had passed those days spent waiting

for the Painted People, and in spite of all that she had suffered, they had been days of joy for Arite. She had not stood apart from the tribes as they gathered together, determined to seek what pleasure and beauty they could in the last days. She had joined freely in the song and the dance, grateful once more for the life she had led, for the bravery she had shown, in battle and in love, in living and in dying.

Now, from amongst the revellers, Arite looked up towards the Painted People. Not with the warrior's eye, searching for the champions that must be killed, the weak places where an army might be broken. She searched only for some last glimpse of her son.

There was a surge in her heart as she saw little figures trailing behind that horde. For she saw soon enough that they were children leading mules and wagons – bent-backed and exhausted, tottering on their feet, boys and girls put to the miserable work of slaves. Perhaps they were not trusted yet to be killers. Perhaps there was still a chance for them to be saved.

For she saw that the Painted People stood frozen upon the hillside before her. That horde of oathsworn killers who knew no fear in battle could not now take a single step forward. Their captains screamed orders at them, sounded out the old songs of war and death, but still the horde would not advance.

It seemed as though the Painted People, those worshippers of death, now saw something before them that they half remembered – men and women who walked in a waking nightmare, glimpsing a dream into which they might escape.

A shiver passed through them, their spears trembling like trees in a storm. There before them, written in the flesh of the People of the Dream, perhaps they could see memories of the lives they had once lived. The simple joys of feasting by the fire and watching the wheeling stars above them, the pleasure of the hunt and the peaceful kinship of the tribes as they had once been, and could be again.

For a moment, it seemed that the dream might do what a hundred warbands could not. For a moment, she thought that the Painted People might break and scatter and return to their homes, and think no more of death.

But then she could see a figure, rising above the rest. A tall man, upon a tall horse.

It was Corvus, the Maimed King, who rode back and forth along lines of his warriors – his cloak cast from his shoulders and thrown open to the wind, and he rode naked before them, pointing to his terrible scars, reminding them of all that they had given and all that they had done.

It must have been so much easier not to think, not to wake from the nightmare. The Painted People were so steeped in blood already, perhaps it was more frightening for them to turn aside from what they had begun. She saw their spears begin to hold steady, and that fell legion began its march forward once more, hopeless and death-besotted, as inevitable and pitiless as the tide drawing in across the sand.

Arite turned to those who were gathered behind her, the dancers and singers, the lovers and the dreamers. 'It is time,' she said.

They answered her at once – no phalanx or shield wall did they form, but a simple line, their hands linked, swaying gently back and forth like trees in the wind. And, even with their deaths marching before them, still those people sang.

A moment where they stood alone against an army, where

the singing of the People of the Dream sought to drown out the war songs of the Painted People. A moment without hope, and yet even so, it was beautiful.

Then above the songs a voice was calling out – Mor's voice. And the chieftain of the Votadini was screaming in joy as he pointed to the north, laughing and weeping and calling his praise to the long-dead gods of that island.

For there upon the horizon, two horsemen rode.

The sun shone brilliantly upon them at first and made them creatures of light and shadow, as though they were heroes come from the Otherlands to witness the death of their kin. Closer they came, galloping like madmen, the horses gasping and weary beneath them, and Arite could see two riders dressed for war, wearing the shining armour of the Sarmatians, long war spears in their hands. And there were calls of hungry joy from the Painted People when they saw warriors clad for war, worthy opponents and not dreamers for them to fight and kill.

But those war cries fell silent when the riders came closer still. For they could see those riders clearly now. They could see what one of them held in his hands.

The Burning Cauldron, the tomb of the dead gods, the greatest treasure of the Painted People.

Arite could see the man who held it – Kai, his skin now a terrible, ghostly white, as though he were a man risen from the dead, one of those heroes from the old stories who crawl from the grave for one last battle.

And though beside her Mor laughed and wept for joy to see those riders, she felt only the cold feeling that came in the presence of death. The knowledge, deep and wordless, that the cauldron had been won at a terrible price.

★

From atop the hill, Kai stared down at the Painted People and those who opposed them, upon a nightmare and a dream.

He had won that vision with a desperate journey. They had fled from the sacred grove upon the Island of the Spears, casting burning brands into the saplings behind them. They had listened to the howls of grief and betrayal that echoed from the cliffs and rose to the sky like the songs of wolves. He remembered stealing a boat of the Painted People, the oars biting his palms as they rowed away, as the wind and the tide carried them back to the mainland, back to the land of men and the living, away from that burning island of dead gods and soulless men.

And it would all have been for nothing, if it was not for the sight that had greeted them upon the shore. The shadows that waited for them, tall proud figures who stared watchfully out into the sea – the horses of the Sarmatians, not roaming wild and free but lined up in close order, oathsworn warriors awaiting their captain's commands.

Kai could not say what compelled the horses to come back and wait for them – love or duty, a silent oath kept by the horses in their own particular way. But all that mattered was that they were there. And so Kai and Lucius had ridden to the south, night and day, following the burning trail of the Painted People until it brought them to this place.

Now he looked out upon the sea of faces that stared up at him, their voices melding together – cries of joy and hate, pleading and cursing, all blending in his ears. And a sudden weakness stole through Kai then, as the dead gods, perhaps knowing his intention, gave an unearthly weight to the black iron in his hands. The knife wound in his side burned and throbbed with fever, and the metal felt wonderfully cool against his skin. He found himself afraid to part with that cauldron then, afraid to do what had to be done.

But Lucius's hand was upon his, offering his strength to share the burden. On his skin Kai could see the markings he had made the night before from the ash of the Burning Cauldron. Not the signs of war, the chimeric predators of the Sarmatians or the warrior eagles of Rome, but the charms of peace and play – childlike sketches of deer and songbirds, paintings of sun and moon and stars, crude etchings that stood as symbols of the people they loved. They had taken that ash from the Burning Cauldron, which had been meant to bring war and death to the southlands, and they had made something beautiful instead.

Seeing those marks of the things that they fought for, Kai felt his courage return. He lifted the cauldron above his head, holding that great and terrible darkness in the air for all to see. And the Painted People were wailing in terror then, their hands reaching up as though hoping they could somehow hold up that cauldron from afar, that through force of will alone they might reach through half a mile of empty air to fix it in place.

But it was already too late. Kai upended the cauldron, and he sent the last of the ash pouring away – a hundred years of evil magic, scattered to the wind in a moment. And then, like a vengeful god casting down a thunderbolt, he reared back and threw the cauldron down.

It struck a stone and rang like a bell, the note warping and shifting as the metal cracked, the iron spalling from the impact in a little puff of black dust. But still, that iron held strong. And perhaps, on its own, that would not have been omen enough to make a difference.

But the cauldron rolled back to the feet of Kai's horse – a tall, proud horse of the Sarmatian steppe, a warrior and a prince of its people. And with a single disdainful stamp of its feet, it broke the cracked cauldron into pieces.

Silence followed. The most terrible silence that he had ever heard, and there was no telling what the Painted People would do now. They might scatter silently to the winds, freed from their blood oaths. They might slaughter all that they saw, driven on by sacred revenge for decades to come.

And then Kai heard it – the sound of a woman laughing. A haunting, echoing sound that rang across the fells, familiar and wonderful and terrible all at once. The sound of his sister laughing.

He saw her there amongst the Painted People – Laimei, her skin marked by fresh tattoos, a great spear in her hand, dressed once more with strands of red felt that hung from the haft like ceaseless torrents of blood. Her eyes were upon Kai, and she raised that spear towards him. The warrior's salute, the highest honour that she could give.

And he was calling to her then, screaming and weeping, begging her to stop, to wait. For he knew her heart then, better than he ever had before – their minds as one, the same blood beating in their veins. For the first and last time, he truly knew her.

But it had always been impossible to turn her aside from what she chose to do. She served a great master faithfully, the same one that she had always served – the nameless Sarmatian god of war and death.

Her lips were moving, and though he could not hear what

she said, he did not need to. It was as though she spoke the words in his mind or whispered them in his ear – no words of love or forgiveness, no last message to her kin and companions, just the words of the proverb that had guided her life, the whispered motto that had gifted the Sarmatians courage and victory, had led them to wrack and ruin.

'Though our lives be short, let our fame be great.'

And then her voice was raised loud enough for him to hear. They were not words that she spoke but some wordless battle song, an echoing cry of hate and pain and joy. And as she called up to the gods to witness her, she raised her spear and drove it into the man next to her.

His scream sounded out, echoed from the tall cliffs like the pealing of a bell. And then, as one, as though issued a command by the sounding of a horn or the cry of a commander or an omen from a vengeful god, the Painted People went to war against themselves.

Kai saw it all – a red-haired warrior pulling a man who must have been his brother to the ground and opening his throat without hesitation. A woman, her skin a mess of scars and tattoos, who snatched up her knife and plunged it again and again into her own chest, laughing and weeping as though taking revenge on a hated enemy. A pair of warriors who, with a strange kind of courtesy, ran each other through at the same instant, each dying with his head resting upon the other's shoulder, an embrace of flesh and iron.

And he could see Corvus too – the Maimed King, pushing and struggling and battling his way through the mob, his eyes wide and white and rolling in terror as he saw the monster he had unleashed. He was almost out, almost free, when the hands of the Painted People were upon him, pulling him back, throwing him down. He was ordering them to stop, cursing them with vengeance from the dead gods, begging them for mercy.

But they were people that had been taught to make a god of death, and this was the final, beautifully simple form of that worship – the knives rising as one, like a row of teeth, before they plunged down over and over again, the Painted People devouring their king.

Beyond the army of the Painted People, Kai saw the little figures guiding the mules and carts who did not join in the slaughter. Those children, newly marked with the tattoos of the Painted People but not yet made into killers, who looked about themselves and pleaded for guidance. And yet they too must have felt the call of death – perhaps already, they had seen and done such terrible things that the darkness might come as a blessing. Kai saw them begin to drift towards the killing ground, and knew that there was no time left.

One last time, he set his horse to the charge. And, exhausted as he was, he found the strength to gallop forwards, found the courage to charge once more towards death.

Galloping hoofbeats echoed nearby as Lucius followed close behind, and from the gathered tribes of the southlands, from the ranks of the Sarmatians and the Votadini, a single rider came forth to join them. Even at the gallop, Kai could see the braids of gold and silver hair that took flight with every strike of the horse's hooves as Arite rode out to try to save their child.

Kai cast his useless spear to the ground, for he had no need of weapons, not any more. And he was crying out then – not a war song or a curse upon his enemies, but simply a name, over and over again. Akkas, the name of his son, the child that he had never seen.

Children they were, but still they fought. Some bayed war cries at him, and one slashed at Kai with a jagged knife as he passed. But he did not fear the blade, not any more, not with the wound in his side that ached and burned and festered. Lucius and Arite were at his side, driving their way through and calling out that same name over and over again – *Akkas, Akkas, Akkas*. And then the children, frightened of Kai's horse and the rider that seemed to know no fear, were breaking and scattering before him.

All save for one. Almost unseen amongst the others, for this was a boy of no more than five summers – his hair thick and black, his coppery skin newly marked with the tattoos of the Painted People. And when that child looked up at Kai his grey eyes could have been those of Laimei, those of Kai's sister.

A moment too where it seemed as though that child would take the same path as Laimei. That he would go bravely into death, ashamed and broken and seeing no other choice left to him. But the child looked at Kai, and though they had never seen one another before, it seemed that Akkas understood who he was. A glimpse of his own reflection in still water, a figure he might have seen in his dreams of longing – what gave that understanding, Kai did not know. But the boy recognised his father, and he leapt up into Kai's outstretched arms.

The horses, once free of the battlefield, would go no further. Arite, Kai, Lucius, and Akkas – each held on to the other, bowing their heads together, a tribe of four once more. No words spoken, just the ragged, exhausted, sobbing breaths of those who have fought and suffered, though not a single one of them had struck a blow that day.

Arite's hands were upon Kai then, but it was no lover's touch. By the fear in her eyes he knew that she had seen it all – the reddish lines that spread across skin hot to the touch, the knife wound in his side that seeped blackly through his tunic. As a woman of the steppe, a warrior of the warbands, she would know well enough what those signs meant.

But there was no time to think on that now. There was another death that mattered much more. For when Kai looked back, just for a moment he saw Laimei there amongst the Painted People, one last time.

She was high above the others, her great horse rearing towards the sky – skin painted in blood, her face carved open into a terrible smile of teeth and bone, her shattered spear raised above her like a triumphant banner. One last, exultant scream, like an eagle as it stoops and plunges down upon a dove, and then she was lost in the dying horde.

Kai knew that his people would speak that story forever, of how Laimei had stood alone and destroyed the Painted People single-handed. He knew that a champion could not ask for a better life, a better death, a better story to be told of her. And yet, as he clutched his friend and his lover and his child close to him, he could not help but wish Laimei had found a way to live instead, so that he would not have to go on without her.

But he knew that it did not matter. He knew, as his wound burned and bled deep within him, that he would join her soon enough.

28

For the Painted People, there was no end to their self-slaughter during the day. They fought even when their spears were broken and knives were dull and they lacked the strength to lift them. At last the sun fell from the sky, and as though some spell had been broken with the coming of the night, the few survivors slunk away into the darkness. They returned to their homelands and sought to forget what they had done, what they had become. Hoping that, in time, they would be forgiven.

When the sun rose again the next day, it rose only upon the dreamers and the dead.

As quickly as they had come together, the People of the Dream broke apart once more. Some lingered in that place, going about the grim work of burying and burning the corpses of the Painted People. Others returned to their hunting runs and sacred places, to the homes that they had saved. The old feuds would break open soon enough between those tribes; the love they had found for each other would be forgotten within a single cycle of the moon. Even so, they knew that it had been beautiful while it lasted. Perhaps some part of it lingered on within them all – in the fragment of a memory, in a glimpse of a dream.

The tribes struck out to the east and the west and the south. Only four riders headed northwards.

Kai and Lucius, Arite and Akkas rode north upon their proud Sarmatian horses with the breaking of the dawn. They made no farewells and departed with no ceremony, the way that a band of Sarmatians might suddenly break from their tribe without a word being spoken, driven by some compulsion to seek new lands and new companions with the restless, wandering urge that had always marked their people.

Though the battle was over and a great victory won, the cauldron broken and the Painted People destroyed, those four rode north with the solemn and proud air of warriors riding towards their deaths.

For one of them, at least, it was true.

The first day.

The four of them travelled through an empty, shattered land. The rolling hills were emptied of the herds that should have teemed upon them, the lowland farms burned black, the wolves moving openly through the heather in search of the dead to feast upon. But everywhere those four riders went, they saw the signs of life returning – a band of ash-covered children stealing out of the forests to forage amongst the ruins, an old man and a braying donkey patiently beginning to till a burned field, a gathering of tribesmen in the ruins of a Roman amphitheatre. A land wounded, but not broken. A people determined to live once more.

Lucius kept his eyes forward as he rode, sitting as stiff and straight in his saddle as though he were upon a parade ground before the eyes of an emperor. Behind him, he could hear the gasping breaths that Kai took as the wound fever ran through him.

A part of him had known that Kai was dying, even as they made their desperate journey south with the cauldron – there had been no time to think on it then, with death so close to them both. What did it matter that Kai shook and trembled with the fever as they rode day and night, that his wound suppurated and would not close? Neither of them had expected to live beyond those next few days.

But on that first night after the battle with the Painted People, when they gathered about the campfire, Kai had turned to him – his eyes ablaze with the fever, looking for all the world like a prophet touched by the words of a god.

'Lucius?' he had said.

'Yes?'

'Will you come with me?'

'Where will you go?' Lucius had asked.

'North of the Wall.'

'To go beyond Roman lands.'

Kai had nodded. 'Just so.'

To die beyond Roman lands – that was what remained unspoken. There was no need to say it.

Now they had no enemy in sight, nothing but the wild open country, boundless and beautiful. But Lucius was frightened as he rode, more fearful than he had ever been before a battle – afraid of what Kai might say in those last few days. And, even more than that, afraid of what he himself might fail to say, before the end.

But Kai seemed to have no desire to speak. No sense of urgency, even as the fever grew stronger and bent him double with pain. He simply watched the landscape as he rode, his eyes tracing the swooping motion of a kestrel above them, a great herd of deer that moved like a wave across the hillside, the patterns the rain left upon the dark stone crags that they passed. And when at last he opened his mouth, he did no more than ask each of them to sing with him – Lucius, Arite, and Akkas, sharing the old travelling music of the Sarmatian steppe, a Roman marching song, the poetry of myths that Akkas loved so much.

That was how the first day passed – trading songs as the Roman road rang beneath their horses' hooves. It was only in the evening, about the campfire, that Kai spoke of something else.

Akkas was asleep, his head resting in his father's lap as Kai gently stroked the boy's long dark hair. Arite lay still in the darkness – she was sleeping too, perhaps, or merely pretending to. And Lucius heard Kai speak softly then, over the crackling of the fire.

'Have I done enough?' he said.

Lucius made no answer.

Then even softer, as though he spoke only to himself, Kai said: 'Can I be forgiven?'

When Lucius stole a glance at Kai, he saw the Sarmatian looking into the fire – waiting, perhaps, to see if any of his companions would answer him.

More than anything, Lucius wanted to speak then – of all that they had shared and done together, of the memories of courage that Kai would leave behind him. Of the pain, too, but the love that had been at the root of that pain. Of forgiveness, above all else.

But Lucius could not find the words that he needed, that he could trust to carry all of that weight. And so, to his shame, he kept his silence, and let that moment slip away.

The second day.

Arite rose early, just before the dawn. She woke Akkas and led him down the river close to the road, the boy mumbling and still half asleep. Stripping off his filthy clothes, she plunged him into the water and washed the filth of the road and the battle away.

She looked upon his fresh tattoos, those crude inkings of the Painted People that would mark his skin forever. She searched for wounds, and found them – his feet raw from days of walking, marks upon his hands and shoulders from where he had dragged and carried arrows and spears, working like a slave for the Painted People. And she looked for other wounds too, in the way he would not meet her eye or laugh when she splashed water upon him, in how he merely looked to the horizon with an absent, hunted look that she knew all too well. Either he would heal, or he would become one of those broken children of war that she had seen so many times before, the survivors of raids and feuds who always found some quiet way to die. For Akkas, only time would tell.

She felt eyes upon her skin then. Turning from her son, she saw Kai sitting upon the side of the road, watching them both.

He made no attempt to approach, to play the father to his

son or a husband to her. He just gave a little smile and a wave of the hand, and then he went back to the horses – impatient, it seemed, to be on the move.

'Let us not ride upon the road today,' he said, when she and Akkas joined him at last. 'We shall find a way through the land instead.'

She glanced at Lucius. 'But...' she began, unwilling to voice the thought.

'Do not worry,' Kai answered. 'It is not my time yet. It shall not be today.'

And so they turned from the Roman road and plunged into the hillsides, tracing their way through the sheep tracks and the little streams that cut through the bracken and the heather – the pathways that were made and lost and made again with the turning of the seasons, that had come and gone for a thousand years before the Romans conquered that land.

At once there was rain, swirling down from the sky in great misty columns and drumming upon the broad leaves of the trees. Kai turned his head up towards the sky, eyes closed, and said: 'Is it too much to ask for three clear days in this cursed land?' But Arite saw that he smiled as he spoke – the rain must have been a cool blessing against his skin.

A strange pain about the heart to see him so content, a pain that she did not understand or know how to answer. And so Arite stirred her horse forward, seeking that peace in motion that the Sarmatians had always known, the blessed forgetfulness of a nomad on the move with no past and no future.

It was Akkas who rode beside Kai that day – shy and uncertain, with this strange, dying stranger so close to him, smelling of sweat and rot and death. All of that day, he and Kai spoke together. The boy asked of war and battles, but no longer with the foolish eagerness of a child who knows nothing of death. Akkas was akin to an old soldier now, his youth taken from him in the score of days he had spent with the Painted People, and Kai spoke to him as such – stories not of valour but of suffering, and of what came from the suffering afterwards, the beautiful and terrible relics of war. Brotherhood and grief, bravery and shame.

They passed most of the day this way – a father and a son, given one single day to act as such. It was only at midday, when they paused to rest and water the horses, that Arite heard Kai approach her. There was no mistaking the sound of him for any of the others, for Kai walked with the heavy, laboured steps of the sick or the dying.

'May I speak?' she heard him say. 'Or do you prefer the silence?'

And in spite of herself she smiled to hear that particular chivalry of the steppe, that asked honestly without demand. 'You may speak, Kai,' she answered.

But for a long time he said nothing. They sat together in the shadow of a lone sycamore tree, the first seedpods drifting down upon them like falling snow, and they let the silence speak for them. Together, they watched Lucius with Akkas, as man and boy tended to the horses with all of the nomad's love.

After a time, Kai asked: 'They are close, Lucius and Akkas?' And there was a catch in his voice as he spoke.

'They are. But more as brothers, strange as that may seem. Not as a father and son.'

Kai nodded slowly. 'Seeing them together, it reminds me of my daughter, Tomyris.'

Silence for a time, as both of them remembered that wild-eyed girl Kai had been forced to leave behind upon the steppe, many years before – the child he would never see again.

'Lucius has been kind to you?' Kai said.

'Aye,' Arite answered. 'He has been a brother to me as well. Does that sadden you or please you?'

'I would not have you lonely,' Kai answered softly. 'Nor him. Was it your choice or his?'

'Oh, his, I should think. I did not go looking for love, but he would have been a fine enough choice. Handsome for a Roman. Kind as well. And he keeps his word.'

She thought perhaps those last words might wound Kai. But he cocked his head to the side, seeming to turn the words over in his mind as though they were a puzzle to be solved.

'I have spent my life in oaths and promises,' he said. 'Keeping most, breaking some. A few of them were well spoken, and they let me be brave. But only a few.'

'You wish you had done otherwise?'

'No. For to be here, at the end, with you all – I do not regret that my promises have brought me to this place.'

She thought that she understood then why he had wished to abandon the road and ride through the wild and open country. Here, it was easy to imagine that they were back upon the steppe, travellers free to wander where they wished. As though they rode into the past, away from the pain they had caused one another.

'I am glad for the time we spent together,' she heard him say.

'So am I,' she said quietly. And, to her surprise, she found that she spoke truly.

'I am sorry for the wounds I caused.'

She held her hand up, watching the firelight catch upon the old scars, the marks of war and of life that traced over her skin. 'They heal,' she said. 'They do heal, in time.'

Kai smiled then, and she knew that smile all too well – the mad, wolfish grin with which the Sarmatians had always tried to confront death. 'But I have no time left.'

She let her eyes wander towards the north. Somewhere out there lay the Wall, their journey's end, little more than a day's ride away. A part of her longed to see the Wall tomorrow, for all of this to be ended. And another part of her longed to never see the white stone rising before them – to live the nomad's dream, and have this journey last forever.

The third day.

Kai did not wake with the rising of the sun, for he had not slept at all. He had lain there and waited for the dawn, his wounds pulsing in agony. And more than the pain, it was his fear that had kept him awake, a terror that was now close to madness.

He had tried to keep it from his companions, with smiles and with song. After looking once at the wound in his side – a yellowing, blackened sight that threatened to unman him – he had not dared to look at it again in that journey north. He had tried to be carefree as he spoke, when all he wished for was to scream in terror, to beg them to speak to him of forgiveness, to offer him some final gift of love.

He had not kept his fear hidden out of shame. But that fear seemed almost an evil, living thing to him, a figure that stalked and hunted them on the journey north. A monster from which he should protect them, an enemy for him to face alone. To speak of it was to grant it power, to make them a part of his fight, and that he could not do.

But now, it seemed, that enemy had won. For it seemed impossible that he would rise again.

Kai had lived his whole life in the presence of death, yet it had always seemed somehow distant – the silhouette of a rider glimpsed upon a hillside, a war song heard echoing from a neighbouring valley. Now it was sitting there beside him, jeering and mocking, close enough to smell and taste and touch. And in his fever, he heard it speak – telling him of all the foolish mistakes he had made in his life, all the people he had wounded and betrayed. Telling him that he had no time left.

When Kai lifted his head, he saw the others gathered about him. Akkas had pure terror etched upon his face, for Kai must have seemed monstrous to him in that moment, twisted and broken as he was with the fever. Arite and Lucius masked their feelings well enough, but he knew that they must both believe that he could not rise again.

In a gesture that took half the strength he had left, he raised a trembling, shaking hand. With the other half of that strength he forced himself to smile, to speak.

'I cannot stand,' he said, 'but I can still ride. It is not yet time.'

And so they helped him up, his horse still and patient as he fought his way into the saddle, the way a drowning man might fight his way onto the wreckage of his ship. For the code of the Sarmatians was that a man who could not ride was dead already, with nothing to him but the merciful stroke of a sword that would send him to the next world. And Kai would have one more day of life, no matter how hard he had to fight for it.

Each step of the horse brought pain, but that pain spoke of life to him. The beautiful things in his life had always been bordered by pain, it seemed to him now – the suffering of battle where he had learned to be brave, the pain of love that had made the tender moments matter so much more, the pain of his broken bonds with Lucius, Bahadur, and Arite that made him treasure what they had once known together.

No more songs for him, no kind words or shared memories. Just the pain and the journey, step by agonising step, tracing a slow, inevitable way to the north as the sun drifted through the sky above them. For once, there was no rain – one final, beautiful day of light falling upon the open country.

At last, he saw the Wall towering on the horizon before them, the sun shining on the white stone, bright and brilliant. The edge of the Empire, the boundary of the Roman world. Now it marked a different kind of boundary.

Kai was eager now, almost hurrying. For it seemed to him that he had never wanted anything so much as to be back beyond that Wall, to go to a place where the Roman Empire held no hold and could not touch him.

But then a set of hooves fell silent upon the road behind him. And when Kai turned his head he saw Lucius there, his horse standing still beneath him.

'What is it?' Kai asked.

'I cannot go further,' Lucius answered.

Kai tried a smile. 'Afraid of the barbarians beyond the Wall?'

'I am afraid. But not of that.'

No one spoke for a time. They waited there, together, until Lucius found the courage to speak again.

'I know what you will ask of me,' he said quietly.

Kai nodded. 'You remember the story of my father?'

'I do,' Lucius answered. For many years before, Kai's father had grown too old and weak to ride a horse or steady a spear. A killing circle had gathered, all of his kin and companions there to witness an honourable death, and it had fallen to Kai to take up his sword and kill him. The duty of the eldest son.

'I could not do it,' Kai said. 'But you have always been braver than me. Will you be brave for me, one last time?'

Lucius did not answer for a time. Grey-faced, his eyes upon the Wall as though he faced some terrible, unstoppable enemy. All his courage spent, it seemed, on the journey north – none left to take those last few steps.

Kai stirred his horse towards the Roman. He leaned forward and whispered: 'It should be my son that kills me. But I cannot make him do it. Will you spare him that?'

At this, Lucius closed his eyes – a steadying then, a stillness settling, the way Kai had seen Lucius gather himself before a battle, that secret, private way in which each warrior found courage. In the end, the Sarmatians always said, it was a choice between fighting for hate or for love. And Kai knew which Lucius would choose.

'I will do it,' Lucius said at last.

And together, they rode through the shattered gates and fire-blackened stone. Beyond the Wall, to lands free of the touch of Rome – no cities or walls or forts to be seen, just the rolling hills and distant mountains, the music of the river in his ears and the birds wheeling in the sky above.

And once they were through, Kai could go no further.

He fell from the saddle as soon as he was through the gate – the pain doubling, and doubling once more, the world washed grey in his sight.

The others were close about him then, and he would have given anything to see their faces clearly – how much time he had wasted, it seemed to him now, how many moments he had lost with those that he loved. But he could only close his eyes against the pain, and gasp: 'The river. Please. The river.'

They carried him there. One arm he curled against his wound, the other scooped water up to his lips – he drank and drank and drank from the river, but it did not quench his thirst.

He could not stand, or ride, or drink. And so, at last, he knew that it was time.

A kiss he gave to each of them upon the forehead, and one by one he saw them flinch from the touch – his lips must have felt as fire against their skin. He hoped that they might find some kind of godly blessing in that feverish kiss, for the Sarmatian gods were only to be found into the sword, and the fire.

Then he heard the soft sound of iron against leather. The sound of a sword being drawn.

With that sword, Lucius had killed the last king of the Sarmatians, far to the east. A sacred weapon, or so it was said amongst Kai's people, and Kai felt his fear fade a little at the sight of it. As though the iron whispered words of comfort to him, and told him not to be afraid.

He saw Lucius trace out a circle with that blade – slowly, reluctantly, pacing one full revolution, the point of the blade cutting against the earth. Only Arite and Akkas were standing in witness, but all at once Kai could see others gathered there: Laimei and Bahadur, Saratos and Tasius, Corvus and Zanticus, his father and the mother he had never known. All the companions he had lost, all the men that he had killed, they were all there in that killing circle. Fever visions, ghosts beckoning from the Otherlands, bearing witness to what was to come.

And he could hear them too – singing the songs of war, offering the clash of shield against sword, calling for him to be brave and show no fear. But Kai did not look upon the dead, for his eyes were upon Arite and Akkas. He knew that it was a simple thing to be brave in the company of those that he loved.

The sword rose in the air and the sunlight caught it, sharp and blinding and beautiful against the blade. He saw that light dance and shake, as Lucius's hands trembled.

Then the blade hung still in the air, like a hawk above its mark.

It steadied, stooped, and fell.

29

There was no screaming or raging, no curses against the gods or wails of grief echoing against the broken Wall. For Arite, there was only the hollowing sense of grief, the still peace that sometimes followed death. Beside her Akkas stared at the bloody ground, his face pale but steady, marking a moment he would remember for the rest of his life, for good or for ill. And at the centre of that killing circle, Arite watched as Lucius slowly knelt upon the ground and took Kai's hand in his own.

Arite began the rituals of the dead, covering Kai first with a handful of earth and then her cloak, stabbing her sword into the ground beside him to mark the place, to let the gods know to come and take a warrior to the Otherlands. Akkas watched her, his hands aping his mother's movements, his lips silently repeating the prayers that she spoke. Perhaps the child already knew that he would have to do this many times himself, that his life would be spent in confrontation of death, in defiance of grief, and that these rituals were part of that defiance.

At last, when all was done and Arite took her place beside Lucius, she heard him speak.

'I should have said more to him,' Lucius said. 'We had three days together – why did I say so little?'

'There was no need to speak it,' she said. 'He knew it all, here at the end.'

A whisper from beside her: 'Did it have to be done?' Akkas said.

'He was dying,' she answered. 'It was a good death.' But her voice shook as she spoke.

Beside her, Lucius stared at the sword in his hand as though seeing it for the first time. With it, he had killed a king and saved the Sarmatian people, led them halfway across the world. With it, he had stolen the Burning Cauldron and destroyed the Painted People. With it, he had killed his friend.

The sun shone upon the blade one last time as he raised it up and sent it spinning through the air. And there was a moment after it landed in the river where the current twisted the hilt back towards the bank, as though some unseen spirit were holding it up and offering it back to Lucius, tempting him to take it up just one more time. Then the water carried it down, carried it away, and it was lost forever.

'A shame,' a voice said, from close by. 'There was magic in that sword.'

And Arite saw him then – in the shadow of the Wall, framed by the blackened stone and fallen towers, stood Mor, chieftain of the Votadini.

'An evil magic,' Lucius said. 'I am glad to be rid of it.'

'Perhaps so,' Mor answered. 'Perhaps it is a different kind of magic that we need now. Of peace, and not of war.'

'You followed us here?' Arite said.

Mor nodded. 'It was not my place to travel with you. He did not love me the way that he loved the three of you. But still, I wished to be here, at the end.' He knelt with them and laid a gentle hand upon the dead man, as though asking for his forgiveness. Then he said: 'I came to say that I was wrong.'

'About what?'

'About many things, but Kai and Laimei most of all.' Mor settled beside them, cross-legged like a storyteller around a fire, and said: 'Long before, when they came to speak to me of the Painted People, I thought they were bringing my death with them. I could see it there, a shadow they carried with them, waiting to be spoken and birthed into the world. I knew that there would be a sacrifice. And I chased it gladly, for I thought that it would be me.'

'Gladly?' Arite said.

Mor laughed, caught. 'Yes, perhaps that is a lie. I am no hero. I was afraid. Afraid to die. For I think that there is a world beyond this one, but it is a world of shadows and dust, and I do not wish to hurry towards it. But I would have done it anyway, for them. They taught me to be brave, and I shall always remember that.' The chieftain of the Votadini sighed. 'But it was not my death that each of them carried that day. It was their own.'

'They would call it a good death,' Lucius whispered.

'Yes, they would. So perhaps we shall be the sacrifice after all – those left behind to grieve, to live in a world made empty without them, a world diminished.' Mor looked at Lucius then, and said: 'What is to be done now, in this empty world of ours?'

'You ask this of me?' Lucius answered, his voice weary.

'Of course. You could be a high king of these lands now,

if you chose it.' A dry chuckle. 'Easier if you still had that sword, but you could have this entire island bend the knee to you. It would be but the work of a season for you to become our king.'

King. Arite knew that word was a curse amongst the Romans. Even though their emperor was a king amongst kings in all but name, still they thought the title a relic of the barbarous peoples, a mark of the primitive. Yet here it was, a crown offered to him as though he had been born to it – what man might say no to such a thing?

But Lucius shook his head. 'I want no crown upon my head,' he said softly. 'The Maimed King is dead, and I shall not take his place. This land has seen enough of kings and emperors.'

Mor nodded, and seemed content – perhaps some last, secret test had been passed, one final omen fulfilled. 'It is an empty world that you and I must live in,' he said, 'without Kai and Laimei. But we shall make that empty world as beautiful as we can for our people. Together, in this place. Can you do this with me?' And it was to Arite he spoke then.

A chill touch upon Arite's skin. 'What part am I to play in this?' she said.

'You have not heard the stories that I have heard,' Mor answered. 'The Sarmatians and the People of the Dream, they call you a witch, a warrior, a queen. They say that you brought the tribes together, vanquished the Painted People with a word and a spell.'

'That is *your* story, I think,' she said.

'Perhaps.' And a shadow crossed Mor's face as he stared down at the body beside them, shrouded in its cloak. 'I would give the dead their due if I could. But we need our champions living. For it is killing that comes easily to our three people – the Sarmatians, the Romans, the many tribes of this island. We must learn to live long, and in peace. Can you both help me to do that?'

Lucius looked towards the northlands, lost for a time, it seemed, in memory and longing. Then he said: 'The Votadini will take their lands once more. Your war with Rome is finished. That I can do, now that Caerellius is dead.'

'It shall be so,' Mor said. 'There is much to be rebuilt, north and south of the Wall. I may do my part in the north.'

'I shall do so in the south,' Lucius answered. 'And what of you, Arite?'

'What?'

'The Sarmatian soldiers, they shall serve their years in this place. Another twenty years of service – they swore their oaths to Rome, and I know they shall not break them.' Once more he laid a hand upon Kai, who lay there in silent witness. 'But you swore no oath,' Lucius said. 'You could go home, if you wanted to. Back to the steppe of Sarmatia. Will you go?'

A moment where she thought of the land she had been born in. The wildflowers and tall grass dancing in the wind, the interlacing rivers that she knew every curve of, the stars above where she might read the stories of her gods and heroes, a land that was untouched by the tombs the Romans called fortresses, the scars of stone that they called roads. A memory that was now like a dream – she knew it mattered to her, she knew that it had been beautiful. But for all that she tried to hold on to it, the memory seemed to slip away from her.

She reached out to touch the earth beside her, the earth where her husband was buried, where Akkas's father would now be buried. And she looked at her son, and said: 'Do you wish to go, my child, or stay?'

Akkas thought on it for a long time, and at last, some of those scars of war seemed to slip away. He had been raised on stories of the open steppe, wild and beautiful and free. He was, for a brief moment at least, a child once more, dreaming of a home that he longed for, that had been promised to him, and that he had never seen.

Akkas looked around them then, upon that hard, wild, beautiful land around the Wall, filled with the dead and the dreaming. And at last, smiling shyly, he said: 'What is home to me, if not here?'

THE FREE

AD 200

30

Many years later, there was another rare, brilliant day in the northlands – scarcely a single cloud to be seen in the sky, as the sun beat down upon the white stone of the Wall.

Those stones were especially white at Cilurnum, the Fort of the River and Pool. After the Painted People had come burning and pillaging to the south almost twenty years before, the fort had been rebuilt. The years had weathered it a little, but it shone in the sunlight that day, bright and proud and with the promise of all new things.

It was a busy day for the garrison of that fort. The gates were open, traders and travellers from the south and the north moving freely from one side to another. Those who passed through the gates bore the tattoos of many tribes – the Votadini, the Brigantes, the dozen different tribes of the northlands. Sometimes, peering closely, one might even see a tattoo that had been altered decades before, a faded mark of one of the Painted People.

But if the soldiers of the Wall saw such markings, they made no comment upon them. There was ribald chatter between the sentries and the travellers – the merchants muttering about the taxes (and the bribes) that they had to pay, yet still trading songs and stories with the Romans, calling out to men they knew not just as soldiers and conquerors but as friends. They would bicker and haggle and bribe and cheat one another by day, and share a cup in the wine shops of the *vicus* at night.

For it had been two decades of peace, there in the northlands. Two decades spent trying to forget their hate, learn a little of friendship – perhaps even a little of love.

The sun fell low in the sky. The horns blew, announcing the changing of the guard, and there was a flurry of movement up on the Wall, sentries who were half asleep at their posts coming to life once more as they made their way from their posts. Some went to the barracks, in search of sleep or the company of their friends. Others headed towards the *vicus* for wine and dice. All trying, for a few hours, to forget that they would be back upon the Wall the next day, and the next, and the next, for as long as any man could reckon into the future.

But there was one of those men who did not go with the rest of his companions. An old soldier, grey-streaked hair spilling out from beneath his helm, his skin marked with tattoos unlike any tribe of Britannia, inked animals that spoke of a distant land far to the east – the twisting, chimeric predators of the Sarmatians. And when the horn sounded, that man simply walked from his post with a careless ease, casting aside his spear and tossing his helmet to the ground.

It was a shocking breach of discipline, and a centurion strode up to that warrior at once, face purpling with rage, ready to bellow a reprimand and order the man flogged. But when he saw the face revealed beneath that helm, the centurion fell silent. And though it was but a simple soldier of the auxiliaries that stood there before him, it was the centurion that offered the salute first.

'Good luck, Mordos,' said the centurion.

The Sarmatian smiled, and did not answer the salute in kind. He gave a clasp of the arm and the touch of the heart, the greeting and farewell of the people of the steppe. 'Thank you, sir,' he said.

He limped through the crowded streets of the fort with an uneven gait that betrayed some old wound, and he rubbed his knuckles incessantly, for long years in the saddle had left those hands aching, the fingers bowed over like claws. A man of forty or fifty years perhaps, but walking like one half again as old, a man made ancient by war. But the eyes were bright, and Mordos still walked with a soldier's pride as he went towards the commander's quarters at the heart of the fort.

He had some time to wait before he was seen. A long queue of supplicants to the overworked Prefect – a wine-shop owner ranting about drunken soldiers damaging his wares, a cobbler complaining of forged coins, a soldier come to beg leave to see his sweetheart – and behind them Mordos shifted impatiently from foot to foot. Twenty-five years he had spent in service to Rome, twenty-five years spent watching from the Wall, and yet still he had not lost the nomad's restless longing for a journey, the hatred of staying for too long in a single place.

The bored Prefect barely looked up as the warrior hobbled forward to his desk – it was merely another burdensome task for that day, and it meant nothing to him. The ritual words were spoken, a chisel tapped against copper as the scribe marked the tablet that would give Mordos his citizenship and his freedom. But, frowning at the last moment, the Prefect looked down at an empty place upon the copper tablet. 'You must take a Roman name.'

A wry smile from the barbarian. 'My own is not good enough?' he said.

'Not to be a Roman citizen.'

The Sarmatian thought for a time, while the Prefect tapped his finger impatiently upon the desk. At last, he leaned forward and whispered his answer.

'Very well,' the Prefect answered shortly. His scribe made the last scratches upon the tablet, stamped it and handed it to the man before him – no longer a Sarmatian soldier, but a free citizen of Rome. 'It is done.'

The Sarmatian stood there, irresolute. A moment so long waited for, and it seemed that he did not know what to do with it. No more was he bound to the shouted commands of centurion and prefect, his time measured by water clock and hourglass, his life pledged to his conquerors. But something more was needed, some ritual or piece of magic to truly set him free.

The sound of footsteps rang out against the tiles – a soldier's steady, even tread, only slowed a little by age. For another man was coming forward then, stooped and weary, marked and scarred. His hair was mostly silver, and only here and there, if one peered closely, might there be seen a few strands of reddish gold remaining. It was Lucius Artorius Castus who strode to stand beside the Sarmatian; Lucius, though he no longer bore any mark of rank upon him, who was there to give one final command.

'Rome thanks you,' Lucius said. 'I thank you. Now go, and be free.'

Mordos offered the salute. 'Thank you, sir,' he said.

'What name did you choose?' Lucius asked as they walked to the courtyard outside the commander's quarters, once more under the brilliant light of the sun.

'Artorius, of course,' Mordos said.

Lucius shook his head. 'Will you tell me why?'

'It is part of your name, is it not?'

'It is. But I mean, why not take Lucius as your name?'

'I am not worthy of it,' Mordos said simply. 'For I am not a hero such as you are. I merely stood beside a hero, once or twice.'

No answer to be made to that. No answer but a bowed head, the silvery trail of tears that ran down Lucius's cheeks, that found the deep furrows of wrinkle and scar, that settled and shone upon the whitened beard.

'Soon enough there shall be hundreds of us with that name,' Mordos said, 'all of them in honour of you. You have no children of your own left?'

Silent, Lucius shook his head.

'Well, no matter.' Mordos chuckled to himself. 'You will have a brood that even the champions of the old stories might be proud of, lustful bastards that they were.'

'There were five thousand Sarmatians that came to this island,' Lucius said. 'Now, only a few hundred are left to go free as citizens of Rome.'

'More than could be hoped for,' Mordos answered, 'after twenty-five years of service. Wars and rebellions. And age.' He lifted up his clawlike hands, warped by countless winters spent clutching cold reins. 'I never dreamed to live so long,' he said. 'Upon the steppe, my son would be sharpening his blade, ready to give me the stroke of mercy.' He hesitated. 'But I am glad. I am glad to live. Gladder still to be free of Rome. I shall see what I may do with the years that are left to me.'

'Where shall your fortune take you now?' asked Lucius.

A wolfish grin – the way that all the Sarmatians seemed to smile, reckless and dangerous, loving and brave, the kind of smile that Lucius loved so much but had never managed to learn himself. 'Right now,' said Mordos, 'it shall take me to the wine shop by the south gate. Join me there? The others will come too, in time. A few of them took their citizenship after last night's watch, and they'll have been drinking all day.'

'I shall join you soon enough,' Lucius said. 'But there is something else that I must do, first. Someone else that I wait for.'

One last salute, the last that Mordos would ever give in his life. And then the Sarmatian was gone, whistling merrily as he went – some song of his own devising that seemed to blend one of the old songs of the steppe with the marching music of the Roman Legion.

Lucius took his place upon the bench in the courtyard – grateful to sit, for he too was old now, and weary. He waited.

From time to time soldiers would pass, each of them offering Lucius a salute (much, or so he thought, to the annoyance of the Prefect sitting at his desk). The sun rolled through the sky and Lucius sat there patiently, lost in his memories, until a shadow fell across him.

A woman's voice spoke. 'I knew that I would find you here,' Arite said.

'And I knew that you would come,' Lucius answered, and gestured to the bench beside him.

She sat down gratefully – the years hung heavy on her too. 'I passed some Sarmatians in the wine shop on my way here.'

'Oh yes?'

'Four men,' she said, a smile on her face, 'and each of them called Artorius. What do you think of that?'

'That it sounds like the beginning of a joke.'

'Oh, it is no joke to them.'

'How did they seem to you?' Lucius asked.

'Happy.' The smile fell away from her face then. 'And free.' She looked at the Prefect, sitting at his desk with the doors still open, the roster roll of the fort open beside him – names crossed off as men retired, or died. Blank spaces ready for those who would soon be newly sworn to the service.

'Perhaps he will not come,' Lucius said.

'He will come,' she answered. 'He is too much his father's son not to.'

'I wish he had not chosen this path,' Lucius said softly. 'I tried to talk him out of it.'

'I know. But when have young men ever listened to old men? Or to their mothers?'

And he could hear them approach as though in answer to those words, the quick and brash footsteps of young men, and soon a band of them came into view, whooping and hollering. Some of them were children of the Sarmatians, others were men from the Votadini or the Brigantes, all of them choosing not to be farmers or hunters or shepherds for the rest of their lives, but to take up the trade of their fathers, to become soldiers of Rome. And at their head, leading the way like a captain or a champion, was Akkas.

'Do you wish it were otherwise?' Lucius said to Arite.

She laughed then – for a moment the years were gone from her, and she was young and merry once more. 'You know so little of our people,' she said, 'even after all these years. Why should I fear for him, as a soldier of Rome? He may die of a fever in winter, step on a nail and be taken by lockjaw. Death waits for him in every place. There is no use fearing it.'

Lucius looked away from her then. 'You have lost so much already.'

'We all have,' she said quietly. 'But it is a miracle that he lives – by all the odds he should have died when he was a boy, at the hands of the Painted People. Every day since then, I count as a blessing.' She hesitated, and then said: 'I used to think that the gods sought to break me with sadness, to kill me with grief. And so I lived in defiance of them. But I discovered that there is a beauty in grief too.' And she fell silent, as she looked once more upon her son.

Akkas had grown tall and lean and rangy, tattoos thick upon his copper skin. That ink was a mixture of designs – some Sarmatian, others in the patterns that the Votadini loved. And Lucius knew that buried deep beneath them were the old tattoos that the Painted People had marked him with when he was a child, that Akkas would carry with him all his life.

He had a wild, determined look to him – even as he laughed and joked with his companions, he kept his gaze fixed upon the Prefect, fixed upon his goal. Even as he patiently waited in the line, Lucius could see that restless hunger to find his place in the world.

A shiver across the skin at the sight, the echoing memory of a friend long since lost. 'He will be a fine warrior,' Lucius said. 'Like his father.'

'Yes,' Arite answered, 'he will. Though he has much still to learn. I only wish you would be here to teach him.'

Lucius started at that, as though struck. 'Why should I not be here? I am not so old as I look.'

'Oh, you never could lie well, Lucius,' she said. 'It is one of the things that I love about you.' She looked at him then, with a keen and testing gaze. 'I see it in the restless way that you pace about the streets. That look in your eyes, soft and needful, as though you peered into some other world that you longed to travel to. The whispers that you speak to your horse. I know well the signs of a man falling in love with the journey that he plans to take.'

Lucius nodded slowly. 'Yes,' he said, 'it is true.'

'And I think I know where you shall go,' she said. 'Kai could not go home, and so you shall travel in his place. You will go back to Sarmatia to look for his daughter, Tomyris?'

'I will.'

Arite looked away. 'She may be dead, you know. Twenty-five years is a lifetime on the steppe. A feud, or childbirth, or a winter fever. Death is always close to us there too.'

'I shall find her spirit, then.'

'You would have to die there to speak with her spirit,' she said. And then, more softly, 'But I think that you mean to.'

'Perhaps,' he said. 'In a feud, or a winter fever, as you say. But not the Roman way, not by my own hand. I would like to see the Sarmatian steppe one last time before I die.'

'And if you do find her, what shall you say to her? That her father died well?'

'I shall tell her that he lived well,' Lucius said. Then: 'I shall tell her that I loved him.'

A silence then. For those young men had reached the

front of the line. There, in turn, Lucius and Arite watched as each of them gave their oaths to Rome.

The words the same, but for each one a different meaning, a different, silent promise made to themselves. To be brave, to be powerful, to die well – each would have his own dream that he fought to bring into the world.

'You could come with me,' Lucius said abruptly. 'See the steppe one last time before...' His voice trailed away.

Arite smiled gently. 'See it one last time before I die?' she said. 'Do I look so old or sick to you? Be mindful of your own grey hair, and let me worry about mine.' And she was solemn then, as solemn as her son making ready to swear his oath. 'We have always been a travelling people,' she said. 'Our home is where we lay our heads to rest each night. We came from a wild open country at the edge of the Empire, and that is where we are now. You did as you promised. The men I loved lie buried in this land. I shall join them one day. But I have no need to see the steppe again. What I love is here.'

Akkas was stepping forward, making ready to speak the words of his oath. But then, just for a moment, Lucius saw him hesitate.

A single beating of the heart – a moment, perhaps, where Akkas saw half a hundred different ways that his life could go. Hunter or shepherd, thief or bandit, lover or hero or fool. A moment for him to be certain that he made the right choice. A moment, perhaps, where he thought of the father he had known for but a few days, many years ago.

Then the words were pouring from his mouth, the oath spoken clearly and proudly – twenty-five years of his life, gifted away to Rome in a moment. He and his companions stood solemnly before the Prefect, like statues of warriors proudly carved in stone, a monument to bravery and foolishness and the dreams of the young.

Then they were children once more – tumbling out of the courtyard, laughing and squabbling and brawling like seabirds fighting and dancing around their nests upon the cliffs. Lucius heard them speaking of the great deeds they would do, and of the glorious heroes who had come before them. He heard stories of warriors fighting gods upon a frozen river, of a champion who fought with a spear of fire and burned away a monstrous horde in the shadow of a wall, of a sacred sword cast into a river even as a hero died beside it.

They went out into the fort, and they carried those stories – false and beautiful and brilliant and true – out into the world with them.

After a time, Arite stood without ceremony and went to follow her son. Not a word or glance was exchanged between her and Lucius, though they knew they would never see each other again – that beautiful, carefree farewell of the steppe.

He waited there alone, until the torches were lit and the sun had fallen from the sky. He waited until the deepest part of the night before he made his way to where his horse was stabled, to begin the long, final journey to the other side of the Empire, the farthest edge of the world as he knew it.

For that deepest part of night was when the dead were said to break from their world and walk amongst the living, and he hoped, more than anything else, that the dead might travel with him on that long journey home. That in the shadows of the night and beneath the light of the moon, he might see Kai riding beside him one last time.

Historical Note

This is a work of fiction. Relatively little is known for certain about the Sarmatians, a primarily nomadic people with no written record of their own left behind and a minimal archaeological footprint. What we do know of them is pieced together from written Greek and Roman sources such as Strabo, Cassius Dio, Ovid, and Herodotus, as well as the archaeological finds that survive (mostly from graves). So what we have is limited in scope and unreliable in nature – frustrating for the historian, but exciting for the novelist (and, I hope, the reader).

We do know that there was a war with the Roman Empire in AD 175 or so, a battle upon the frozen Danube, and eventually a peace settlement which sent thousands of Sarmatian heavy cavalry to the north of Britain. Much more than that remains mysterious, but the Sarmatians are pleasingly connected to many myths, ranging from that of the Amazon warrior women to that of our own King Arthur.

If you'd like to read further, I recommend *The Sarmatians* (Tadeusz Sulimirski, 1970) and *Sarmatians* (Eszter Istvánovits and Valéria Kulcsár, 2017) as excellent summaries of the archaeological and written record, and *Tales of the Narts* (John Colarusso and Tamirlan Salbiev, 2016), and *From Scythia to Camelot* (C. Scott Littleton and Linda Malcor, 2000) for more on the mythological links.

Acknowledgements

And so, at last, the end.

It's been a long journey to reach the end of this trilogy. Writing is a lonely trade, but I've been very fortunate to have good company at every step of the way. Enormous thanks, as always, go to my agent, Caroline Wood, and everyone else at Felicity Bryan for all that they've done to get these books out into the world, and especially to Caroline for her support and brilliant instinct for what makes a good story.

I also owe tremendous thanks to the good folks at Head of Zeus for taking a chance on this project. In particular, thanks go to Nic Cheetham for the initial inspiration and drive to commit to this story, to Greg Rees for his thoughtful editing and steady guidance through the process, to Polly Grice for her work in getting the book out to readers, Mark Swan for the gorgeous cover, and Camilla Rockwood for a precise copyedit.

No writer is an island (as much as we like to pretend otherwise), and I owe a great debt to my friends and family, to my students and colleagues at the Warwick Writing Programme. In particular, I'd like to thank my parents, Gill and Michael, for being my first readers, and to Sara for steadying my nerves with her kind words about the book in its early stages.

This book is dedicated to my sisters, Emma, Sarah, and Kathy. I knew early on that I wanted to have a brother/sister relationship at the heart of this trilogy, to try to capture some of that beautiful, tender, fiery, and squabbling kind of love that siblings know so well. Each of them, in their own particular way, stand as an inspiration to me – I love you all.